D1102322

THE INFERNAL CITY

An Elder Scrolls Novel

THE INFERNAL CITY

An Elder Scrolls Novel

GREG KEYES

TITAN BOOKS

The Infernal City: An Elder Scrolls Novel
ISBN 9781848567160

Published by Titan Books
A division of Titan Publishing Group
144 Southwark Street
London
SE1 0UP

First Edition June 2010

5 7 9 10 8 6 4

Copyright © 2010 ZeniMax Media Inc. ZeniMax, Bethesda Softworks,
Bethesda Game Studios, The Elder Scrolls, Oblivion and Morrowind are
trademarks or registered trademarks of ZeniMax Media Inc. in the US
and/or other countries. Used under license. All Rights Reserved.

Book design by Liz Cosgrove.

Visit our website www.titanbooks.com

Did you enjoy this book? We love to hear from
our readers. Please email us at readerfeedback@titanemail.com
or write to us at Reader Feedback at the above address.

To receive advance information, news, competitions, and exclusive
Titan offers online, please register as a member by clicking the "sign up"
button on our website: www.titanbooks.com

No part of this book may be reproduced, stored in a retrieval system,
or transmitted, in any form or by any means without the prior written
permission of the publisher, nor be otherwise circulated in any form of
binding or cover other than that in which it is published and without
similar condition being imposed on the subsequent purchaser.

A CIP catalogue record for this title is available from the British Library.

Printed and bound in Great Britain by CPI Group UK Ltd.

For my daughter,
Dorothy Nellah Joyce Keyes.
Welcome, Nellah.

ACKNOWLEDGMENTS

I would first like to thank everyone involved in The Elder Scrolls for such rich material to work with. Specifically, thanks to Kurt Kuhlmann, Bruce Nesmith, Pete Hines, and Todd Howard for their input and guidance. I would be remiss to neglect mentioning the Imperial Library website, which was also an invaluable resource in writing this book.

As always, thanks to my agent, Richard Curtis. Thanks to my friend Annaïg Houesnard for being a good sport about me lifting her name.

Thanks also to my editor, Tricia Narwani, editorial assistant Mike Braff, and copy editor Peter Weissman, production manager Erin Bekowies, production editor Shona McCarthy, marketing manager Ali T. Kokmen, publicist David Moench, and, of course, the publisher, Scott Shannon. For the wonderful cover, thanks go out to illustrator Paul Youll and designer Dreu Pennington-McNeil.

THE INFERNAL CITY

An Elder Scrolls Novel

PROLOGUE

———————

When Iffech felt the sea shudder, he knew. The wind had already fallen like a dead thing from the sky, gasping as it succumbed upon the iron swells, breathing its last to his mariner's ears. The sky always knew first; the sea was slow—dreadful slow—to come around.

The sea shook again—or, rather, seemed to drag beneath their keel. Up in the crow's nest Keem screamed as he was tossed out like a kitten. Iffech watched him twist and almost impossibly catch the rigging with those Cathay Raht claws of his.

"Stendarr!" Grayne swore, in her South Niben twang. "What was that? A tsunami?" Her feeble human gaze searched out through the dusk.

"No," Iffech murmured. "I was off the Summerset Isles when the sea tried to swallow them, and I felt one of those pass under us. And another, when I was younger, off the coast of Morrowind. In deep water you don't feel much. This is deep water."

"Then what?" She brushed her silver and gray bangs off her useless eyes.

Iffech twitched his shoulders in imitation of a human shrug and ran his claws through the patchy fur of his forearm. The still air smelled sweet, like rotting fruit.

"See anything, Keem?" he called up.

"My own death, nearly," the Ne Quin-alian cat shouted back, his voice rasping hollow, as if the ship was in a box. He lithely hauled his sleek body back into the nest. "Nothing on the sea," he continued after a moment.

"Under it, then," Grayne said nervously.

Iffech shook his head. "The wind," he said.

And then he saw it, in the south, a sudden blackness, a crackle of green lightning, and then a form like a tall thunderhead billowed into being.

"Hold on!" he shouted.

And now came a clap like thunder but forty times louder, and a new fist of wind that snapped the mainmast, taking poor Keem to the death he had nearly seen. Then all was still again, except for the roaring in his damaged ears.

"By the gods, what can it be?" he barely heard Grayne ask.

"The sea doesn't care," Iffech said, watching the dark mass move toward them. He looked around his ship. All of the masts were broken, and it appeared that half the crew was already gone.

"What?"

"Not many Khajiit take to the sea," he said. "They'll bear it for trade, to move skooma around, but few there are who love her. But I've adored her since I could mewl. And I love her because she doesn't care what the gods or daedra think. She's another world, with her own rules."

"What are you going on about?"

"I'm not sure," he admitted. "I feel it, I don't think it. But don't you think—doesn't it feel like . . ." He didn't finish. He didn't need to.

Grayne stared out toward the thing.

"I see it, now," she said.

"Yes."

"I saw an Oblivion gate open once," she said. "When my father worked in Leyawiin. I saw things—it feels a little like that. But Martin's sacrifice—they say it can't happen again. And it doesn't look like a gate."

It wasn't shaped like a thunderhead, Iffech realized. More like a fat cone, point down.

Another wind was starting up, and on it something unbelievably foul.

"It doesn't matter what it is," he said. "Not to us."

And a few instants later it didn't.

Sul's throat hurt, so he knew he had been screaming. He was soaked with sweat, his chest ached, and his limbs were trembling. He opened his eyes and forced his head up so he could see where he was.

A man stood in the doorway with a drawn sword. His eyes were very wide and blue beneath a shock of curly, barley-colored hair. Swearing, Sul reached for his own weapon where it hung on the bedpost.

"Just hold on there," the fellow said, backing up. "It's just you've been hollering so, I was worried something was happening to you."

The dreamlight was still fading, but his mind was starting to turn. If the fellow had wanted him dead, he probably would be.

"Where am I?" he asked, taking a grip on his longsword, despite his reasoning.

"In the Lank Fellow Inn," the man replied. And then, after a pause, "In Chorrol."

Chorrol. Right.

"*Are* you okay?"

"I'm fine," Sul said. "Nothing to concern you."

"Ah, yes." The man looked uncomfortable, "Do you, umm, scream like that every—"

"I won't be here tonight," Sul cut him off. "I'm moving on."

"I didn't mean to offend."

"You didn't," Sul replied.

"The breakfast is out, down there."

"Thank you. Please leave me."

The man closed the door. Sul sat there for a moment rubbing the lines in his forehead. "Azura," he murmured. He always knew the prince's touch, even when it was light. This had not been light.

He closed his eyes and tried to feel the sea jump beneath him, to hear the old Khajiit captain's words, see again through his eyes. That thing, appearing in the sky—everything about it stank of Oblivion. After spending twenty years there, he ought to know the smell.

"Vuhon," he sighed. "It must be you, Vuhon, I think. Why else would the prince send me such a vision? What else would matter to me?"

No one answered, of course.

He remembered a little more, after the Khajiit had died. He had seen Ilzheven as he last saw her, pale and lifeless, and the smoking shatterlands that had once been Morrowind. Those were always there in his dreams, whether Azura meddled with them or not. But there had been another face, a young man, Colovian probably, with a slight bend in his nose. He seemed familiar, as if they had met somewhere.

"That's all I get?" Sul asked. "I don't even know which ocean to look in." The question was directed at Azura, but he knew it was rhetorical. He also knew he was lucky to get even that. He dragged his wiry gray body out of bed and went over to the washbasin to splash water in his face and blink red eyes at himself in the mirror. He started to turn away when he noticed, behind him in the reflection, a couple of books propped in an otherwise empty shelf. He turned, walked over, and lifted the first.

TALES OF SOUTHERN WATERS, it announced.

He nodded his head and opened the second.

THE MOST CURRENT AND HIGH ADVENTURES OF PRINCE ATTREBUS, this one read.

And there, on the frontispiece, was an engraving of a young man's face with a slightly crooked nose.

For the first time in years Sul uttered a hoarse laugh. "Well, there you go," he said. "I'm sorry I doubted you, my Prince."

An hour later, armed and armored, he rode south and east, toward madness, retribution, and death. And though he had long ago forgotten what happiness was, he imagined it must have been a bit like what he felt now.

PART I

ARRIVAL

ONE

―――――

A pale young woman with long ebon curls, and a male with muddy green scales and chocolate spines, crouched on the high rafters of a rotting villa in Lilmoth, known by some as the Festering Jewel of Black Marsh.

"You're finally going to kill me," the reptile told the woman. His tone was thoughtful, his saurian features composed in the faint light bleeding down through the cracked slate roof.

"Not so much kill you as get you killed," she answered, pushing the tight rings of her hair off her face and pressing her slightly aquiline nose and gray-green gaze toward the vast open space beneath them.

"It works out the same," the other hissed.

―――――

"Come on, Glim," Annaïg said, tossing herself into her father's huge leather chair and clasping her hands behind her neck. "We can't pass this up."

"Oh, I think it can be safely said that we can," Mere-Glim replied. He lounged on a low weavecane couch, one arm draped so as to suspend over a cypress end table whose surface was supported by the figure of a crouching Khajiit warrior. The Argonian was all silhouette, because behind him the white curtains that draped the massive bay windows of the study were soaked in sunlight.

"Here are some things we could do instead." He ticked one glossy black claw on the table.

"Stay here in your father's villa and drink his wine." A second claw came down. "Take some of your father's wine down to the docks and drink it there." The third. "Drink some here and some down at the docks . . ."

"Glim, how long has it been since we had an adventure?"

His lazy lizard gaze traveled over her face.

"If by adventure you mean some tiring or dangerous exercise, not that long. Not long enough anyway." He wiggled the fingers of both hands as if trying to shake something sticky off them, a peculiarly Lilmothian expression of agitation. The membranes between his digits shone translucent green. "Have you been reading again?"

He made it sound like an accusation, as if "reading" was another way of referring to, say, infanticide.

"A bit," she admitted. "What else am I to do? It's so boring here. Nothing ever happens."

"Not for lack of your trying," Mere-Glim replied. "We very nearly got arrested during your last little adventure."

"Yes, and didn't you feel alive?" she said.

"I don't need to 'feel' alive," the Argonian replied. "I *am* alive. Which state I would prefer to retain."

"You know what I mean."

"*Hff.* That's a bold assertion," he sniffed.

"I'm a bold girl." She sat forward. "Come on, Glim. He's a were-crocodile. I'm certain of it. And we can get the proof."

"First of all," Mere-Glim said, "there's no such thing as a were-crocodile. Second, if there were, why on earth would we care to prove it?"

"Because . . . well, because people would want to know. We'd be famous. And he's dangerous. People around there are always disappearing."

"In Pusbottom? Of course they are. It's one of the dodgiest parts of town."

"Look," she said. "They've found people bitten in half. What else could do that?"

"A regular crocodile. Lots of things, really. With some effort, I might be able to do it, too." He fidgeted again. "Look, if you're so sure about this, get your father to talk Underwarden Ethten into sending some guards down there."

"Well, what if I'm wrong? Father would look stupid. That's what I'm saying, Glim. I need to know for sure. I must find some sort of proof. I've been following him—"

"You've what?" He gaped his mouth in incredulity.

"He looks human, Glim, but he comes and goes out of the canal like an Argonian. That's how I noticed him. And when I looked where he came out—I'm sure the first few steps were made by a crocodile, and after that by a man."

Glim closed his mouth and shook his head.

"Or a man stepped in some crocodile tracks," he said. "There are potions and amulets that let even you gaspers breathe under-water."

"But he does it all the time. Why would he do that? Help me be sure, Glim."

Her friend sibilated a long hiss. "*Then* can we drink your father's wine?"

"If he hasn't drunk it all."

"Fine."

She clapped her hands in delight. "Excellent! I know his routine. He won't be back in his lair until nightfall, so we should go now."

"Lair?"

"Sure. That's what it would be, wouldn't it? A lair."

"Fine, a lair. Lead on."

————

And now here we are, Annaïg thought.

They had made their way from the hills of the old Imperial quarter into the ancient, gangrenous heart of Lilmoth—Pusbottom. Imperials had dwelt here, too, in the early days when the Empire had first imposed its will and architecture on the lizard people of Black Marsh. Now only the desperate and sinister dwelt here, where patrols rarely came: the poorest of the poor, political enemies of the Argonian An-Xileel party that now dominated the city, criminals and monsters.

They found the lair easily enough, which turned out to be a livable corner of a manse so ancient the first floor was entirely silted up. What remained was vastly cavernous and rickety and not that unusual in this part of town. What was odd was that it wasn't full of squatters—there was just the one. He had furnished the place with mostly junk, but there were a few nice chairs and a decent bed.

That's about all they got to see before they heard the voices, coming in the same way they had—which was to say the only way. Annaïg and Glim were backed up in the corner, and here the walls were stone. The only way to go was up an old staircase and then even farther, using the ancient frame of the house as a ladder. Annaïg wondered what sort of wood—if wood it was—could resist decomposition for so long. The wall- and floorboards here had been made of something else, and were almost like paper.

So they had to take care to stay on the beams.

Glim hushed himself; the figures in the group below were gazing up—not at them, but in their vague direction.

Annaïg took a small vial from the left pocket of her double-breasted jacket and drank its contents. It tasted a bit like melon, but very bitter.

She felt her lungs fill and empty, the elastic pull of her body around her bones. Her heart seemed to be vibrating instead of beating, and the oddest thing was, she couldn't tell if this was fear.

The faint noises below suddenly became much louder, as if she was standing among them.

"Where is he?" one of the figures asked. They were hard to make out in the dim light, but this one looked darker than the rest, possibly a Dunmer.

"He'll be here," another said. He—or maybe she—was obviously a Khajiit—everything about the way he moved was feline.

"He will," a third voice said. Annaïg watched as the man she had been following for the last few days approached the others. Like them, he was too far away to see, but she knew him by the hump of his back, and her memory filled in the details of his brutish face and long, unkempt hair.

"Do you have it?" the Khajiit asked.

"Just brought it in under the river."

"Seems like a lot of trouble," the Khajiit said. "I've always wondered why you don't use an Argonian for that."

"I don't trust 'em. Besides, they have ripper eels trained to hunt Argonians trying to cross the outer canal. They're not so good at spotting me, especially if I rub myself with eel-slime first."

"Disgusting. You can keep your end of the job."

"Just as long as I get paid for it." He pulled off his shirt and removed his hump. "Have a look. Have a taste, if you want."

"Oh, daedra and Divines," Annaïg swore, from the beam they crouched on. "He's not a were-croc. He's a skooma smuggler."

"You're finally going to kill me," Glim said.

"Not so much kill you as get you killed."

"It works out the same."

And now Annaïg was quite sure that what she felt was fear. Bright, terrible, animal fear.

"By the way," the Khajiit below said, lowering his voice. "Who are those two in the rafters?"

The man looked up. "Xhuth! if I know," he said. "None of mine."

"I hope not. I sent Patch and Flichs up to kill them."

"Oh, kaoc'," Annaïg hissed. "Come on, Glim."

As she stood, something wisped through the air near her, and a shriek tore out of her throat.

"I knew it," Glim snapped.

"Just—come on, we have to get to the roof."

They ran across the beams, and someone behind her shouted. She could hear their footfalls now—why hadn't she before? An enchantment of some sort?

"There." Glim said. She saw it; part of the roof had caved in and was resting on the rafters, forming a ramp. They scrambled up it. Something hot and wet was trying to pull out of her chest, and she hysterically wondered if an arrow hadn't hit her, if she wasn't bleeding inside.

But they made it to the roof.

And a fifty-foot fall.

She pulled out two vials and handed one to Mere-Glim.

"Drink this and jump," she said.

"What? What is it?"

"It's—I'm not sure. It's supposed to make us fly."

"Supposed to? Where did you get it?"

"Why is that important?"

"Oh, Thtal, you made it didn't you? Without a formula. Remember that stuff that was supposed to make me invisible?"

"It made you sort of invisible."

"It made my skin translucent. I looked like a bag of offal walking around."

She drank hers. "No time, Glim. It's our only hope."

Their pursuers were coming up the ramp, so she jumped, wondering if she should flap her arms or . . .

But what she did was fall, and shriek.

But then she wasn't falling so fast, and then she was sort of drifting, so the wind actually pushed her like a soap bubble. She heard the men hollering from the roof, and turned to see Glim floating just behind her.

"See?" she said. "You need to have a little faith in me."

She barely got the sentence out before they were falling again.

———

Later, battered, sore, and stinking of the trash pile that broke their final fall, they returned to her father's villa. They found him passed out in the same chair Annaïg had been in earlier that morning. She stood looking at him for a moment, at his pale fingers clutched on a wine bottle, at his thinning gray hair. She was trying to remember the man he had been before her mother died, before the An-Xileel wrested Lilmoth from the Empire and looted their estates.

She couldn't see him.

"Come on," she told Glim.

They took three bottles of wine from the cellar and wound their way up the spiral stair to the upper balcony. She lit a small paper lantern and in its light poured full two delicate crystal goblets.

"To us," she said.

They drank.

Old Imperial Lilmoth spread below them, crumbling hulks of villas festooned with vines and grounds overgrown with sleeping palms and bamboo, all dark now as if cut from black velvet, except where illumined by the pale phosphorescences of lucan mold or the wispy yellow airborne shines, harmless cousins of the deadly will-o'-wisps in the deep swamps.

"There now," she said, refilling her glass. "Don't you feel more alive?"

He blinked his eyes, very slowly. "Well, I certainly feel more aware of the contrast between life and death," he replied.

"That's a start," she said.

A small moment passed.

"We were lucky," Glim said.

"I know," she replied. "But . . ."

"What?"

"Well, it's no were-croc, but we can at least report the skooma dealers to the underwarden."

"They'll have moved by then. And even if they catch them, that's a drop of water in the ocean. There's no stopping the skooma trade."

"There certainly isn't if no one tries," she replied. "No offense, Glim, but I wish we were still in the Empire."

"No doubt. Then your father would still be a wealthy man, and not a poorly paid advisor to the An-Xileel."

"It's not that," she said. "I just—there was justice under the Empire. There was honor."

"You weren't even born."

"Yes, but I can read, Mere-Glim."

"But who wrote those books? Bretons. Imperials."

"And that's An-Xileel propaganda. The Empire is rebuilding itself. Titus Mede started it, and now his son Attrebus is at his side. They're bringing order back to the world, and we're just— just dreaming ourselves away here, waiting for things to get better by themselves."

The Argonian gave his imitation shrug. "There are worse places than Lilmoth."

"There are better places, too. Places we could go, places where we could make a difference."

"Is this your Imperial City speech again? I like it here, Nn. It's my home. We've known each other since we were hatchlings, yes, and if you didn't already know you could talk me into almost anything, you do now. But leaving Black Marsh—that you won't get me to do. Don't even try."

"Don't you want more out of life, Glim?"

"Food, drink, good times—why should anyone want more than that? It's people wanting to 'make a difference' causing all the troubles in the world. People who think they know what's better for everyone else, people who believe they know what other people need but never bother to ask. That's what your Titus Mede is spreading around—his version of how things ought to be, right?"

"There is such a thing as right and wrong, Glim. Good and evil."

"If you say so."

"Prince Attrebus rescued an entire colony of your people from slavery. How do you think they feel about the Empire?"

"My people knew slavery under the old Empire. We knew it pretty well."

"Yes, but that was ending when the Oblivion crisis happened. Look, even you have to admit that if Mehrunes Dagon had won, if Martin hadn't beaten him—"

"Martin and the Empire didn't beat him in Black Marsh," Glim said, his voice rising. "The An-Xileel did. When the gates opened, Argonians poured into Oblivion with such fury and might, Dagon's lieutenants had to close them."

Annaïg realized that she was leaning away from her friend and that her pulse had picked up. She smelled something sharp and faintly sulfurous. Amazed, she regarded him for a moment.

"Yes," she finally said, when the scent diminished, "but without Martin's sacrifice, Dagon would have eventually taken Black Marsh, too, and made this world his sportground."

Glim shifted and held out his glass to be refilled.

"I don't want to argue about this," he said. "I don't see that it's important."

"You sounded as if you thought so for a second there, old friend. I thought I heard a little passion in your voice. And you smelled like you were spoiling for a fight."

"It's just the wine," he muttered, waving it off. "And all of the excitement. For the rest of the night, can we just celebrate that your 'flying' potion wasn't a complete failure?"

She was starting to feel warm in her belly, the wine at its business.

"Well, yes," she said. "I suppose that's worth a toast or two."

They drank those, and then Glim looked a little sidewise at her.

"Anyway—" he began, then stopped.

"What?"

He grinned his lizard grin and shook his head.

"You may not have to go looking for trouble. From what I heard, it might be coming for us."

"What's this?"

"The *Wind Oracle* put into port today."

"Your cousin Ixtah-Nasha's boat."

"Yah. Says he saw something out on the deep, something coming this way."

"Something?"

"That's the crazy part. He said it looked like an island with a city on it."

"An uncharted island?"

"An unmoored island. Floating in the air. Flying."

Annaïg frowned, set her glass down and wagged a finger at him. "That's not funny, Glim. You're teasing me."

"No, I wasn't going to tell you. But the wine . . ."

She sat up straighter in her chair. "You're serious. Coming this way?"

"'Swat he said."

"Huh," she replied, taking up the wine again and sinking back into her chair. "I'll have to think about that. A flying city. Sounds like something left over from the Merithic era. Or before." She felt her ample mouth pull in a huge smile. "Exciting. I'd better go see Hecua tomorrow."

And so they finished that bottle, and opened another—an expensive one—and outside the rains came, as they always did, a moving curtain, glittering in the lamplight, clean and wet, washing away, for the moment, Lilmoth's scent of mildew and decay.

TWO

A boy was once born with a knife instead of a right hand, or so Colin had heard. Rape and attempted murder planted him in his mother, but she had lived and turned all of her thoughts toward vengeance. She laughed when he carved his way out of her and went gleefully into the world to slaughter all who had wronged her and many who had not. And when his victims were drowning in their own blood, they might ask, "Who are you?" and he would answer simply, "Dalk," which in the northern tongue is an old word for knife.

According to the legend, it happened in Skyrim, but assassins liked the story, and it wasn't that uncommon for a brash young up-and-coming killer to take that alias and daydream of making that cryptic reply.

The knife in Colin's hand didn't feel remotely a part of him. The handle was slick and clammy, and it made his arm feel huge and obvious, hanging by his side just under the edge of his cloak.

Why hadn't the man noticed him? He was just standing there, leaning against the banister of the bridge, staring off toward the lighthouse. He came here each Loredas, after visiting his horse at the stables. Often he met someone here; there was a brief conversation, and they would part. He never spoke to the same person twice.

Colin continued toward him. There was traffic on the bridge—mostly folks from Weye going home for the night with their wagons and the things they hadn't sold at market, lovers trying to find a nice place to be secret.

But it was thinning out. They were almost alone.

"There you are," the man said.

His face was hard to see, as it was cast in shadow by a watch-light a little farther up. Colin knew it well, though. It was long and bony. His hair was black with a little gray, his eyes startling blue.

"Here I am," Colin replied, his mouth feeling dry.

"Come on over."

A few steps and Colin was standing next to him. A group of students from the College of Whispers were loudly approaching.

"I like this place," the man said. "I like to hear the bells of the ships and see the light. It reminds me of the sea. Do you know the sea?"

Shut up! Colin thought. Please don't talk to me.

The students were dithering, pointing at something in the hills northwest.

"I'm from Anvil," Colin said, unable to think of anything but the truth.

"Ah, nice town, Anvil. What's that place, the one with the dark beer?"

"The Undertow."

The man smiled. "Right. I like that place." He sighed and ran his fingers through his hair. "What times, eh? I used to have a beautiful villa on the headland off Topal Bay. I had a little boat, two sails, just for plying near the coast. Now . . ." He raised his hands and let them drop. "But you didn't come here for any of that, did you?"

The students were finally moving off, talking busily in what sounded like a made-up language.

"I guess not," Colin agreed. His arm felt larger than ever, the knife like a stone in his hand.

"No. Well, it's simple today. You can tell them there's nothing new. And if anyone asks, tell them that no food, no wine, no lover's kiss is as beautiful as a long, deep, breath."

"What?"

"*Astorie*, book three. Chapter— What are you holding there?"

Stupidly, Colin looked down at the knife, which had slipped from the folds of his cloak and gleamed in the lamplight.

Their eyes met.

"No!" the man shouted.

So Colin stabbed him—or tried. The man's palms came up and the knife cut into them. Colin reached with his left hand to try to slap them aside and thrust again, this time slicing deep into the forearm.

"Just stop it!" the man gasped. "Wait a minute, talk—"

The knife slipped past the thrashing limbs and sank into his solar plexus. His mouth still working, the fellow staggered back, staring at his hand and arm.

"What are you doing?" he asked.

Colin took a step toward the man, who slumped against the banister.

"Don't," he wheezed.

"I have to," Colin whispered. He stooped down. The man's arms came up, too weak now to stop Colin from cutting his throat.

The corpse slipped to a sitting position. Colin slid down next to him and watched the students, distant now, entirely unaware of what had just happened.

Unlike the two men coming from the city, who were walking purposefully toward him. Colin put his arms around the dead man's shoulders, as if the fellow had passed out from drinking and he was keeping him warm.

But there wasn't any need for that. One of the pair was a tall bald man with angular features, the other an almost snoutless Khajiit. Arcus and Khasha.

"Into the river with him now," Arcus said.

"Just catching my breath, sir."

"Yes, I saw. Quite a fracas, when all we asked you to do was slit his throat."

"He . . . he fought."

"You were careless."

"First time, Arcus," Khasha said, smoothing his whiskers and twitching his tail impatiently. "How slick were you? Let's get him in the river and be gone."

"Fine. Lift, Inspector."

When Colin didn't move, Arcus snapped his fingers.

"Sir? You meant me?"

"I meant you. Sloppily done, but you did do it. You're one of us now."

Colin took the dead man's legs, and together they heaved him over. He hit the water and lay there, floating, staring up at Colin.

Inspector. He'd been waiting three years to be called that.

Now it sounded like just another word.

"Put on this robe," Khasha said. "Hide the blood until we get you cleaned up."

"Right," Colin said dully.

———

He got his documents the next day, from Intendant Marall, a round-faced man with an odd ruff of beard beneath his chin.

"You'll lodge in the Telhall," Marall told him. "I believe they already have a case for you." He put down the pen and looked hard at Colin. "Are you well, son? You look haggard."

"Couldn't sleep, sir."

The intendant nodded.

"Who was he, sir?" Colin blurted out. "What did he do?"

"You don't want to know that, son," Marall said. "I advise you not to try and find out."

"But sir—"

"What does it matter?" Marall said. "If I told you he was responsible for the kidnapping and murder of sixteen toddlers, would that make you happy?"

"No, sir."

"What if I told you his crime was to make a treasonous joke about her majesty's thighs?"

Colin blinked. "I can't imagine—"

"You're not supposed to imagine, son. Yours is not the power of life and death. That lies far above you. It comes, in essence, from the authority of the Emperor. There is always a reason, and it is always a good one, and it is not your business, do you understand? You do not imagine, you do not think. You do what you're told. "

"But I've been trained to *think*, sir. This office trained me to think."

"Yes, and you do it very well. All of your instructors agree on that. You're a very bright young man, or the Penitus Oculatus would not have approached you in the first place, and you have done very well here. But any thinking you do, you see, is in service to your job. If you're asked to find a spy in the Emperor's guard, you must use every bit of logic at your disposal. If you're asked to quietly discover which of Count Caro's daughters has been poisoning his guests, again, use your forensic training. But if you're given a clear order to steal, injure, poison, stab, or generally do murder, your brain is only to help you with the method and the execution. You are an instrument, a utensil of the Empire."

"I know that, sir."

"Not well enough, or you wouldn't be asking these questions." He stood up. "You're from Anvil, I seem to remember. One of the city guardsmen recommended you for testing."

"Regin Oprenus, yes sir."

"Without his recommendation, what would you be doing right now?"

"I don't know, sir."

But he did, in a general way. His father was dead, his mother barely got by doing laundry for the better off. He'd managed to teach himself to read, but his education wouldn't have gone much further than that, and if it had, it wouldn't have been of any use to him. At best he might have worked in the shipyard or managed to hire onto a ship. The Imperial invitation had been a dream come true, offering him everything he'd wanted as a young boy.

And that was still the case, despite . . . this. And now he would draw a salary. He could send his mother some of that before she worked herself to death.

"This is the test, isn't it?" he said. "Not last night. Now."

The intendant ghosted a little smile. "Both were tests, son. And this isn't the last, just the last official one. Every day on this job is a new challenge. If you're not up to it, the time to say so is now, before you're in over your head."

"I'm up to it, sir," Colin said.

"Very well, then, Inspector. Take the rest of the day off. Report for duty tomorrow."

Colin nodded and walked away, in search of his new lodgings.

THREE

———◆———

When Annaïg awoke, Mere-Glim was still sprawled on the floor, his breath rasping loudly.

"Oh!" she muttered as she rose, pressing her throbbing temples, feeling her belly turn.

How much wine had they drunk?

She stumbled her way to the kitchen, winced at the sun as she unshuttered the windows. She built a fire in the stove, then opened the walk-in pantry in the diffuse light and considered the sausages hanging in bundles, the long blades of salted pogfish, barrels of flour, salt, sugar, rice, the pitiful basket of mostly wilted vegetables.

There were eggs on the counter, still warm, so Tai-Tai must be up and doing his job, which wasn't always the case.

And there was her mother's antique leather-bound spice case with its seventy-eight bottles of seeds and dried leaves.

Everything she needed.

Mere-Glim wandered in a few minutes after the garlic and chilies hit the oil and the air went sharp and pungent.

"I'm too sick to eat," he complained.

"You'll eat this," Annaïg told him. "And you'll like it. Old Tenny used to make this for Dad, before we couldn't afford her anymore."

"If that's so, why is it different every time you make it? Last time it had peanuts and pickled pork, not chilies and garlic."

"We don't have any pork pickle," she replied. "It's not the specific ingredients that matter—it's the principles of composition, the balance of essences, flavors, oils, and herbs."

Saying that, she emptied the spices she had ground a bit before with mortar and pestle, and the earthy scents of coriander, cardamom, lady's mantel seeds, and ginger wafted about the kitchen. She added two handfuls of crushed rice, stirred that a bit, covered it with a finger of coconut milk, and set it to simmer with a lid on the pot. When the porridge was done, she ladled it into bowls and added slices of venison sausage, red ham, and pickled watermelon rind.

"That looks disgusting," Mere-Glim said.

"Not done yet," she said. She broke two eggs and dropped them, raw, into each bowl.

Glim perked up and his tongue licked out. "Goose eggs?"

"Uh-huh."

"Maybe I will try it."

She set a bowl in front of him, and after an experimental bite, he began downing it with gusto. Annaïg tucked into her own.

"I already feel better," Mere-Glim said.

"See?"

"Yes, yes."

She took another bite.

"So tell me more about this 'floating city,'" she said. "When is it supposed to be here?"

"Ix said they outpaced it for three days and it never changed course before they finally got the wind they needed to really leave it behind. It was headed straight here, he said, and will arrive sometime early tomorrow at the pace it's coming."

"So what did he figure it was?"

"A big chunk of rock, shaped like a top. They could see buildings on the rim. The ship's wind-caller didn't like it. Quit the minute they got into port and left town, fast, on a horse."

"What didn't the wind-caller like?"

"He kept saying it wasn't right, that none of his magicks could tell him anything about it. Said it smelled like death."

"Did anyone take word to the Organism?"

"I can never understand you two when you're together," a soft voice wisped. She turned her gaze to the door and found her father standing there. "That smells good," he went on. "Is there any for me?"

"Sure, Taig," she said. "I made plenty."

She ladled him up a bowl and passed it. He took a spoonful and closed his eyes.

"Better than Tenithar's," he said. "Always in the kitchen, weren't you? You learned well."

"Do you know anything about this?" Annaïg said, a bit impatiently. It always bothered her, talking to her father, and she knew it shouldn't, and that bothered her twice. But he sounded so soul-weak, as if most of his spirit had leaked out of him.

"I wasn't kidding," he said. "You've been like this since you were children. I recognize a few words here and there . . ."

Annaïg waved the old complaint aside. "This—flying city that's supposed to be heading toward us. Do you know anything about that?"

"I know the stories," he sighed, picking at the stew. "It started with Urvwen—"

Annaïg rolled her eyes. "Crazy old Psijic priest. Or whatever they call themselves."

"Said he felt something out in the deep water, a movement of some kind. So, yes, he's crazy and the An-Xileel are irritated by him, especially Archwarden Qajalil, so he was dismissed. But then there were the reports from the sea, and the Organism sent out some exploratory ships."

"And?"

"They're still out there, looking for a phantom probably. After all, Urvwen has been spreading his message down at the docks. No wonder if sailors are seeing things."

"My cousin's ship put to sea from Anvil three weeks ago," Mere-Glim said. "He did not talk to Urvwen."

Her father's face tightened oddly, the way it did when he was trying to hide something.

"Taig!" she said.

"Nothing," he replied. "It's nothing to worry about. If it's dangerous the An-Xileel will meet it with the same might that drove the Empire out of Black Marsh and the Dunmer out of Morrowind. But what would a flying city want with Lilmoth?"

"What do the Hist say?" Annaïg asked.

The spoon hesitated halfway up to her father's lips, then continued. He chewed and swallowed.

"Taig!"

"The city tree said it was nothing to worry about."

Mere-Glim made a high, scratchy humming sound and fluttered his eyes. "What do you mean? The 'city' tree?" He hesitated, as if he had said too much.

"Lorkhan's bits, Glim," Annaïg said. "We're not visitors here, you know."

He nodded. She hated how he was when he spoke straight Tamrielic. He didn't sound like himself.

"It's just, the Hist, they are all—connected. Of the same mind. So why mention the city tree in particular?"

Her father's eyes searched about a bit aimlessly, and he sighed again. "The An-Xileel in Lilmoth talk only to the city tree."

"What's the difference?" Annaïg said. "Like Glim said, they're all connected at the root, right? So what the city tree says is what they all say."

Glim's face was like stone. "Maybe not," he said.

"What's that mean?"

"Annaïg—" her father started. His voice sounded strained.

When he didn't continue for a moment, she raised her hands. "What, Taig?"

"Thistle, this might be a good time for you to visit your aunt in Leyawiin. I've been thinking you ought to anyway. I went so far as to set aside money for the voyage, and there is a ship leaving at dawn."

"That sounds worried to me, Taig. It sounds like you think something's wrong."

"You're all that's left me that matters," the old man said. "Even if the risk is small . . ." He opened his hands but would not meet her eye. Then his forehead smoothed and he stood. "I have to go. I am called to the Organism this morning. I will see you tonight, and we can discuss this further. Why don't you pack, in case you decide to take the trip?"

For a moment she saw farther; Leyawiin was an ocean voyage away, but from there she could reach the Imperial City, even if all she had were her own two feet. Maybe . . .

"Can Glim go?"

"I'm sorry, I've only money for one passage," he replied.

"I wouldn't go anyway," Glim said.

"Right, then," her father said. "I'll be off. I'll have dinner brought from the Coquina, Thistle. No need to cook tonight. And we'll talk about this."

"Right, Taig," she said.

As soon as he was out of earshot, she leveled a finger at Mere-Glim. "You go down to the docks and see what that crazy priest has to say, and anything else you can find out. I'm going to Hecua's."

"Why Hecua's?"

"I need to fine-tune my new invention."

"Your falling potion, you mean?"

"It saved our lives," she pointed out.

"On a related note," Glim said, "why, by the rotting wells, are you worried about flying at this time?"

"How else are we going to get up on a flying island, by catapult?"

"Ahh . . ." Mere-Glim sighed. "Ah, no."

"Look at me, Glim," Annaïg said.

Slowly, reluctantly, he did so.

"I love you, and I'd love to have you along, but if you don't want to go, no worries. I'm not going to give you a hard time. But I'm going, Xhu?"

He held her gaze for a moment, and then his nostrils contracted.

"Xhu," he said.

"Meet you here at noon."

———

As Mere-Glim followed Lilmoth's long slump to the bay Imperials named Oliis, he felt the cloud-rippled sky gently pressing on him, on the trees, on the ancient ballast-stone paving. He wondered, which is to say that he gave his mind its way, let it slip away from speech into the obscure nimbus of pure thinking.

Words hammered thought into shape, put it in cages, bound it in chains. Jel—the tongue of his ancestors—was the closest speech to real thought, but even Annaïg—who knew as much Jel as anyone not of the root—her throat couldn't make all the right sounds, couldn't shade the meanings enough for him to really converse with her.

He was four people, really. Mere-Glim the Argonian, when he spoke the language of the Empire, which cut his thoughts into human shapes. When he spoke to his mother or siblings he was

Wuthilul the Saxhleel. When he spoke with a Saxhleel from the deep forest, or even with a member of the An-Xileel, he was a Lukiul, "assimilated," because his family had been living under Imperial ways for so long.

When he spoke with Annaïg he was something else, not between the two, but something very different from either. Glim.

But even their shared language was far from true thought.

True thought was close to the root.

The Hist were many, and they were one. Their roots burrowed deep beneath the black soil and soft white stone of Black Marsh, connecting them all, and thus connecting all Saxhleel, all Argonians. The Hist gave his people life, form, purpose. It was the Hist who had seen through the shadows to the Oblivion crisis, who called all of the people back to the marsh, defeated the forces of Mehrunes Dagon, drove the Empire into the sea, and laid waste to their ancient enemies in Morrowind.

The Hist were of one mind, but just as he was four beings, the mind of the Hist could sometimes escape itself. It had happened before. It had happened in Lilmoth.

If the city tree had separated itself, and the An-Xileel with it, what did that mean?

And why was he going to do what Annaïg had asked him to do rather than trying to discover what was happening to the tree whose sap had molded him?

But he was, wasn't he?

He stopped and stared into the bulbous stone eyes of Xhon-Mehl the Fisher, once Ascendant Organ Lord of Lilmoth. Now all that was visible of him was his lower snout up to his head. The rest of him was sunken, like most of ancient Lilmoth, into the soft, shifting soil the city had been built on. If one could swim through mud and earth, there were many Lilmoths to discover beneath one's webbed feet.

An image arose behind his eyes; the great stepped pyramid of

Ixtaxh-thtithil-meht. Only the topmost chamber still jutted above the silt, but the An-Xileel had excavated it, room by room, pumping it out and laying magicks to keep the water from returning. As if they wanted to go back, not forward. As if something were pulling them back to that ancient Lilmoth . . .

He stopped, realizing he was still walking without knowing exactly where he was going, but then he knew. The undertow of his thoughts had brought him here.

To the tree. Or part of it. The city tree was said to be three hundred years old, and its roots and tendrils pushed and wound through most of lower Lilmoth, and here was a root the size of his thigh, twisting its way out of a stone wall. Everything else around him had become waterish, blurred, but as he laid his webbed hand on the rough surface, the colors sharpened and focused.

He stood there, no longer seeing the crumbling, rotted Imperial warehouses, but instead a city of monstrous stone ziggurats and statues pushing up to the sky, a place of glory and madness. He felt it tremor around him, smelled anise and burning cinnamon, and heard chanting in antique tongues. His heart thumped oddly as he watched the two moons heave themselves through the low mist of smoke and fog that rolled through the streets, and the waters surged beneath them, around them, beyond the sky.

His thoughts melted together.

He wasn't sure how long it was before his mind complicated itself again, but his hand was still on the root. He lifted it and backed away, and after a few long breaths he began walking, and in the thick night around him, the massive structures softened, thinned, and went mostly away, until he was once again in the Lilmoth where his body was born.

Mostly away. But he felt it now, the call the An-Xileel felt, and he realized that a part of him had already known it.

He knew something else, too. The tree had cut him off from the vision before it had run its course.

That was troubling.

Gulls swarmed the streets like rats near the waterfront, most of them too greedy or stupid to even move out of his way as he picked his way through fish offal, shattered crabs, jellyfish, and seaweed. Barnacles went halfway up the buildings here. This part of town had sunk so low that when a double tide came, it flooded deep. The docks themselves floated, attached to a massive long stone quay whose foundations were as ancient as time and whose upper layer of limestone had been added last year. He made his way up the central ramp to the top of it. Here was a city in itself; since the An-Xileel forbade all but licensed foreigners in the city, the markets had all crowded themselves here. Here, a fishmonger held a flounder up by the tail, selling from a single crate of silver-skinned harvest. There, a long line of sheds with the Colovian Traders banner hawked trinkets of silver and brass, cooking pots, cutlery, wine, cloth. He had worked here, for a while. A group of his matriline cousins had set up a business selling Theilul, a liquor made of distilled sugarcane. They'd originally sold the cane, but since their fields were twenty miles from town, they'd found it easier to transport a few cases of bottles than many wagonloads of cane—and far more profitable.

He knew where to find Urvwen; right in the thick of it all, where the great stone cross that was the waterfront joined.

The Psijic wasn't yelling, as usual. He was just sitting there, looking through the crowd and past the colorful masts of the ships to the south, toward where the bay came to the sea. His bone-colored skin seemed paler than usual, but when the silvery eyes found Mere-Glim approaching, they were full of life.

"You want to know, don't you?" he said.

For a moment Mere-Glim had trouble responding, the experience with the tree had been so powerful. But he let words shape his thoughts again.

"My cousin said he saw something out at sea."

"Yes, he did. It's nearly here."

"What is nearly here?"

The old priest shrugged. "Do you know anything about my order?"

"Not much."

"Few do. We don't teach our beliefs to outsiders. We counsel, we help."

"Help with what?"

"Change."

Mere-Glim blinked, trying to find his answer there.

"Change is inevitable," Urvwen went on. "Indeed, change is sacred. But it is not to be unguided. I came here to guide; the An-Xileel—and the city council—the 'Organism' that they so thoroughly control—do not listen."

"They have a guide—the Hist."

"Yes. And their guide brings change, but not the sort that ought to be encouraged. But they do not listen to me. Truth be told, no one here listens to me, but I try. Every day I come here and try to have some effect."

"What's coming?" Mere-Glim persisted.

"Do you know of Arteum?" the old man asked.

"The island you Psijics come from," Glim answered him.

"It was removed from the world once. Did you know that?"

"I did not."

"Such things happen." He nodded, more to himself, it seemed, than to Mere-Glim.

"Has something been removed from the world?" he asked.

"No," Urvwen said, lowering his voice. "Something has been removed from another world. And it has come here."

"What will it do?"

"I don't know. But I think it will be very bad."

"Why?"

"It's too complicated to explain," he sighed. "And even if

you understood my explanation, it wouldn't help. Mundus—the world—is a very delicate thing, you know. Only certain rules keep it from returning to the Is/Is Not."

"I don't understand."

The Psijic waved his hands. "Those boats out there—to sail and not founder—the sails and the ropes that hoist them, control them—tension must be just so, they must adjust as the winds change, if a storm comes they may even have to be taken down . . ." He shook his head. "No, no—I feel the ropes of the world, and they have become too tight. They pull in the wrong directions. And that is never good. That is what happened in the days before the Dragonfires first burned—"

"Are you talking about Oblivion? I thought we can't be invaded by Oblivion anymore. I thought Emperor Martin—"

"Yes, yes. But nothing is so simple. There are always loopholes, you see."

"Even if there aren't loops?"

Urvwen grinned at that but didn't reply.

"So this—city," Mere-Glim said. "It's from Oblivion."

The priest shook his head, so violently Mere-Glim thought it might come off.

"No, no, no—or yes. I can't explain. I can't—go away. Just go away."

Mere-Glim's head was already hurting from the conversation. He didn't need to be told twice, although technically he had been.

He wandered off to find his cousins and procure a bottle of Theilul. Annaïg could wait a bit.

FOUR

———

Hecua's single eye crawled its regard over Annaïg's list of ingredients. Her wrinkled dark brow knotted in a little frown.

"Last try didn't work, did it?"

Annaïg puffed her lips and lifted her shoulders. "It worked," she said, "just not exactly the way I wanted it to."

The Redguard shook her head. "You've the knack, there's no doubt about that. But I've never heard of any formula that can make a person fly—not from anywhere. And this list—this just looks like a mess waiting to happen."

"I've heard Lazarum of the Synod worked out a way to fly," Annaïg said.

"Hmm. And maybe if there was a Synod conclave within four hundred miles of here, you might have a chance of learning that, after a few years paying their dues. But that's a spell, not a synthesis. A badly put-together spell likely won't work at all— alchemy gone wrong can be poison."

"I know all of that," Annaïg said. "I'm not afraid—nothing I've ever made turned out too bad."

"It took me a week to give Mere-Glim his skin back."

"He had his skin," Annaïg pointed out. "It was just translucent, that's all. It didn't *hurt* him."

Hecua buzzed her lips together in disdain. "Well, there's no talking to the young, is there?" She held up the list and began picking through the bottles, boxes, and canisters on the shelves that made up the walls of the place.

While she did so, Annaïg wandered around the shelves, too, studying their contents. She knew she didn't have everything she needed. It was like cooking; there was one more taste needed to pull everything together. She just didn't have any idea what it was.

Hecua's place was huge. It had once been the local Mages' Guild hall, and there were still three or four doddering practitioners who were in and out of the rooms upstairs. Hecua honored their memberships, even though there was no such organization as the Mages' Guild anymore. No one much cared; the An-Xileel didn't care, and neither the College of Whispers nor the Synod—the two Imperially recognized institutions of magic—had representatives in Lilmoth, so they hadn't anything to say about it either.

She opened bottles and sniffed the powders, distillations, and essences, but nothing spoke to her. Nothing, that is, until she lifted a small, fat bottle wrapped tightly in black paper. Touching it sent a faint tingle traveling up her arm, across her clavicle, and up into the back of her throat.

"What is it?" Hecua asked, and Annaïg realized her gasp must have been audible.

She held the container up.

The old woman came and peered down her nose at it.

"Oh, that," she said. "I'm really not sure, to tell you the truth. It's been there for ages."

"I've never seen it before."

"I pulled it from the back, while I was dusting."

"And you don't know what it is?"

She shrugged. "A fellow came in here years ago, a few months after the Oblivion crisis. He was sick with something and needed some things, but he didn't have money to pay. But he had that. He claimed he'd taken it from a fortress in Oblivion itself. There was a lot of that back then; we had a big influx of daedra hearts and void salts and the like."

"But he didn't say what it was?"

She shook her head. "I felt sorry for him, that's all. I imagine it's not much of anything."

"And you never opened it to find out?"

Hecua paused. "Well, no, you can see the paper is intact."

"May I?"

"I don't see why not."

Annaïg broke the paper with her thumbnail, revealing the stopper beneath. It was tight, but a good twist brought it out.

The feeling in the back of her throat intensified and became a taste, a smell, bright as sunlight but cold, like eucalyptus or mint.

"That's it," she said, as she felt it all meld together.

"What? You know what it is?"

"No. But I want some."

"Annaïg—"

"I'll be careful, Aunt Hec. I'll run some virtue tests on it."

"Those tests aren't well proven yet. They miss things."

"I'll be careful, I said."

"*Hmf*," the old woman replied dubiously.

———

The house, as usual, was empty, so she went to the small attic room where she had all of her alchemical gear and went to work. She did the virtue tests and found the primary virtue was restorative and the secondary was—more promisingly—one of alteration. The tertiary and quaternary virtues didn't reveal themselves even so vaguely.

But she knew, knew right to her bones, that this was right. And so she passed hours with her calcinator, and in the end she was turning a flask containing a pale amber fluid that bent light oddly, as if it were a half a mile of liquid instead of a few inches.

"Well," she said, sniffing it. Then she sighed. It felt right, smelled right—but Hecua's warning was not to be taken lightly. This could be poison as easily as anything. Maybe if she just tasted a little . . .

At that moment she heard a sound on the stairs. She stayed still, listening for it to repeat itself.

"Annaïg?"

She sighed in relief. It was only her father. She remembered he had been bringing food home, and a glance out her small window proved it was near dinnertime.

"Coming, Taig," she called, corking the potion and stuffing it in her right skirt pocket. She started up, then paused.

Where was Glim? He'd been gone an awfully long time.

She went to a polished cypress cabinet and withdrew two small objects wrapped in soft gecko skin. She unwrapped them carefully, revealing a locket on a chain and a life-sized likeness of a sparrow constructed of a fine metal the color of brass but as light as paper. Each individual feather had been fashioned exquisitely and separately, and its eyes were garnets set in ovals of some darker metal.

As her fingers touched it, it stirred, ruffling its metal wings.

"Hey, Coo," she whispered.

She hesitated then. Coo was the only thing of value her mother had left her that hadn't been stolen or sold. Sending her out was a risk she didn't often take. But Glim had had more than enough time to get to the waterfront and back, hours and hours more. It was probably nothing—maybe he was drinking with his cousins or something—but she was eager to find out what the Psijic priest had to say.

"Go find Glim," she whispered to the bird, conjuring the image of her friend in her secret eye. "Speak only to him, hear only at his touch."

She purred, lifted her wings, and drifted more than flew out of the open window.

"Annaïg?"

Her father's voice again, nearer. She went out, closing the door behind her.

She met him near the top of the winding flight. He was red in the face from wine or exertion or probably both.

"Why didn't you just ring the bell, Taig?" she asked.

"Sometimes you don't come down right away," he said, stepping aside. "After you."

"What's the rush?" she asked, descending past him.

"We were going to talk," he said.

"About the trip to Leyawiin?"

"That, and other things," he replied.

The stair came to a landing, and then continued down.

"What other things?"

"I haven't been a very good father, Thistle. I know that. Since your mother died—"

There was that annoying tone again. "It's been fine, Taig. I've got no complaints."

"Well, you should. I know that. I tell myself that I've been doing what's needed to keep us alive, to keep this house . . ." He sighed. "And in the end, all meaningless."

They passed the next landing.

"What do you mean, meaningless?" she asked. "I love this house."

"You think I don't know anything about you," he said. "I do. You pine to leave here, this place. You dream of the Imperial City, of studying there."

"I know we don't have the money, Taig."

He nodded. "That's been the problem, yes. But I've sold some things."

"Like what?"

"The house, for one."

"What?" She stopped with her foot on the floor of the ante-chamber, just noticing the men there, four of them—an Imperial with a knobby nose, an orc with dark green hide and low, brushy brows, and two Bosmeri who might have been twins with their fine, narrow faces. She recognized the orc and the Imperial as members of the Thtachalxan, or "Drykillers," the only non-Argonian guard unit in Lilmoth.

"What's going on, Taig?" she whispered.

He rested his hand on her shoulder. "I wish I had more time, Thistle," he murmured. "I wish I could go with you, but this is how it is. Your aunt will see you get to the Imperial City. She has friends there."

"What's happening, Taig? What do you know?"

"It doesn't matter," he said. "Best you not find out."

She brushed his hand from her shoulder. "I'm not going to Leyawiin," she said. "Certainly not without a better explanation and certainly not without you—and Glim."

"Glim . . ." He exhaled, then his face changed into a visage utterly alien to her. "Don't worry about Glim," he said. "There's nothing to be done there."

"What do you mean?"

She could hear the panic building in her voice. It was as if it had pulled itself outside of her and become a thing of its own.

"Tell me!"

When he didn't answer, she turned and strode for the door.

The orc stepped in her way.

"Don't hurt her," her father said.

Annaïg turned and ran, ran as fast as she could toward the kitchen and other door, the one that led to the garden.

She was only halfway there when hard, callused hands clamped on her arm.

"I owe yer father," the orc growled. "So you'll be coming with me, girl."

She writhed in his grasp, but the others were all around her.

Her father leaned in and kissed her forehead. He stank of black rice wine.

"I love you," he said. "Try to remember that, in the days and years to come. That in the end I did right by you."

———

With half a bottle of Theilul sloshing in his belly, Mere-Glim made his wobbly way back toward the old Imperial district. He knew Annaïg was going to be irritated with him for not returning sooner, but at the moment he didn't care that much. Anyway, it wasn't much fun watching her concoct her smelly compounds, which is what she had surely been doing all afternoon. He hadn't spent much time with his cousins lately—or with anyone except Annaïg, really. If he had, he might have known he wasn't alone in feeling a bit cut off from the tree, that only the An-Xileel and other, even wilder people from the deep swamps seemed to enjoy complete rapport with it.

That was bothersome in a lot of ways, and perhaps most bothersome was that his mind—like many of his people—had a hard time believing in coincidence. If the tree was doing something strange at the same time a flying city appeared from nowhere, it seemed impossible that there wasn't some connection.

Maybe Annaïg's father was right—after all, the old man did work with the An-Xileel. Maybe it was time to go, away from Lilmoth and its rogue tree.

If it was rogue. If all the Hist weren't involved. Because if they were, he would have to get out of Black Marsh entirely.

A light rain began splattering the mud-covered path as he passed beneath the pocked, eroded limestone arch that had once marked the boundary of the Imperial quarter. He whirl-jumped as a fluttering motion at the edge of his vision opened ancient templates—but what he saw there wasn't a venin-bat or blood-moth. It took him a moment to sort out that it was Annaïg's metal bird, Coo.

She must really be irritated, he thought. She rarely used Coo for anything.

He blew out some of the water that had collected in his nose and flipped open the little hatch that covered the mirror.

He didn't find Annaïg gazing back at him, though. It was dark, which meant the locket was closed.

But it was emitting faint sounds.

He pressed the bird nearer his ear. At first he didn't hear much—breathing, the muffled voices of two men. But then suddenly a man was shouting, and a woman shrieked.

He knew that shriek like he knew his own—it was Annaïg.

"Back here, girl!" a hoarse voice growled.

"Just tell my father you put me on the ship!" he heard Annaïg shout. "He'll never know the difference."

"Maybe he wouldn't," Hoarse Voice grunted. "But I would, yeah? So on the boat you go."

Annaïg then vented a string of profanities, some of which she almost certainly had made up on the spot, because Mere-Glim hadn't heard them before, and he had pretty much heard all of her arsenal of swear-words and phrases—or thought he had.

With a grunt he turned around and started back down toward the docks. It seemed Annaïg's father did know something, something so bad he'd had his own daughter kidnapped to get her out of town.

Well, that was great. Now he felt worse about everything.

He began to run.

FIVE

———

Annaïg thought she would have a chance to escape when they reached the ship, but her father's thugs—and his money—seemed to convince the captain, an Argonian so old that patches of his scales had become translucent. She and her things were placed in a small stateroom—about the size of a closet, actually—and that was bolted from the outside, with the promise that she would be free to wander the ship once they were a few leagues from land.

That didn't stop her from trying to find a way out, of course. The small window was no help, since she couldn't shape-shift into a cat or ferret. She tried screaming for help, but they were facing away from the docks, so there was no one to hear her above the general din. She couldn't find a way through the door, and as it turned out, if someone had built any sort of secret doors or panels into the bulkhead, they were far too clever for her.

That left crying, which she actually started before completing her search. Her tears were thoroughly mixed—anger, grief, and terror. Her father would never think of treating her like this unless he was certain that remaining meant death. So why had he decided to stay and die? Why did he get that choice and not her?

Once she got past the noisy stage of crying and settled into more dignified, ladylike sniffling, she realized someone was saying her name. She looked at the door and window, but the sound was funny, very small . . .

And then she remembered, and felt really stupid.

She took off the locket and opened it up and there was Glim's familiar face. His mouth was slightly open and his teeth were showing, indicating his agitation.

"Glim!" she whispered.

"Where are you?" he asked.

"I'm on a ship—"

"Did you get the name?"

"The *Tsonashap*—'Swimming Frog.'"

The tiny figure of his head turned this way and that.

"I see it," he said at last. "It's making ready."

"I'm in a small stateroom near the bow," she told him. "There's a short corridor—" She stopped and bit her lip. "Glim, don't try it," she said at last. "I think . . . I think something really awful is about to happen. Trying to get me out of here—you'll only get caught. Get out of Lilmoth, as far and as fast as you can."

Glim blinked slowly.

"I'm going to close the bird and put it away now," he said.

"Glim—" But the image vanished.

Annaïg sighed, shut the locket and her eyes. She felt tired, hungry, worn-out.

Glim was coming, wasn't he?

The first hour, she waited anxiously, preparing herself to spring into action. But then she felt the boat moving on the water. She looked out the window and saw the lanterns on the quay receding.

"*Xhuth!*" she swore. "Waxhuthi! Kaoc'!"

But the lights, uninterested in her expletives, continued to dim and dwindle.

She opened the locket, but no image greeted her. She held it up to her ear, but she didn't hear anything, either.

Had he heeded her advice, or had he been caught, injured, murdered? In her whirling thoughts he was all of them. Glim, missing an arm; Glim, headless; Glim bound in chains and about to be thrown overboard . . .

Something rattled at her door, and her heart actually skipped a beat. She'd always thought that was just an expression. She stood, fingers knotted in fists she didn't really know how to use, waiting.

The door opened, a snout appeared, and large reptilian eyes that sagged deep in their wrinkled sockets.

"Captain," she said, making her voice as cold as possible.

"We're in deep water," he grated. "Don't be foolish and try to swim for it. You'll not make it, not with the sea-drakes hereabouts."

He glanced down at her clenched hands and flashed his own claws, shaking his head.

"Never think that," he said. "I'd see you safe to your destination, but no one attacks a captain on his ship and doesn't pay hard. It's law."

"Law? Kidnapping is against the law!"

"This isn't kidnapping, it's your father's wish—and you aren't old enough to go against his wish, at least not in this sort of matter. So best resign."

He hadn't said anything about Glim, and she was afraid to ask.

She loosened her fingers. "Very well. I'm free to move about the ship?"

"Within reason."

"Right. Here's me moving, then."

She pushed past him into the brief hall, up the steps, and onto the deck.

Above her, sails billowed and snapped in the plentiful wind that always drove off the coast early in the night, and the bow cut a furrow through a sea lacquered in silver and bronze by the two great moons above. For a moment her fear and dismay were overcome by an unexpected rush of joy at the beauty of it, the adventure it seemed to promise. Across the sea to the Empire, and everything she'd always wanted. Her father's last, best—almost only—gift to her.

She went and stood with her hands braced on the bulward and looked out across the waters. They were sailing south, out of the bay, and then they would go west, along the mangroved coast of Black Marsh, until they reached the Topal Sea, and then they would turn north.

Or she could throw herself in the water and swim what she guessed to be west, brave the sea-drakes, and with more luck than she deserved reach land. But by the time she made it back to Lilmoth, it would be too late. The city—or whatever it was—was supposed to arrive in the morning.

Still . . .

"Hold your breath," someone whispered behind her, and then she was lifted and falling, and a blink afterward stunned and wet. She gasped for air and clawed at her captor, trying to climb up on his head, but a strong hand clamped over her nose and mouth before she could so much as scream, and suddenly she was beneath, enclosed by the sea, moving though it in powerful pulses. She knew she shouldn't breathe, but after a few moments she had to try, to suck in something, anything, to make the need stop.

But she couldn't do it, even when she wanted to.

She woke with air whistling in and a voice behind her.

"Keep quiet," he said. "We're behind them, but a keen eye will spot us."

"Glim?"

"Yes."

"Are you rescuing me or trying to kill me?"

"I'm not sure myself," he said.

"The captain said something about sea-drakes."

"A distinct possibility," he said. "So here's what we'll do. You hang tight to my shoulders. Don't kick or try to help—let me swim for both of us. Try to keep your head under if you can, but I'll be shallow enough so you can lift it out for a few breaths when you need to. Right?"

"Okay."

"Let's go, then."

Glim began digging at the water then, and after finding his pace with a human clinging to his back, he settled into a powerful, almost gliding measure. On land, Glim was strong, but here he seemed really powerful—a crocodile, a dolphin. After a few panicked moments, she had her head bobbing in and out of the water in rhythm with him and was actually beginning to enjoy the ride. She had never been a good swimmer, and the sea always seemed somehow deeply unfriendly, but now she felt almost a part of it.

It was just then, as the last of her fears melted away, that Glim rolled and turned so quickly that she nearly lost her grip. The cadence broken, she gulped water, only barely managing not to inhale.

Then the water itself seemed to slap at them. Glim was going even faster now, weaving and rolling, not giving her any chance to breathe at all. Again, a vortex seemed to jerk at them, and as they spun she caught a glimpse of an immense dark shape against the moonlight glowing down through the water—something like a crocodile, but with paddles instead of legs.

And much, much bigger.

Glim dove deeper, and her lungs began to scream again, but just as suddenly, he turned back up and in an instant they broke free of the sea's grasp, hurling into the air, where the black gas in her chest found its way out and one sweet sip of the good stuff got in before they struck once more down through the silvery surface. Agony ripped along her leg, and then Glim was doing his crazy dance again, and something scraped at her arm and she screamed bubbles into the water as her fingers began to lose their grip.

But then they stopped, and Glim was hauling her up out of the water. He sat her down on something hard, and she sagged there, gasping, tears of pain seeping from her eyes.

"Are you okay?" Glim asked.

She felt her leg. Her hand came away sticky.

"I think it bit me," she said.

"No," he said, squatting to examine her. "If it had, you wouldn't have a leg. You must have scraped against the reef."

"Reef?" She brushed her eyes and looked around.

They weren't on land—at least, not the mainland. Instead they rested on a tiny island hardly more than a few inches above the water. Indeed, at high tide it would certainly be below water.

"She's too big to follow us in here," he said. "Looks like the captain wasn't kidding about sea-drakes."

"I guess not."

"Well, from here on out we only have sharks to worry about."

"Yes, well at least I'm bleeding," Annaïg managed to quip.

"Yah. So maybe the next half mile won't be boring."

But if there were sharks around, they didn't fancy the taste of Breton blood, because they made it to the shore without incident. If shore it could be called—it was actually a nearly impenetrable wall of mangroves, crouched in the water like thousands of giant spiders with their legs interlocked. Annaïg was pleased with the image until she remembered that it was from an Argonian folktale, one which claimed that's exactly what mangroves had once been, before they earned the wrath of the Hist in some ancient altercation and were transformed.

Somehow Glim found them a way through the mess, and finally to the sinking remnants of a raised road.

"How far do you think we are from Lilmoth?" she asked.

"Ten miles, maybe," Glim replied. "But I'm not sure we're well-advised to go back there."

"My father's there, Glim. And your family, too."

"I don't think there's anything we can do for them."

"What's happening? Do you know?"

"I think the city tree has gone rogue, just as it did in ancient times. A lot of people say this one grew from a single fragment of the root that survived the elder's killing, more than three hundred years ago."

"Rogue? How?"

"It doesn't talk to us anymore. Only to the An-Xileel and the Wild Ones. But I think it must be talking to this thing coming from the sea."

"That doesn't make any sense."

"Only because we don't know everything."

"So you think we should just abandon the town?"

He did his imitation of a human shrug.

"You know I can't," she said.

"I know you want to be a hero like those people in your books. Like Attrebus Mede and Martin Septim. But look at us—we aren't armed, even if we knew how to fight, which we don't. We can't handle this, Nn."

"We can warn people."

"How? If the predictions are true, the flying island will reach Lilmoth before we do, by hours."

She hung her head and nodded. "You're right."

"I am."

She held the image of her father for a moment. "But we don't know what's going to happen. We still might be able to help."

"Nn—"

"Wait a minute," she said. "Wait. It's coming from the south, right?"

"Oh, no."

"We have to find high ground. We have to be able see where it is."

"No, really, we don't." She gave him the look, and he sighed. "I just rescued you. How determined are you to die, anyway?"

"You know better than that."

"Fine. I think I know a place."

———

The place was an upthrust of rock that towered more than a hundred feet above the jungle floor. It seemed unclimbable, but that proved not to be a problem when Glim led her to a cave opening in the base of the soft limestone. It led steadily upward, and in some places stairs had been carved. Faded paintings that resembled coiled snakes, blooming flowers, and more often than not nothing recognizable at all decorated the climb, and an occasional side gallery held often bizarre stone carvings of half-tree, half-Argonian figures.

"You've been here before, I take it?" she asked.

"Yes," he replied, and made no other comment, even when she began hinting that one ought to be forthcoming.

Rose was blooming in the east by the time they scaled the last of the stairs and stood on the moss and low ferns on the flat summit of the tabletop. It was quiet, dreamlike, and everything suddenly seemed turned around and impossible. What was she doing here, chasing this fantasy? Nothing was happening, nothing ever happened . . .

"Xhuth!" Glim breathed, just as the bright line of the sun lit the bay on fire.

Her first impression was of a vast jellyfish, its massive dark body trailing hundreds of impossibly slender, glowing tentacles. But then she saw the solidity of it, the mountain ripped from its base and turned over. The mass of it, the terrifying size.

She had been picturing a perfect cone, but this had crevasses and crags, crude, sharp, unweathered angles, as if it had just been torn from the ground the day before. The top seemed mostly as flat as the summit they stood upon, but there were shapes there, towers and arches—and most strangely, a long, drooping fringe depending from the upper edge like an immense lace collar, but twisted about by the wind and then frozen in its disheveled state. It was still south of them and a bit west, but its movement was clear enough.

She watched it, frozen, unable to find a response.

Something faint broke the silence, a sort of susurrus, a buzzing. She fumbled in the pockets of her dress, found the vial marked with an ear, and took a draft.

The hum sharpened into not one voice, but many. Vague, gibbering cries, unholy shrieks of agony and fear, babbling in languages she did not know. It sent scorpions down her back.

"What . . . ?" She strained at the jungle floor below the island, where the sounds seemed to be coming from, but couldn't make anything out through morning haze, distance, and thick vegetation.

She turned her attention back to the island, to the glowing strands it trailed. They might have been spider silk spun from lightning, some flashing briefly brighter than others. She realized they weren't trailing, but dropping down from the center of the base, vanishing into the treetops, flashing white and then withdrawn into the island's belly. As some came up, others descended, creating her original impression of a constant train of them.

Amidst the bright strands, something darker moved.

Swarms of something—they might have been hornets or bees, but given the distance, that would make them huge—emerged from the stone walls and hurtled toward the jungle below. But at some invisible line a few hundred feet below the island, they suddenly dissolved into streamers of black smoke, then vanished into the treetops. Unlike the threads, they did not reappear.

"Glim—" she whispered.

She turned and saw him going back down the steps. Only his head was visible.

"No, Glim, I've changed my mind," she said, trying to keep her voice low, despite the distance. "We'll wait for it to pass. It's doing something—"

Glim's head vanished from view.

Seized with fresh terror, she bolted after him. He was easily caught—he wasn't moving fast—but when she did catch him, his eyes were oddly blank.

"Glim, what is it?"

"Going back, back to start over," he murmured vaguely. Or at least that's what she thought he meant, because he was speaking in Jen, a deeply ambiguous tongue. He might have been saying, "Going back to be born," or any of ten other things that made no sense.

"Something's wrong," she said. "What is it?"

"Back," he replied. He kept walking.

For another ten steps she watched him go, trying to understand, but then she knew she didn't have time to understand, because the howling and screaming was beneath them now, echoing up through the caverns.

Whatever they were, they were coming.

She caught up with him and tickled him under the jaw. When his mouth gaped reflexively—she'd had a lot of fun with that when they were kids—she poured the contents of a vial into it. He closed his mouth and coughed.

She drank her own dose. It felt like a cold iron rod was being pushed down her esophagus, and she coughed, violently.

The world spun dizzily . . .

No, it wasn't the world. It was her. She and Glim were out of the cave and ten feet above the summit, then twenty, but spinning crazily. She thrashed, trying to catch his hand before they drifted too far apart, and finally got his wrist.

That stabilized them a bit, which was good, but now they were picking up speed, and they were aimed straight at the floating island.

"Turn!" she shouted, but nothing happened. As the stone loomed nearer and nearer, she desperately tried to imagine another destination—her house, her father's house back in Lilmoth.

That worked, for they turned, slightly, then a bit more. But then Glim grunted, trying to shake himself free, and they were suddenly yanked back toward the thing. Annaïg felt her grip breaking, and knew even if she managed to turn, she was going to lose Glim. He wanted to go down, but more than that, he wanted to go to that thing.

So she picked the deepest crevasse she could see and focused on it, and the wind became a thunder in her ears. Glim's will appeared to relent, and they began to pick up speed. Something seemed to draw through her, as if she had somehow passed through a sieve and not been shredded, and then that, too, was past. Walls of black stone reached around her like an immense cloak, and then she felt weight return, and the sure grip of the world renew.

SIX

—————————

Annaïg stirred and pushed up with aching limbs. Her arms seemed spindly and weak, her legs boneless.

Her palms were pressed against thick-grained basalt, and she saw she rested at the base of the vertical crevasse she had aimed for; a sliver of light was visible, relatively narrow but rising hundreds of feet. It felt somehow as if she were in a temple, and the sky itself some holy image.

Glim was a few yards away, thrashing feebly.

"Glim," she hissed. Echoes took up even that faint cry.

"Nn?" His head twisted in her direction. He seemed to be back in his eyes.

"You break anything?" she asked him.

He rolled into a sitting position and shook his head. "I don't think so," he said. "Where are we?"

"We're on the thing. The flying island."

"How?"

"You don't remember anything, do you?"

"No, I—I remember climbing the spur. And then . . ."

His pupils rapidly dilated and shrank, as if he was trying to focus on something that wasn't there.

"The Hist," he said. "The tree. It was talking to me, filling me up. I couldn't hear anything else."

"You were pretty out of it," she confirmed.

"I've never felt like that," he said. "There were a lot of us, all walking in the same direction, all with the same mind."

"Walking where?"

"Toward something."

"This place, maybe?"

"I don't know."

"Well, we're here now. What is the tree telling you now?"

"Nothing," he murmured. "Nothing at all. I've never felt that, either. It's always there, in the background, like the weather. Now . . ." He looked out at the light. "They say if you go far enough from Black Marsh, you can barely hear the Hist. But this—it's like I've been cut away from the tree. There's not even a whisper."

"Maybe it's something about this place," she said.

"This place," he repeated, as if he couldn't imagine anything else to say.

"We flew up here," she said.

"Your gunk worked."

"It did."

"Congratulations."

"That I'm not so sure about," she murmured.

"But this is what you wanted, yes, to be up here?"

"I changed my mind," she said. "In the end it was you who wanted to come here—only you wanted to go beneath, down to the ground. I wanted to go back to town. This was the compromise."

A sudden snap and flurry sounded behind them, and they turned just in time to see a handful of dark figures come hurtling out of some dark apertures in the stone wall. At first her only impression was of wings rushing by, but one of the things circled tight, came back, and beat around their heads before settling on long, insectile legs.

It resembled a moth, albeit a moth nearly her size. Its wings were voluptuous, velvety, dark green and black. Its head was merely a black polished globe with a long, wickedly sharp needle projecting out like a nose. Its six legs, ticking nervously beneath it, ended in similar points.

It leaned toward her and seemed to sniff, making a low fluting noise. Then it smelled Glim.

The moment stretched, and Annaïg tried to keep her panic in a little box, way in the back of her head.

Nothing to see here, she thought at it. *We're not intruders, nothing of the kind. I was born right here, on this very spot . . .*

Its wings beat and it flew off with preternatural speed.

Annaïg realized she had been holding her breath, and let it out.

"What the Iyorth was that?" Glim snarled.

"I've no idea," she replied. She stood and limped toward the light, where the things had flown. Glim followed.

A few steps brought them to the aperture, which turned out to be only about twelve feet wide. Below was a cliff that was more than sheer, it actually curved to vanish beneath them.

"I reckon we're somewhere on the bottom third of the cone," she said.

Farther below was jungle, and not much to see, but the space between the island and the treetops was pretty busy.

Near the island, the air was full of the moth-things flying in baroque patterns, like some crazy aerial dance. As she watched, some peeled away and dove straight down, and as they passed a certain altitude they suddenly became vague and smokelike, and she now recognized them as the things she had seen from the spur.

She saw, too, the bright threads, following the flying creatures down into the trees and then suddenly licking back up, vanishing somewhere beneath them.

"What am I seeing?" she wondered aloud.

"I think it's what we're *not* seeing," he replied. "What's down there beneath the trees."

"I fear you're right."

The day waxed on. Now and then more fliers went past them, and occasionally they had a glimpse down through the canopy, where something was moving, but the opening was never enough to discern what.

And then, inevitably, they reached the rice plantations south of Lilmoth, and finally they had a fuller picture.

The distance fooled her, at first, and she thought she was seeing some sort of ant, or insect, as if maybe the fliers were transforming into a land-bound form.

Then she adjusted scale and understood that they were mostly Argonians and humans, although there were a large number of crawling horrors that must have come out of the sea. She recognized some of them as Dreughs, from her books. Others resembled huge slugs and crabs with hundreds of tentacle-limbs, but for these she had no names.

Many of them were marching all in the same direction, but others ran off in swarms. It was all very abstract and puzzling, until they reached a village Annaïg guessed to be Hereguard Plantation, one of the few farms still run mostly by Bretons. She could see a group of them, drawn up behind a barricade.

It wasn't long before they were fighting, and Annaïg's horror mounted. She wanted desperately to look away, but it was as if she no longer controlled her muscles.

She saw a wave of Argonians and sea monsters wash over the barricade, and like arrows of mist, the moth-things plunged into the fray. Wherever they fell, a silvery thread followed, striking the body and reeling back up, brighter. The moths simply vanished.

The wave passed, leaving the bodies of the dead Bretons behind, pushing on into the village.

But then the dead stirred. They came to their feet and joined the march.

Annaïg was sick then, and although there was little in her belly to lose, she bent double, retching. It spent her, and she lay trembling, unable to watch more.

"So," she heard Glim say after a moment. "So this is what the tree wanted."

She heard the pain in her friend's voice, and despite how she felt, dragged herself back to the edge and opened her eyes.

Again her first impression failed her. She imagined she was seeing an Argonian army, standing shoulder-to-shoulder, ready to slay this foul enemy as they had the forces of Dagon in times past.

But then she got it.

"They're just standing there. They aren't fighting."

Glim nodded. "Yes."

The air was thick with fliers and threads.

"I don't understand," Annaïg wailed. "Why does the tree want your people to die?"

"Not all of us," Glim whispered. "Just the Lukiul. The assimilated. The tainted. The An-Xileel, the Wild Ones—they've gone away. They'll come back, after this is over, and every Imperial taint will be scoured."

"It's mad," she said. "We have to do something."

"What? In three hours every living thing in Lilmoth will be dead. Worse than dead."

"Look, we're here. We're the only ones who have any chance of doing anything. We have to try!"

Glim watched the slaughter below for another few breaths, and in that moment she feared he was going to fling himself down to join his people.

But then he let out the long, undulating hiss that signified resignation.

"Okay," he repeated in Tamrielic. "Let's see what we can do."

———

They left the edge and walked back into the crack. The holes that the fliers had come through were high, and the climb looked difficult, but the split in the island continued back, gradually sloping down. Daylight was soon behind them, and while the ghost of it followed them for a while, eventually they were in near complete darkness. She wished she'd foreseen this—one of her earliest concoctions had been to help her see at night. But without any proper materials or equipment, there wasn't any way to make one now.

The going was easy enough, though—the walls remained about twice her shoulder-width apart, so it was easy enough to keep a hand on each rough surface. The floor was a little uneven, but after a few stumbles her feet grew cautious enough.

She could hear Glim breathing, but after they left the ledge, he hadn't said anything, which was just as well, because not only would it be foolish to make any more noise than necessary, she didn't feel like talking, either.

She reckoned they had gone a few hundred yards when she saw light once again, at first just a veneer on the stone, but soon enough to see where they were stepping again. A good thing, too, because the path led them to another cliff.

This one opened in the belly of the mountain, a vast, dome-shaped cavity open at the bottom so they could once more see the destruction of Lilmoth. They were already over the old Imperial quarter, where her house was.

"Taig," she whispered.

"I'm sure he left," Glim hissed. "The tree couldn't affect him."

She just shook her head and turned her sight away, and through tear-gleamed eyes she saw masses of the threads shooting down—so many it looked almost like rain. She followed their course and saw them, thousands of them, in every nook and cranny of the stone. She couldn't make out much; they, too, seemed vaguely insectile, but she saw the thin, stone-colored tubes the threads issued from, because the rest of whatever-they-were were concealed in circular masses of what appeared to be the same material. They looked a lot like spider egg sacs, but larger, much larger.

"Here," Glim murmured.

She had almost forgotten him. She turned to follow his pointing knuckles and saw steps hewn into the stone, leading up.

There wasn't any other way to go except back, and so Annaïg started up, filled with a sudden, panicked determination. She had to *do* something, didn't she? If she could get up there, cut those things loose, maybe the horror would end.

The steps wound up a few feet and vanished back into another tunnel. This one was illuminated with a palpable phosphorescence. It twisted to curve steeply skyward, and Annaïg realized they were making their way up above the domed space. Almost immediately it began branching, but she kept to her left, and after several breathless moments they came to a silvery-white cable, emerging from the stone below them and vanishing into the ceiling.

"It looks like the threads," she whispered. "Only bigger."

"Not bigger," Glim said. "More."

A little closer, she saw what he meant. The cable was composed of hundreds of threads wound together.

She reached out to touch it.

"Well, that's not smart," Glim said.

"I know," she replied, trying to sound brave. Closing her eyes, she touched the back of her hand to it.

Something whirred about in her head and she felt a sudden giddy surge.

She saw now that the hole was larger than the cable that came up through it and, lying flat she was able to make out the jungle floor again. Below her, the ropelike structure unwound itself, sending threads off in every direction. She could see some of them vanishing into the web sacs.

"If we cut this, we'll get a lot of them," she said.

"What do you mean, 'get' them? What do you think will happen?"

"They're all connected here."

"Okay."

"Then if we cut it . . ." She flailed off, gesturing.

"You think it will, what, shut this whole thing down? Destroy this island?"

"It might. Glim, we have to do something."

"You keep saying that." He sighed. "What will you cut it with?"

"Try your claws."

He blinked, then stepped forward and experimentally raked his claws across the thing. He shivered and stepped back, then hit it again, with such force that the cord vibrated.

It wasn't scratched.

"Any other ideas?"

"Maybe if we can find a sharp rock—" She broke off. "Do you hear that?"

Glim nodded.

"Xhuth!"

Because somewhere in the passages, she could hear voices shouting, several of them.

"Come on," she said, and started up another branch of the tunnel.

They kept going, taking random branches, but the voices were gradually growing louder, and there was little doubt in her mind now that they were being pursued.

Whenever they came to a turn that seemed to go down, she took it, reasoning that so far they hadn't been bothered by anything from that direction, but inevitably the passages seemed to move them upward.

She couldn't have known, could she? How big this was all going to be, how utterly beyond her? It was ridiculous.

As if the gods had decided to punctuate that thought, the tunnel suddenly debouched onto a steep ledge that vanished into the interior space of the island.

She drew up short, panting, but Glim grabbed her arm and they were suddenly skittering down the tilted surface. Her surprise was so complete that all thought was pushed from her brain by white light, so when the Argonian caught a knob at the edge and swung them sharply down and under, she had nothing to be relieved about. She found herself on a rounded, springy surface.

It was one of the web sacs.

Glim pulled her up to where the thing was anchored to the stone, the sloping shelf now a ceiling above them, and they crouched there, trying to calm their breathing for many long moments.

A voice suddenly spoke above them, in a tongue that sounded teasingly familiar. The voice might have been that of a man or mer. Another, stranger voice replied. This time she caught a few words; it was Merish dialect of some sort. She closed her eyes, focusing on the sounds.

"—could be dead already," she made out.

"We can't take that chance. He'll have our heads if another vehrumas gets them."

"Who else is looking for them?"

"Word gets around fast. Come on, let's try this way."

The two continued talking, but the sounds grew gradually more distant until they faded away.

As the voices diminished, she heard Mere-Glim resume breathing.

"I don't suppose you understood any of that?" he asked.

"Remember how you used to make fun of me for studying old Ehlnofex?" she asked.

"A dead language? Yes." His throat expanded and he huffed. "They were speaking Ehlnofex?"

"No, but it was enough like it for me to understand it."

"And?"

"Someone saw us fly up here. They're searching for us."

"Who?"

"Whoever lives here. There was a word I didn't understand—vehrumas—but it sounds like there are more than one bunch trying to find us."

"Wonderful. So what do we do?"

To her surprise, she suddenly knew.

She fumbled in her jacket and pulled out Coo.

"Go to the Imperial City," she said, her voice surprisingly steady. "Find Crown Prince Attrebus. Speak only to him, hear only in his presence. He will help us." She saw him in her mind's eye, her own imagining based on the portraits she had seen.

Coo clicked and tinged, and then flew off, dodging gracefully through the filaments, diminishing, a speck, gone.

"How does that help us?" Glim asked. "Why should Attrebus care what happens to us?"

"This thing isn't stopping at Lilmoth," she told him. "It'll go on, through all of Tamriel. And you're right, we can't stop it, you and I. Most likely we'll die or be captured. But if we can survive a little while, until Coo reaches Attrebus—"

"Listen to yourself."

"—if Coo reaches him, and at least one of us survives, we can tell him what's happening. Attrebus has armies, battlemages, the resources of an empire. What he doesn't have is any information about this place."

"Neither do we. And it will be days, at least, before Coo

reaches the Imperial City—if he does."

"Then we have to survive," she said. "Survive and learn."

"Survive what? We don't even know what we're up against."

"Well, then let's find out."

"I have a better idea," Glim said, pointing to the oily black snout emerging from the cocoon. "Let's grab onto one of those strands and ride it to the ground."

Annaïg frowned. "They're moving too fast. Anyway, then we'd just be down there where everything is dying."

He paused, looked at her as if she was crazy, and then rolled his eyes.

"You were kidding," she said.

"I was kidding," he confirmed.

————

The filaments that anchored the web sacs to the stone gave them purchase to climb down to the next ledge, where they found another tunnel. They went in quietly, mindful of what had happened before. As before, the way tended either upward and outward or back into the vault. After perhaps an hour they came across one of the now familiar cables.

Less familiar was the person licking it.

He hadn't seen them yet.

It was a man, naked from the waist up and clad in loose, dirty trousers rolled tight at his waist. His shape and features were those of a human or mer, except that his eyes were a bit larger than normal and recessed more deeply into his face. His hair was unkempt, greasy, and dingy yellow.

She motioned Glim back, but the fellow's gaze snapped over to them, and he stopped licking the cable.

"Lady!" he exclaimed, in the same dialect she'd heard before, bending his head and battering his forehead with his knuckles.

"Lady, this isn't at all what it looks like!"

Annaïg just stared for a moment.

"Lady?" the man repeated. She saw fear in his eyes, but puzzlement as well. Clearly he thought he knew who—or more likely, what—she was.

The man's eyes widened further and he stepped back as Glim emerged.

"What is it, then?" Annaïg asked, trying to sound haughty. "What is it if it's not what it looks like?"

"Mistress," the man replied. "I hope you understand what you saw just now was just appearances. I wouldn't actually—"

"Lick the cable? That's exactly what it looked like you were doing."

The man's eyes narrowed. "That's a funny accent, lady. Some of the words are strange. I've never heard them. And your companion . . ."

"Who are you?" Annaïg asked, feeling her feeble attempt at a bluff crumbling.

"Wemreddle," the man replied. "Wemreddle of the Bolster Midden, in fact, if you must know." He lifted a finger and shook it. "You're not supposed to be here either." He waved violently at Glim. "And there's no such thing as you, you know. No. No such thing as you. You're the ones they're talking about. The ones from outside. From down there."

"Look," Annaïg said, "we don't mean anyone any harm—"

"No, listen," Wemreddle said. "I'm of the Bolster Midden, didn't I tell you? What business do I have with them upstairs? Sump take them and *keep* them. But come on now. I'll get you safe and cozy. Come on with me."

"He's not armed," Glim lisped, in their private cant. "I can kill him."

"You've never killed anyone."

"I can do it." There was a new hardness in his voice.

Wemreddle stepped back. "I mean to help."

"Why?"

"Because I hate all this," he said. "I hate them at the top of the chutes. And you—you might be able to help with them."

"Why do you say that?"

"This new place. You know things about it? The plants, the minerals, the ways of things. They say you flew here without wings."

"I know a little," she said.

"Yes. That's powerful knowledge. Enough to change things. Will you come?"

Annaïg looked sidewise at Glim, but his expression offered no opinion.

"This might be what we're looking for," she told him.

"I can't follow him. What's he saying?"

"I think he's with some disenchanted group, a resistance maybe. They want our help against another faction. We can exploit this, as Irenbis did the various factions of Cheydinhal."

"Irenbis?"

"Irenbis Songblade."

"That's from a book, isn't it?"

"It's a chance, Glim. You agreed we have to do something."

"Something it is, then," he replied.

SEVEN

———————————

"What *is* that?" Annaïg asked, trying not to gag at the stench. Her belly was already empty and her throat and chest ached.

"That's the Midden," Wemreddle said. "Of the four lower Middens, Bolster has the richest scent."

"Rich?" Annaïg drew another breath, this one worse than the last. "I wouldn't describe it as rich. How far away is it?"

"We've still some way to go," Wemreddle said. Then, defensively, "If you wouldn't say rich, then what? Savor the layers of complexity, the contrast of ripe, rotten, and almost raw, the depth and diversity of it."

"I—"

"No, no, wait. When we're there you'll understand better. Appreciation will come."

Annaïg somehow doubted that. It seemed more likely that her lungs would close themselves and suffocate her rather than take in any more of the waxing stench. As they progressed, the floor and walls of the tunnels became first slick and then coated in a dank, putrid sheen, and she began to picture herself climbing up through the bowels of some enormous beast.

"What is this place?" she asked. "Where is it from?"

"This place?"

"The whole—island. Floating mountain, whatever you want to call it.

"Oh. You mean Umbriel."

"Umbriel?"

"Yes, Umbriel, it's called."

"And why is it here?"

Again he looked puzzled. "Here is *here*," he said.

"No, I mean why have you come to my world? Why are you attacking it?"

"Well, I'm not, am I? I'm just in the Bolster Midden."

"Yes, but why has Umbriel come here?" she persisted.

"I've no idea. Does it matter?"

"People are dying down there. There must be a reason."

He stopped and scratched his head. "Well, yes, Umbriel needs souls. Lots and lots of souls—there's no secret there. But he could get those plenty of places. If you're asking why here in particular, I'm afraid I've no way of knowing that."

"You mean it's just *feeding*?" Annaïg asked, incredulous.

"Well, we've lots of mouths to feed, don't we," he replied with an air of diffidence.

"Why do they become—if their souls are taken up here— why do their bodies keep going?"

"Do I really have to explain this?"

"If I'm going to help you, I think I deserve whatever explanation you can give me."

"Oh, very well. Look, something beneath us dies. The soul-spinners nick the soul with their lines, and then the larvae fly down and get all snug in the bodies—which then harvest more souls. You see?"

"The larvae have wings and round heads?"

"Yes. See, you do know this."

"I saw one of them," she replied. "It seemed like it should have been perfectly capable of murder on its own."

"In Umbriel, sure. But they have to leave Umbriel to find souls, which means they lose their substance."

"So that's what I saw," Annaïg said. "But why?"

"Why what?"

"Why do they become ethereal?"

"That's a big word," Wemreddle said.

"Yes, but—"

"I don't know," Wemreddle said. "I've never thought about it. You fall in water, you get wet. Stray from Umbriel, you lose substance. It's just how things are."

Annaïg digested that for a moment.

"Very well. But how does it start? I mean, if larvae can't kill anything unless they have a soulless body to steal, how do the first ones get bodies?"

"I don't know that either."

"And what becomes of the souls?"

"Most go to the ingenium, which keeps Umbriel aloft and moving. Some go to the vehrumasas."

"I don't know that word," she said. "What does it mean?"

"The place where they prepare food. Where the furnaces are."

"Kitchens? You people eat souls?"

"Not all of us. I don't—I'm not that elevated. But them at the top, and Umbriel himself, or course—well, they like their delicacies. We don't see that in the Middens, do we?"

"And yet you were licking the cable," she said.

He blushed. "It's not against nature to want a taste, is it? Just a little taste?"

Annaïg had a sudden, unpleasant thought.

"Are the lords—are *you*—daedra?"

"What's a daedra?" Wemreddle asked.

"You've never heard of daedra?" she asked. "But didn't this city come from Oblivion?"

Wemreddle just looked blankly at her.

"There are sixteen daedric princes," Annaïg explained. "Some are just—well, evil. Mehrunes Dagon, for instance—he tried to destroy our world, back before I was born. Others—like Azura—aren't supposed to be so bad. Some people worship them, especially the Dunmer. But besides the princes, there are all sorts of minor daedra. Some people can conjure them and make them do their bidding."

"We do the bidding of the lords," Wemreddle said. "If I were a daedra, would I know it?"

"Maybe not," Annaïg realized. "What is the name of your highest lord?"

"Umbriel, of course."

"There's no prince that goes by that name," she mused, "although I suppose a daedric prince could be known by any number of names."

Wemreddle seemed entirely disinterested in the conversation, so she let it drop. She had so many new questions now, she didn't know what to ask next, so instead of questioning him further, she filled Glim in on what Wemreddle had been telling her.

"It's horrible," she said. "What if it's really aimless? If our world is being destroyed just so this thing can keep in the air? What if there is no other agenda?"

"There must be more to it than that," Glim responded. "There has to be. Otherwise why would Umbriel ally with the city tree? Why would it spare anyone?"

"Maybe it didn't. If the tree is insane, as you think, it might have just imagined an alliance."

"It's possible." He snicked his teeth together. "You were right, in a way," he said. "It sounds as if we were to stop the flow of souls to this ingenium of theirs, then this would turn into just another rock."

"Maybe. Could it be that simple?"

"I doubt it will be simple," the Argonian replied.

They walked in silence for a bit, while Annaïg turned it all over in her head.

When they finally reached the Bolster Midden, she was sure of her earlier impression, for she could think of nothing to compare it to other than the gorged, bloated stomach of a giant.

And the smell—well, it was bad. Glim's nictating membranes kept shutting, and Glim could wade through the most noisome fen without really noticing.

But this wasn't a noisome fen, and she was, in fact, beginning to understand Wemreddle's bizarre assertion. Animal was here, sweetly, sulfurously rotten, but there was also blood still so fresh she could taste the iron in the middle of her tongue. She made out rancid oil, buttery cream, old wine-braising liquid, fermenting again with strange yeasts and making pungent vinegars. Fresh herbs mingled with the cloying molder of tubers and onions gone to liquid.

Best of all were the thousand things she didn't recognize, some deeply revolting and some like a welcome home to a place she'd never been. Some smells were more than that, not only engaging the taste buds and nostrils, but sending weird tingles across her skin and shimmering colors when she closed her eyes.

"You see?"

She nodded dumbly and looked around more carefully.

If this was the belly of a giant, he had many esophagi; more stuff fell periodically from five different openings in the vaulted stone ceiling.

In places, the trash moved.

"What's that?" she asked.

"The worms," Wemreddle replied. "They keep the Midden turning, make it all pure to siphon into the Marrow Sump."

"Marrow Sump?"

"It's where everything goes, and where everything comes from."

That seemed like it would take a longer explanation, so she let it go for more immediate concerns.

"What's up there?" she asked, indicating the apertures above.

"The kitchens, of course. What else?" He pointed at each of the holes in turn. "Aghey, Qijne, Lodenpie, and Fexxel."

"And what do you do down here?"

"Hide. Try not to be noticed. They sent us down here a long time ago to tend the worms, but the worms pretty much tend themselves."

"So where is everyone else?"

"In the rock. I'll fetch them. But first let me find you a safe place, yes?"

"That sounds good," Annaïg said.

A narrow ledge went around the Midden like a collar, albeit one whose dog had outgrown it a bit; here and there they found themselves trudging through offal and pools of putrescence. Light came dimly from no obvious source, but she didn't try to make out what they were stepping through.

At last they came to a small cave, rudely furnished with a sleeping mat and not much else.

"You wait here," he said. "Try not to make much sound."

And with that Wemreddle was gone.

———

"I can't breathe this forever," Glim muttered. Their guide had been gone for a long time, although without the sun, moon, or stars, it was hard to tell exactly how long. Annaïg figured it was hours, though.

"At least we're breathing," she pointed out.

"Well, as long as we're settling for the least," he replied.

"Glim . . ." She put a hand on his shoulder.

He snapped his teeth. "I need to eat something," he said.

"Me, too," she said. The wait had given the shock and adrenaline time to wear off, and now she was ravenous. "I can go out there, see what I can sort out."

He shook his head. "That's disgusting."

"Some of it is still food."

"Stay here. You've no idea what those worms might do, or what else might be out there."

"What, then?"

"I've been thinking," he said.

"Not your strong suit."

"Yes. But I've been doing it, nonetheless. Four kitchens above us, and four other Middens. Do you know how much refuse that suggests, if this is even close to typical?"

"A lot."

"Yes. Which suggests that somewhere up there, a lot of people or—something—are doing a lot of eating."

"I did see what looked like a city along the rim."

"I think we're still far below the rim," he said. "Still, I'm thinking there must be thousands on this island, at least."

"Okay."

"And Wemreddle, the trash keeper, wants you to help with some sort of revolution. Against who knows what and who knows how many? There's a daedra prince up there, for all we know. I'm not sure we want to be a part of this."

"So you think we should leave before he gets back."

"I think we should go looking for food. In the kitchens. See what we're up against. We can always come back here if the trash-tender still seems like a good bet."

"How will we know that until we meet the rest of them?"

"Of whom?"

"Whoever he went to get. The underground. The resistance."

"You and your books," Glim muttered. "Resistance."

"Look around you, Glim. When people are forced to live in places like this, there's usually a resistance."

"Lots of people lived like this in Lilmoth," Glim replied. "They didn't resist anything."

"Well, maybe they should have," she retorted. "Maybe then the An-Xileel couldn't have—"

"It was the tree, Nn, not the An-Xileel. The Hist decide."

"The city tree is psychotic."

"Maybe."

"You said it's happened before, one Hist breaking with the others."

"You're changing the subject."

"Fine. We might as well have some options. Do you know how to get to these kitchens?"

"Of course not. But we know where they are." He pointed up.

"Fair enough," she conceded. Her hand still on his shoulder, she pushed up to standing. Then she noticed some figures approaching along the path that had brought them there. "Oops. Too late. Wemreddle's back."

"That's not much of a resistance," Glim noted. "Six besides him."

"At least they're armed."

Like Wemreddle, they all appeared to be human or mer. They wore uniforms—yellow shirts, aprons, black pants—and they carried an assortment of large knives and cleavers. The only one who was dressed differently was a fellow with thick, curly red hair and beard. His shirt was a black-and-yellow tartan pattern.

Wemreddle was trailing the lot. The red-beard spoke.

"It's true, you're really from the world beyond?"

"Yes," Annaïg said.

"And you have knowledge of its plants, animals, herbs, minerals, essences, and so on?"

"Some," she replied. "I have studied the art of alchemy—"

"Come with us, then."

"To where?"

"To my kitchen. Fexxel's kitchen."

"Wemreddle," Annaïg exploded. "You piece of—"

"They'll let me come up," the man simpered. "They'll let me work up there. This is for the best. You'll be protected. You need that."

"Protection from whom?"

"Me, for one," another voice shouted.

A second group was approaching, twice as large as Fexxel's, and just as heavily armed.

Fexxel spun. "You worm," he roared at Wemreddle. "I bargained in good faith with you!"

"I didn't tell her! I swear it!"

Annaïg could make out the newcomer now. She wore a checked indigo-and-lapis shirt, apron, and indigo pants. Her face was angular, drawn, hard, and her teeth gleamed like opals in the dim light.

"He didn't, actually," the woman said. "One of your own betrayed you. More's the pity for the poor worm, because I don't owe him anything."

Wemreddle began a sort of soft wailing.

"I'll have them, Fexxel."

"I have right, Qijne. I have claim."

"The Midden is neutral territory."

"I found them first."

"Well, you can take it up with someone next time you come out of the sump," she replied. "Or you can walk back to your kitchen in the meat you're wearing."

Annaïg could see Fexxel was trembling, whether with fear or

fury, it was hard to say.

"It might be worth it," he said. "You outnumber us, but I'll kill you before I go down."

"Ah, determination," Qijne said, stepping forward, away from her companions. "Passion. Do you really have such passions, Fexxel? Or is this all superficial, like your cooking?"

Her arm whipped out and a bright, bloody line appeared on Fexxel's cheek. His eyes widened and his mouth worked, but for the moment no sound came out.

Annaïg was still trying to understand what had happened. Qijne's hand had been about a foot from Fexxel's face, and she hadn't seen a weapon in it. Nor did she now.

Fexxel found his voice. "You crazy bitch!" he screeched, blood pouring through the fingers he had pressed to his face.

"See?" Qijne said. "Just blood under there, nothing else. Go home, Fexxel, or I'll make a pie of you."

Fexxel heaved several great breaths, but he didn't say anything else. Instead he left, as instructed, and his followers went with him, glancing back often.

Qijne turned her gaze on Annaïg. Her eyes were as black as holes in the night.

"And you, my dear, are the cook?"

"I—I can cook."

"And what is this?" she asked, stabbing a finger toward Glim.

"Mere-Glim. He's an Argonian. He doesn't speak Mer."

Qijne cocked her head. "*Mer*," she said experimentally, then seemed to dismiss the word—and Glim—with a shake of her head. "Well," she said. "Come, then. We'll go to my kitchen."

Annaïg lifted her chin. "Why should I?" she asked.

Qijne blinked again, then leaned in close and spoke in a casual, confidential manner. "I don't need all of you, you know. Your legs, for instance—not very useful to me. More of a problem, really, if I imagined you were prone to running off."

Each word was like an icicle driven in her back. There was no doubt that the woman was serious.

Qijne patted her on the shoulder. "Come along," she said.

And she came, telling herself that this was what she needed to be doing, trying to learn something about the enemy, trying to find out how to stop this unholy thing.

But it was hard to keep that in her head, because she had never in her life been more afraid of anyone than she was of Qijne.

EIGHT

———————

"This isn't a kitchen," Annaïg whispered to Glim. "This is . . ."

But she had no word for it.

Her first impression was of a forge, or furnace, because enormous rectangular pits of almost white-hot stone lined up down the center of a vast chamber carved and polished from the living rock. Above the pits innumerable metal grates, boxes, cages, and baskets depended from chains, and vast sooty hoods sucked most of the heat and fumes up higher still into Umbriel. Left and right, red maws gaped from the walls—ovens, obviously, but really more like furnaces. Between them, beings strange and familiar crowded and hurried about long counters and cabinets, wielding knives, cleavers, pots, pans, saws, awls, and hundreds of unidentifiable implements.

Though the smells here were generally cleaner than those of the Midden, they were just as varied, and decidedly more alien.

So was the staff; many of them resembled the peoples she knew—there were in particular many who looked like mer; there were others for which—like the place itself—she had no name. She saw thick figures with brick-red skin, fierce faces, and small horns on their heads, working next to ghostly pale blue-haired beings, spherical mouselike creatures with stripes, and a veritable horde of monkeylike creatures with goblinesque faces. These last scrambled along the shelves and cabinets, tossing bottles and tins from shelves in the stone that rose sixty feet along the walls, although in most of the room the ceiling crushed down almost to the level of the tallest head.

But Qijne led her through all of this, past searing chunks of meat, huge snakelike creatures battering against the bars of their cages as the heat killed them, cauldrons that smelled of leek and licorice, boiling blood, molasses.

After a hundred paces the cooking pits were replaced by tables crowded with more delicate equipment of glass and bright metal. Some were clearly made for distillation, this made obvious by the coils that rose above; others resembled retorts, parsers, and fermentation vats. Along the walls were what amounted to vaster versions of these things, distilling, parsing, and fermenting tons of material.

It was breathtaking, and for a moment Annaïg forgot her situation in wonder of it.

But then something caught her eye that brought it all back: a cable, the thickest she had seen yet, pulsing with the pearly light of soul stuff and, more specifically, the life force of the people of Lilmoth. It passed through various glass collars filled with liquid and colored gases, and insectile filaments and extremely fine tubing coiled and wound into what might be condensation chambers.

She felt tears forming, and trembled with the effort to keep them back.

For the first time since entering the kitchens, Qijne spoke.

"You like my kitchen," she said. "I see it."

Her throat caught, but then breath came, and something seemed to rise up through her, inflating her. She focused her gaze on Qijne's eyes.

"It's amazing," she admitted. "I don't understand most of it."

"You really know nothing of Umbriel, do you?"

"Only that it is murdering people."

"Murdering? That's a strange word."

"It's the right word. Why? Why is Umbriel doing this?"

"What a meaningless question," Qijne said. "And how unknowable." She took Annaïg's chin between thumb and forefinger. "I'll let you know what questions are worth asking, little thing. Give me all the attention and love you possess, and you will thrive here. Otherwise, it's the sump. Yes?"

"Yes."

"Very well. My kitchen." She opened her arms as if to take it all in. "There are many appetites in Umbriel. Some are coarse—meat and tubers, offal and grain. Other habitants have more spiritual appetites, subsisting on distilled essences, pure elements, tenebrous vapors. The loftiest of our lords require the most refined cuisine, that which has as its basis the very stuff of souls. And above all, they crave novelty. And that, my dear, is where you come in."

"So that's why you want me? To help you invent new dishes?"

"There are many sorts of dishes, dear. Umbriel needs more than raw energy to run. The sump needs tending; the Fringe Gyre needs feeding. Raw materials must be found or created. Poisons, balms, salves, entertainments, are all in great demand. Drugs to numb, to please, to bring fantastic visions. All of these things and more are done in the kitchens. And we must stay ahead of others, you see? Stay in favor. And that means new, better, more powerful, deadlier, more interesting."

Annaïg nodded. "And you believe I can help you."

"We've just passed through a void; we were nearing the end of our resources. Now this whole pantry is open to us, and you know more about it than I do. I can admit that, you see? In the end you have more to learn from me than I from you, but at this moment you are my teacher. And you will help me make my kitchen the strongest."

"What's to stop the other kitchens from kidnapping their own help?"

She shook her head. "Most of us cannot go far from Umbriel without losing our corpus. There are certain, specialized servants we use to collect things from below."

"The walking dead, you mean?"

"Yes, the larvae. Once incorporated, they can be brought here with certain incantations, bearing raw materials, beasts, what have you. But intelligent beings with desirable souls—"

"Are all already dead by the time your gatherers begin their work."

"Did you interrupt me? I'm sure you didn't."

"I'm sorry."

"I'm sorry, *Chef*."

"I'm sorry, Chef."

Qijne nodded. "Yes, that's how it is. And those of us in the kitchens don't have the power to send them farther, or the incantations to bring them back here. Once the gatherers move very far from Umbriel, contact is lost."

This is good, Annaïg thought. I'm learning weaknesses already. Things that will help Attrebus.

"So here we are," she said.

Annaïg looked at the table Qijne was indicating. It was littered with leaves, bark, half-eviscerated animals, roots, stones, and what have you. There was also a ledger, ink, and a pen.

"I want to know about these things. I want you to list and describe every substance you know of that might be of use to me, and describe as well how to find them. You will do this for half of your work period. For the remainder of your shift you will cook—first you will learn how things are down here, then you will create original things. And they had better be original, do you understand?"

"I don't—it's overwhelming, Chef."

"I will assign you a scamp and a hob and put a chef over you.
That is far more than most that come here are given. Count your
fortunes." She waved at one of her gang, a woman with the gray
skin and red eyes of a Dunmer.

"Slyr. Take charge of this one."

Slyr lifted her knife. "Yes, Chef."

Qijne nodded, turned and strode off.

"She's right, you know," Slyr said. "You don't know how
lucky you are."

Annaïg nodded, trying to read the other woman's tone and
expression, but neither told her anything.

A moment later a yellowish, sharp-toothed biped with long
pointy ears walked up.

"This is your scamp," she said. "We use the scamps for hot
work. Fire doesn't bother them very much."

"Hello," Annaïg said.

"They take orders," Slyr said. "They don't talk. You don't
really need it now, so you ought to send it back to the fires. Your
hob—" She snapped her fingers impatiently.

Something dropped through Annaïg's peripheral vision and
she started and found herself staring into a pair of large green
eyes.

It was one of the monkeylike creatures she'd seen on entering
the kitchen. Closer up, she saw that, unlike a monkey, it was hairless. It did have long arms and legs, though, and its fingers were
extraordinarily long, thin, and delicate.

"Me!" it squeaked.

"Name him," Slyr said.

"What?"

"Give him a name to answer to."

The hob opened his mouth, which was both huge and toothless, so that for an instant it resembled an infant—and more specifically looked like her cousin Luc when he was a child. It capered on the table.

"Luc," she said. "You'll be Luc."

"Luc, me," it said.

"I'll be back to get you when it's time to cook," Slyr said. "This you'll do on your own." She glanced askance at Glim. "What about him?"

"He knows as much about these things as I do," Annaïg lied. "I need him."

"Very well." And Slyr, too, walked off to some other task.

Annaïg realized that she and Glim were alone with Luc the hob.

"Now what?" Glim asked.

"They want—"

"I didn't understand the words, but it's pretty clear what they want you to do. But are you going to do it?"

"I don't see I have much choice," she replied.

"Sure. No one is watching us at the moment. We could escape back to the Midden through the garbage chute and then . . ."

"Right," she said. "And then what?"

"Okay," he grumbled. "Use some of this stuff to make another bottle of flying stuff. Then down the chute, back away, gone."

"I thought we were agreed on this."

"But you'll be helping them, don't you see? Helping them destroy our world."

"Glim, I'm learning a lot, and quickly. Think about it—this is the perfect place for me. If I could have asked for a better chance to sabotage Umbriel, I couldn't have thought of anything better. Given a little time, who knows what I can make here?"

"Yes," he said. "I see that. But what about me?"

"Do as I do. Talk to me now and then as if you're telling me something. Write down the things I tell you to."

"What about that?" he asked of the hob.

She considered the thing. "Luc," she said, "fetch me those whitish-green fronds at the far end of the table."

"Yes, Luc me," the hob said, bounding away and back, bearing the leaves.

"This," Annaïg dictated, "is fennel fern. It soothes the stomach. It's used in poultices for thick-eye . . ."

She had almost forgotten where she was when Slyr returned, hours later.

"Time to cook," Slyr said.

Annaïg rubbed her eyes and nodded. She gestured vaguely at some of the nearby equipment. "I'm really interested in distilling essences," she began. "How does this—"

Slyr coughed up an ugly little laugh. "Oh, no, love. You don't start there. You start in the fire."

———

"But there isn't any fire," she complained minutes later as she turned the hot metal wheel. The grill before her rose incrementally.

"More," Slyr snapped. "This is boar, yes?"

"It smells like it," Annaïg replied.

"And this goes to the grounds workers in Prixon Palace, and they don't like it burnt, like they do in the Oroy Mansion, see. So higher, and then send your scamp on the walk up there to swing a cover over it."

Annaïg kept hauling on the wheel. Sweat was pouring from her now, and she was starting to feel herself moving past fatigue into some whole new state of being.

"What did you mean, about there being no fire?" Slyr asked.

"There's not. It's just rocks. Fire is when you burn something. Wood, paper, something."

Slyr frowned. "Yes, I guess fire can mean that, too—like

when grease falls. Right. But why would we cook by burning wood? If we did, all of the trees in the Fringe Gyre would be gone in six days."

"Then what makes the rocks hot?"

"They're hot," Slyr said. "They are, that's all. Okay, send your scamp."

She pointed at the metal hemisphere suspended on a boom from the ceiling, and the scamp scrambled up into the metal beams and wires above the heat. He pushed the dome—which ought to have been searing—and positioned it over the smoking hog carcass. Annaïg kept cranking until the grill came in contact with the dome.

"There," Slyr said. "We're well above the flames. So what else can we put up there? What do we need to cook slowly?"

"We could braise those red roots."

"The Helsh? Yes, we could." She seemed surprised, for a moment, but covered it quickly.

"These little birds—they would cook nicely up there."

"They would, but those are going to Oroy Mansion—"

"—and they like everything burnt there."

"Yes."

Annaïg was sure Slyr almost smiled, but then she was directly back to business.

"So get on with it," she said.

And so she burned, braised, roasted, and seared things for what felt like days, until at last Slyr led her to a dark dormitory with about twenty sleeping mats. A table supported a cauldron, bowls, and spoons. She stood in line, legs shaking with fatigue, helped herself, and then slid down against the wall near the pallet Slyr indicated was hers.

The stew was hot and pungent, unfamiliar meat and odd, nutty grains, and at the moment it seemed like the best thing she had ever eaten.

"When you finish that, I advise you to sleep," Slyr told her. "In six hours you're back to work."

Annaïg nodded, looking around for Glim.

"They've taken your friend," Slyr said.

"What? To where?"

"I don't know. It was obvious he didn't know much about cooking, and there's curiosity about what he is exactly."

"Well, when will they bring him back?"

Slyr's face took on a faintly sympathetic cast. "Never, I should think," she replied.

She left, and Annaïg curled into a ball and wept quietly. She pulled out her pendant and opened it.

"Find Attrebus," she whispered. "Find him."

———

Mere-Glim wondered what would happen if he died. It was generally believed that Argonians had been given their souls by the Hist, and when one died, one's soul returned to them, to be incarnated once more. That seemed reasonable enough, under ordinary circumstances. In the deepest parts of his dreams or profound thinking were images, scents, tastes that the part of him that was sentient could not remember experiencing. The concept the Imperials called "time" did not even have a word in his native language. In fact, the hardest part of learning the language of the Imperials was that they made their verbs different to indicate when something happened, as if the most important thing in the world was to establish a linear sequence of events, as if doing so somehow explained things better than holistic apprehension.

But to his people—at least the most traditional ones—birth and death were the same moment. All of life—all of history—was one moment, and only by ignoring most of its content could one create the illusion of linear progression. The agreement to see things in this limited way was what other peoples called "time."

And yet how did this place, this Umbriel, fit into all of that? Because he was cut off from the Hist. If he died here, where would his soul go? Would it be consumed by the ingenium Wemreddle had spoken of? And what of his people so consumed? Where they gone forever, wrenched from the eternal cycle of birth and death? Or was the cycle, the eternal moment, only the Argonian way of avoiding an even more comprehensive truth?

He decided to stop thinking about it. This sort of thing made his head hurt. Concentrate on the practical and what he really knew; he knew that he'd been overpowered by creatures with massive, crablike arms, snatched away from Annaïg, and brought here. He didn't know why.

Fortunately, someone entered the room, rescuing him from any more attempts at reflection.

The newcomer was a small wiry male and might well have been a Nord, with his fine white hair and ivory, vein-traced skin. And yet there was something about the sqaurish shape of his head and slump of his shoulders that made him seem somehow quite alien. He wore a sort of plain olive frock-coat over a black vest and trousers.

He spoke a few words of gibberish. When Glim didn't answer, he reached into the pocket of his coat and withdrew a small glass vial. He pantomimed drinking it and then handed it to Glim.

Glim took it, wondering how it would feel to kill the man. He surely wouldn't get far . . .

But if they wanted to talk to him, they must want him alive.

He drank the stuff, which tasted like burning orange peel.

The fellow waited for a moment, then cleared his throat. "Can you understand me now?"

"Yes," Mere-Glim said.

"I'll get directly to the point," the man said. "It has been no-ticed that you are of an unknown physical type, or at least one that hasn't been seen in my memory, which is quite long."

"I'm an Argonian," he said.

"A word," the man said. "Not a word that signifies to me."

"That is my race."

"Another word I do not know." The little man cocked his head. "So it is true, then? You are from outside? From someplace other than Umbriel?"

"I'm from here, from Tamriel."

"Exciting. Another meaningless word. This is Umbriel, and no place else."

"Your Umbriel is in my world, in my country, Black Marsh."

"Is it? I daresay it isn't. But as interesting as this subject may be to you, it holds little appeal for me. What I'm interested in is what you are. What part of Umbriel you will become."

"I don't understand."

"You aren't the first newcomer here, but you may be the first with that sort of body. But Umbriel will remember your body, and others with similar corpora will come along in time—many or a few, depending on what use you are."

"What if I'm of no use at all?"

"Then we can't permit Umbriel to learn your form. We must cut your body away from what inhabits it and send it back out into the void."

"Why not simply let me go? Return me to Tamriel? Why kill me?"

"Ah, a soul is too precious for that. We could not think of letting one waste. Now, tell me about this form of yours."

"I am as you see me," he replied.

"Are you some sort of daedra?"

Glim gaped his mouth. "You know what daedra are?" He asked. "The man we talked to below didn't."

"Why should he?" the man said. "We have incorporated daedra in the past, but none exist here now. *Are* you daedra?"

"No."

"Very well, good, that makes things less complicated. Those spines on your head. What is their function?"

"They make me handsome, I suppose, to others of my race. More to some than to others. I try to take care of them."

"And that membrane between your fingers?"

"For swimming."

"Swimming?"

"Propelling oneself through water. My toes are webbed as well."

"You move through water?" The fellow blinked.

"Often."

"Beneath the surface?"

"Yes."

"How long can you remain beneath before having to surface for air?"

"Indefinitely. I can breathe water."

The fellow smiled. "Well, you see, how interesting. What Umbriel lacks, it will seek out."

Glim shifted on his feet, but since he didn't understand what the man was talking about, he didn't answer.

"The sump. Yes, I think you might do well in the sump. But let's finish the interview, shall we? Now, your skin—those are scales, are they not?"

PART II

PURPOSE

ONE

———

He saw the blow coming from the shift of the Redguard's shoulder, but it was fast, so fast his dodge to the right almost didn't succeed, and although the edge didn't bite, the flat skimmed his bicep. He swung his sword at her ribs, but that same quickness danced her just beyond the reach of his blade.

"Right idea, Attrebus," he heard Gulan shout.

She backed off a bit, her gaze fixed on his. "Yes," she said. "Try that again."

"Got your breath yet?"

"I'll have yours in a minute," she replied. She appeared to relax, but then suddenly blurred into motion.

He backpedaled, but once again her speed surprised him. He caught her attack on the flat of his weapon and felt the weight of her steel smack against the guard. Then she was past, and he knew she would take a cut at his head from back there, so he dropped, rolled, and came back up.

He saw it again, that slight slumping before she renewed her attack. Again he parried and broke the distance, but not quite so much.

She circled, he waited. Her shoulders sagged, and he suddenly threw himself forward behind his blade, so that while she was starting to step and lift her weapon, his point hit her solar plexus and she went down, hard.

He followed her and—as his people cheered—put the dull, rounded point in her face.

"Yield?"

She coughed and winced. "Yield," she agreed.

He offered her his hand and she took it.

"Nice attack," she said. "I'm glad we were at blunts."

"You're very fast," he said. "But you have a little tell."

"I do?"

"Well, I'm not sure I want you to know," he said. "Next time it might not be blunts."

She seemed to be favoring one foot, so he offered her his shoulder. He helped her limp over to the edge of the practice ground, where his comrades watched from their ale-benches.

"Bring us each a beer, will you?" he called to Dario the pitcher-boy.

"Aye, Prince," he replied.

He sat her down a bit apart from the others and watched as she unlaced her practice armor.

"What was your name again?" he asked her.

"Radhasa, Prince," she replied.

"And your father was Tralan the Two-Blade, from Cespar?"

"Yes, Prince," she replied.

"He was a good man, one of my father's most valued men."

"Thank you, highness. It's nice to hear that."

He focused his regard on her more frankly as the armor came off. "He was not the handsomest of men. In that, you don't resemble him much."

Her already dark face darkened a bit more, but her eyes stayed fixed boldly on his. "So, you . . . think I'm a handsome man?"

"If you were a man you would be, but I don't see much mannish about you either."

"I've heard the prince is a flatterer."

"Here's our drink," he said as Dario arrived with the beer.

Beer always tasted perfect after a fight, and this time was no different.

"So why do you seek my service instead of my father's?" he asked her. "I'm sure he would receive you well."

She shrugged. "Prince Attrebus, your father sits the throne as Emperor. In his service, I think I would see little in the way of action. With you, I expect rather the opposite."

"Yes," he said, "that is true. The Empire is still reclaiming territory, both literally and figuratively. There are many battles yet to fight before our full glory is reclaimed. If you ride with me, death will always be near. It's not always fun, you know, and it's not a game."

"I don't think that it is," she said.

"Very good," he said. "I like your attitude."

"I hope to please you, Prince."

"You can start pleasing me by calling me simply Attrebus. I do not stand on ceremony with my personal guard."

Her eyes widened. "Does that mean . . . ?"

"Indeed. Finish this beer and then go see Gulan. He will see you equipped, horsed, and boarded. And then, perhaps, you and I shall speak again."

———

Annaïg saw the murder from the corner of her eye.

She was preparing a sauce of clams, butter, and white wine to go on thin sheets of rice noodle. Of course, none of those things were exactly that; the clams were really something called "lampen," but they tasted much like clams. The butter was actually the fat rendered from something which—given Slyr's description—was some sort of pupa. The wine was wine, and it was white, but it wasn't made from any grape she had ever tasted. The noodles were made from a grain a bit like barley and a bit like rice. She was just happy to be doing something more sophisticated than searing meat, and actually enjoying the alien tastes and textures. The possibilities were exciting.

Qijne was at the corner of her vision, and she made a sort of gesture, a quick wave of her arm.

But then something peculiar happened. Oorol, the underchef whose territory was Ghol Manor, suddenly lost his head. Literally—it fell off, and blood jetted in spurts from the still-standing body.

Qijne stepped away from the corpse as a hush fell over the kitchen. She watched what was left of Oorol fold down to the floor.

"Not good," Slyr murmured.

Qijne's voice rose up, a shriek that somehow still carried words in it.

"Lord Ghol was bored by his prandium! For the fourth time in a row!"

She stood there, staring around, her chest heaving and her eyes flickering murderously about the room.

"And now we have a mess to clean up and an underchef to replace."

Her jittering gaze suddenly focused on Annaïg.

"Oh, sumpslurry," Slyr faintly breathed. "No."

"Slyr," Qijne shouted. "Take this station. Bring her with you."

"Yes, Chef!" Slyr shouted back. She turned and began gathering her knives and gear.

"Now we're in it," Slyr said. "Deep in it."

"She k-killed him," Annaïg stuttered.

"Yes, of course."

"What do you mean, 'of course'?"

"Look, we cook for three lords, right? Prixon, Oroy, and

Ghol. Most of what we make is for their staff and slaves. That's all you and I have been cooking—that's all I've ever cooked. That's not too dangerous. But feeding the lords themselves is—it's not easy. It's not only that they are feckless in their tastes, but they compete with one another constantly. Fashions in ingredients, flavor, presentation, color—all these can change very quickly. And now we're cooking for Ghol, who doesn't know what he likes. Oorol was pretty good—he managed to entertain Ghol for the better part of a year."

Annaïg tried to do the calculations in her head; from various conversations, she reckoned the Umbrielian year at just over half a year on Tamriel.

"That's not very long," she said.

"It's not. Hurry, now, we've got to subdue his staff, find out what they know, and have an acceptable dinner for him."

"How did she—what did she kill him with?"

"We call it her filet knife, but no one really knows. You can't see it, can you? And at times it seems longer than others. We're not quite sure how long it can get. Now come along, unless you have more useless questions to slow us down and speed us toward the sump."

"I do have a question. I don't think it's useless."

"What?" the chef snapped impatiently.

"When you say we have to subdue his staff—"

"We'll see. It might mean a fight. Have a knife in your hand, but hold it discreetly."

———

Slyr's previous staff had consisted of six cooks. Their new staff had eight—Annaïg and Slyr made ten.

In this case, "subduing" them simply meant calming them down and getting them to work, which Slyr managed with a minimum of slapping around, so they were soon discussing the lord's tastes, or at least what little seemed consistent about them. To make things even more fun, it turned out he was having another of the lords—one who used another kitchen entirely—over for dinner, and about him, they knew nothing.

"What was the last thing he liked?" Slyr asked Minn, who had been Oorol's second.

"A broth suspire made from some sort of beast the taskers brought," Minn said. "There was an herb, too."

"Ah. From outside."

"Can you describe them?" Annaïg asked. "The beast and the herb?"

"I can show them to you," Minn replied. They walked over to the cutting counter.

"That's a hedgehog," Annaïg said. "The plant"—she crushed the pale green leaves between her fingers and smelled them—"eucalyptus."

"But we used both again today, and you saw the result."

"You reason from that that he's tired of these things?" Slyr asked. "Were they prepared in the same way?"

"Not at all. We toasted the bones to reveal the marrow and infused all with a vapor of the—ah—youcliptus?"

"That doesn't sound good at all," Annaïg said.

Slyr rolled her eyes. "Quickly now, I don't need to say this again, so get it the first time. Some in Umbriel—us, the slaves, the laborers and tenders, farmers and harvesters, fishers and such—we eat things of gross substance. Meat, grain, vegetable matter. The greatest lords of this city dine only on infusions and distillations of spirituous substance. But between us and them there are the lower lords and ladies who still require matter to consume, but also have some degree of *liquor spiritualis* infused in their diet. But because they desire the highest status—which most will never achieve— they pretend to it, preferring to dine mostly on vapors, scents, gases.

Of course, they must consume some amount of substance. They like broths, marrows, gelatins—" She sighed. "Enough. I will explain more later. For now we have to make something." She turned to Minn. "What else can you tell me of his tastes?"

In the end they made a dish of three things: a foam of the roe of an Umbrielian fish, delicate crystals like spherical snowflakes made of sugar and twelve other ingredients that would sublimate on touching the tongue, and a cold, thin broth of sixteen herbs— including the eucalyptus—which had the aroma of each ingredient but tasted like nothing at all.

The servers took it away, leaving Slyr wringing her hands.

With good cause, because as they were all turning in for the night, Qijne found Annaïg and Slyr.

"It bored him," she said. "Again, he's bored. Make it right, will you?"

And then she left.

"We're dead," Slyr moaned. "Dead already."

Annaïg was light-headed, almost to the point of being sick. Her teeth felt on edge from the foreign, probably toxic elements she had been handling. When she closed her eyes, she kept seeing Oorol's head come off, and the blood, and his strange, slow slump to the floor.

In her third hour of sleeplessness, she felt her amulet wake against her skin.

———

The slippery voice of a nightbird drew the sleep from Attrebus and delivered it to the moons. He rose, taking a moment to study Radhasa's slumbering form. Then he went out on the balcony to gaze out at the darkened but still-wondrous city, at the White-Gold Tower rising to meet the stars. He'd chosen this villa for just this view. He loved looking at the palace—not so much being in it.

A glance to the left showed him Gulan's silhouette, at the far end of the balcony, which fronted several rooms.

"Surely you aren't on guard," Attrebus said.

"She's new," his friend answered, nodding his head toward Attrebus's room. "Your father wouldn't approve."

"My father believes that anything between a commander and one of his soldiers weakens his authority. I believe that friends fight better and more loyally than mere employees. I drink with my warriors, share their burdens. You and I are friends. Do you think I'm weak?"

Gulan shook his head. "No, but we are not—ah—so intimate."

Attrebus snorted. "Intimate? You and I are far more intimate that Radhasa and me. Sex is sex, just another kind of fight. I love all of my people equally, you know, but not for all of the same qualities. Radhasa has qualities that inspire a particular kind of friendship."

"So do Corintha, Cellie, and Fury."

"Yes, and there is no jealousy there, no more than if I play cards with Lupo instead of Eiswulf." He cocked his head. "Why bring this up now? Do you know something I don't?"

Gulan shook his head. "No," he replied. "That's just me, a worrier. You're right, they all love you, and she'll be no different."

"Still, it's good you can tell me these worries," Attrebus said. "I'm not afraid to hear what you're thinking, not like my father, surrounded by his flunkies who tell him only what he wants to hear. I love him, Gulan, and I respect him for everything he's done. But it's the things he hasn't done, won't do . . ." He trailed off.

"This is about Arenthia, isn't it?"

"We only need a small force," Attrebus said. "A thousand, let's say. The locals will rise and fight with us, I know they will—and then we gain a foothold in Valenwood."

"Give him time. He may yet come around."

"I'm restless, Gulan. We haven't done anything worthy of us in months. And yet there's so much to be done!"

"Perhaps he has plans for you here, Treb."

"What sort of plans? What have you heard?"

Gulan's lips pulled back from his teeth.

"What?"

"Some say it's time for you to marry."

"Marry? Why in the world would I want to do that? I'm only twenty-two, for pity's sake."

"You're the crown prince. You're expected to produce an heir."

"Has my father talked to you about this? Behind my back? Did he tell you to put this in my ear?"

Gulan drew back a bit. "No, of course not. But there are rumors in the court. I hear them."

"There are always rumors in the court. That's why I hate it so."

"You'll have to get used to it someday."

"Not anytime soon. Maybe never—maybe I'll perish gloriously in battle before it comes to that."

"That's not funny, Treb. You shouldn't talk like that."

"I know," he sighed. "I'll go to court soon, see if he's planning on saying anything to my face. And if he won't give us the men to go to Arenthia, maybe he'll let us go north to train. There are plenty of bandits up around Cheydinhal. It would be something."

Gulan nodded, and Attrebus clapped him on the shoulder.

"I didn't mean to accuse you of anything, old friend. It's just that, when it comes to matters like this, I find myself unaccountably irritated."

"No harm," Gulan said.

"I think I'm okay here," he said. "I've subdued her. Go to bed."

Gulan nodded and vanished into his room. Attrebus stayed at the rail, contemplating the night sky and hoping Gulan was wrong. Marriage? It could be forced on him. Would his father do that? It didn't really matter, he supposed. He wouldn't let a wife keep him home, away from his proper business. If that was his father's intention, he was going to be disappointed.

A faint whir caught his attention, and he turned to find what at first seemed a large insect darting toward him. He leapt back, suppressing a cry, his hand going for a weapon that wasn't there.

But then it settled on the balustrade, and he saw that it was something much more curious—a bird made all of metal. It was exquisite, really. It sat there, staring at him with its artificial eyes. It seemed to be expecting something from him.

He noticed that there was a little hinged door, like an oddly shaped locket.

He reached, then hesitated. It could be some sort of bizarre assassin's device—he might open it to find a poisoned needle pricking him, or some dire magic unleashed.

But that seemed a little complicated. Why not put poison on the bird's talon and have it scratch him? It could have done that if it had wanted to. Still . . .

He went back into his room, found his dagger, and returning with it and standing to the side, flipped the locket open.

The bird chirped a bright little tune, then fell silent. Otherwise, nothing happened. Inside was a dark, glassy surface.

"What are you?" he wondered aloud.

But it didn't answer, so he decided to leave it where it was and have Yerva and Breslin examine it in the morning—they knew a lot more about this sort of thing than he did.

As he turned to go, however, he heard a woman's voice, so faint he couldn't make it out. He thought for a moment it was Radhasa, waking, but it came again, and this time he was sure it was coming from behind him. From the bird.

He went back and peered into the opening.

"Hello?" the voice came.

"Yes, hello," he said. "Who is this?"

"Oh, thank the Divines," the woman said. "I had almost

given up hope. It's been so long."

"Are you—ah— Look, I feel silly talking to a bird. Can you get to that right off? And perhaps talk a bit louder?"

"I'm sorry, I can't talk louder. I don't want to be discovered. That's Coo you have there; she's enchanted, and I have this locket with me, so we can speak to one another. If it were lighter, we could see each other as well. I can sort of make out your head."

"I don't see anything."

"Yes, it's pitch-dark here."

"Where? Where are you?"

"We're still over Black Marsh, I think. I've only had a few glimpses of the outside."

"*Over* Black Marsh?"

"Yes. There's a lot to explain, and it's urgent. I sent Coo to find Prince Attrebus . . ." The voice faltered. "Oh, my. You *are* the prince, aren't you? Or else Coo wouldn't have opened."

"Indeed, I am Prince Attrebus."

"Your highness, forgive me for addressing you in such a familiar manner."

"That's no matter. And who might you be?"

"My name is Annaïg—Annaïg Hoïnart."

"And you're in some sort of captivity?"

"Yes—yes, Prince Attrebus. But it's not me I'm worried about. I have a lot to tell you and not much time before dawn. I believe our entire world is in terrible danger."

"I'm listening," he replied.

And he did listen as her husky lilt carried him through the night across the Cyrodiil and fetid Black Marsh, to a place beyond imagination and a terror the mind shuddered to grasp. And when at last she had to go, and the moons were wan ghosts in a milky sky, he straightened and looked off east. Then he went to his wardrobe-room, where Terz his dresser was just waking.

"I'll be going to court," he told Terz.

———

Titus Mede had been—and was—many things. A soldier in an outlaw army, a warlord in Colovia, a king in Cyrodiil, and Emperor.

And to Attrebus, a father. They looked much alike, having the same lean face and strong chin, the same green eyes. He'd gotten his own slightly crooked nose and blond hair from his mother; his father's hair was auburn, although now it was more than half silver.

His father sat back in his armchair. He removed the circlet from his curly locks, rubbed his thickly lined forehead, and sighed.

"Black Marsh?"

"Black Marsh, Father, that's what she said."

"Black Marsh," he repeated, settling the crown back on his head. "Well, then?"

"Well what, sire?"

"Well, then, why are we discussing this?" He turned his head toward his minister, an odd, pudgy man with thick eyebrows and mild blue eyes. "Hierem, can you tell me why we're discussing this?"

Hierem sniffed. "I've no idea, majesty," he said. "Black Marsh is rather a thorn in our side, isn't it? The Argonians refuse our protection. Let them deal with their problems."

Something swept through Attrebus so strong he couldn't identify it at first. But then he understood: certainty. Before there was a question about who Annaïg might actually be, what her motives were. She could easily have been some sort of sorceress, tricking him to his doom.

He'd wanted to believe her—his every instinct told him she was genuine. Now he knew his instincts were dead-on, once again.

"You already knew about this," he accused.

"We've heard things," the minister replied.

"Heard th . . ." He sputtered off. "Father—a flying city, an army of walking dead—this doesn't concern you?"

"You said they were moving north, toward Morrowind and at a snail's pace. Our reports say the same. So no, I'm not concerned."

"Not even enough to send a reconnaissance?"

"The Synod and College of Whispers have both been tasked to discover what they can," Hierem said. "And of course some specialists are on their way. But there is no need for a military expedition until they threaten our borders—certainly not one led by the crown prince."

"But Annaïg may not survive that long."

"So it's the girl?" Hierem said. "That's why you want to mount an expedition into Black Marsh? For the sake of a girl?"

"Don't speak to me like that, Hierem," Attrebus warned. "I am your prince, after all. You seem to forget that."

"It's not the girl," his father snorted. "It's the *adventure*. It's the book they'll write about it, the songs they will sing."

Attrebus felt his cheeks burn. "Father, that's nonsense. You say it's not our problem, but when it's made everyone in Black Marsh and Morrowind into corpse-warriors, it will then turn on us. Every day we wait its army grows stronger. Why not fight a small battle now rather than a huge one later?"

"Are you now lecturing *me* on strategy and tactics?" his father snapped. "I took this city with under a thousand men. I routed Eddar Olin's northward thrust with barely twice that, and I hammered this empire back together with a handful of rivets. Do not dare to question that I have this situation in hand."

"Besides," Hierem added, "you don't know that it is coming here at all, *Prince*. It seems to have come from nowhere, probably it will return there."

"That's a stupid assumption to make."

"If it comes for any part of the Empire, we will be ready for it," the Emperor said. "You will not chase after this thing. That is my last word on the matter."

The tone was final. Attrebus glared at his father and the minister, then, after the most perfunctory of bows, he spun on his heel and left.

He sat outside on the steps for a few moments, trying to cool off, get his thoughts together. He was almost ready to leave when he looked up at approaching footsteps.

It was a young man with a thin ascetic face, freckles, and red hair. He wore an Imperial uniform.

"Treb!"

Attrebus stood and the two clapped each other in a hug.

"You're thin, Florius," he said. "Your mother's not feeding you anymore?"

"Not so much. It's mostly your father doing that now."

Treb stepped back and regarded his old friend. "You made captain! Congratulations."

"Thank you."

"I should never have let my father have you," Attrebus said. "You should be riding with me."

"I should like that," Florius said. "It's been a long time since we had an adventure together. Do you remember that time we snuck off into the market district—"

"I remember my father's guards dragging us back by the ears," Attrebus said. "But if you want to arrange a transfer . . ."

"I've been assigned to command the garrison at Water's Edge," Florius said. "But maybe when that assignment's done."

"I'll come looking for you," Attrebus said. "Divines, it's good to see you Florius."

"Do you have time for a drink?"

He paused, then shook his head. "No—I need to see to something right now. But I will see you in future."

"Right, then," Florius said, and the two men parted company.

Attrebus nodded to himself and went to meet Gulan. He

found him near the gate.

"How did it go?" Gulan asked.

"Gather everyone at my house in Ione. We can supply there and be on our way by tomorrow. Be quiet about it."

"That well, eh?" He shifted. "You're going against the Emperor's wishes? Are you sure you want to do that?"

"I've done it before."

"Which is why he's likely to suspect, and have you watched."

"Which is why we're being discreet. Disperse the guard as if I've given them a holiday, and have them come individually to Ione. You and I will take the way through the sewers."

Gulan looked doubtful but he nodded.

Attrebus clapped him on the shoulder.

"You'll see, old friend. This will be our greatest victory yet."

TWO

———

"You're the new skraw," the man said. It wasn't a question.

Mere-Glim nodded, trying to size the fellow up. He looked more or less like one of Annaïg's race, although with a noticeable yellowish cast to his skin and eyes. He had a long, doleful face and red hair. He was wearing the same black loincloth that Glim now wore.

"My name is Mere-Glim," he offered.

"Yeah? You can call me Wert. And what are you, Mere-Glim? They say you don't need the vapors."

They'd been walking through a stone corridor, but now they entered a modest cave. Water poured from an opening in the wall, ran in a stream across the floor, and vanished into a pool in the middle of the chamber. Several globes of light were fixed to the ceiling, nearly obscured by the ferns growing around them. The rest of the cave was felted in moss. Mere-Glim found it pleasant.

"Eh?"

Glim realized he'd been asked a question.

"My people call ourselves Saxhleel," he said. "Others call us Argonians. I'm not sure what you mean by vapors."

"You didn't come out of the sump," Wert said. "Nothing like

you has ever come out of the sump. Which means you ain't from Umbriel, ain't that so?"

"It is," Glim replied.

"So I reckon you're one o' them they was searching for, down below."

"They found us."

"Makes you—well, there ain't no word for it, is there? A From-Somewhere-Elser. Well, then, welcome to the sump. Lovely place to work." He chuckled, but that turned abruptly into a nasty cough. He covered his mouth with the back of his hand, and Glim noticed it came away bloody.

"Vapors," Wert explained.

"What are they?"

"Well, see, I'm told you can breathe down there. But none of us can, not without the vapors. We go to the yellow cave, and we breathe 'em in for a while, and then we can stay under until they wear off."

"How long is that?"

"Depends. A few hours, usually. Long enough to get some work done."

"So what do we do?"

"Well, I'm to show you, I am," Wert said. "That's where we're on to right now. I'll go take the vapors—I won't be back here, because if I don't get in the water right away, I'll suffocate. So you just swim out and wait for me. Don't wander by yourself. And please don't try to run away. You won't make it, and I'll pay the price."

He watched Wert go, then walked over to the pool and lowered himself in, letting the mild current take him along. The pool bent into a tube, and he could see light ahead. A moment later he emerged in shallow water, just about as deep as he was tall.

The sump spread out before him, a nearly perfectly circular lake in the bottom of a cone-shaped cavity. Umbriel City climbed up and away from him in all directions. Some of it hung above him. He thought that if crows could build cities, they would look something like this—vain, shiny, lopsided, brash, and bragging.

A few moments later Wert's head appeared a few yards out. He gestured for Glim to follow.

The shallows teemed with strange life: slender, swaying amber rods covered in cilia, swimmers that seemed like some strange cross of fish and butterfly, living nets composed of globes propelling themselves with water-jets and dragging fine webs between them, centipede-things as long as his arm and little shrimplike things no bigger than his thumb-claw.

He stopped when he saw the body. At first he saw only a thick school of silver fish, but they parted at his approach. It had been a woman with dark skin and hair; now bones were showing in places and worms clustered on exposed organs. Shuddering, he turned away, but then he saw another, similar swarm of fish. And another to his right. He started at something in the edge of his vision, but it was only Wert.

"They drop the bodies from above or send them down the slides. This is where they start." His voice was weird, thick with the water in his lungs.

"Why were they killed?"

"What do you mean? Most just died of something or other. I suppose a few mighta been executed. But this is where we all end, ain't it—in the sump." He waved his hand vaguely. "We collect a lot of stuff for the kitchens here. Orchid shrimp, Rejjem sap, Inf fronds. Other things we fish for deeper, especially shear-teeth. You'll learn about that, but mostly you'll work in the deep sump. That's perfect for you. So come on, let's go to the Drop."

They swam on, with the water getting gradually deeper at first. He didn't have to be told what the Drop was—he knew it when he saw it. The sump became a steeply curving cone that drove deep into the stone of Umbriel. And at the very bottom, in the narrowest place, an actinic light flashed, like a ball of lightning.

"What's that?" he asked.

"That's the conduit to the ingenium," Wert said. "The sump takes care of our bodies—the ingenium takes care of our souls and keeps the world running. I'd stay well clear of the conduit, if I was you. Or me, now that I think of it."

Well, Glim thought. There's something Annaïg would want to report to her prince. If only I had some way of talking to her. He glanced at Wert; he seemed not to be a bad fellow, but in the bigger picture—Annaïg's picture—that wouldn't matter. Though Wert could temporarily breathe underwater, his body was clumsy, not built for swimming. Glim knew he could easily escape him. If he killed him first, that would probably give him more time.

But if he survived long enough to find Annaïg and give her this bit of news, then what? How could he hide when he was the only one of his kind on Umbriel? He couldn't. Not for long.

No, before he did something like that he'd need to have a lot more information to pass on. Could the ingenium be damaged from the sump? From anywhere? If so, how?

They descended about two-thirds of the way down the sump, and Wert began moving toward what appeared to be translucent sacs stuck to the wall. There were hundreds of them, maybe thousands, in all shapes and sizes. As he drew nearer, he could make out vague forms within the sacs.

"These are being born," Wert said.

Curious, Glim moved closer, and to his astonishment found himself looking into a face. The eyes were closed, the features not fully formed, but it wasn't a child's face; it was that of an adult—just softer, flabbier than most. It was also hairless.

"I don't understand."

Wert grinned, plucked something from the water, and handed it to Glim. It was a sort of worm, very soft. It pulsed in and out, and with every contraction, a little jet of water squirted from one end of it. Other than that, it was featureless.

"That's a proform," Wert said. "When someone dies, the inge-nium calls one of these down to the conduit and gives it a soul. It comes back up here and attaches to the wall, and someone grows."

"That's interesting," Glim said. He looked at the proform. "You all start as this? No matter what you end up looking like? This is what you really are?"

"You've got funny questions in your head," Wert said. "We are what we are."

"And everyone is born like this?"

"Everyone, from lord and lady to me and—well, not you. At least not yet."

"How are they born?"

"Well, that's one of your jobs—to recognize when one of these is about to start breathing. You can tell by the color of the sac—it gets a sheen, like this one. Then you swim that up to the birth pool—that's another cave up in the shallows."

"What if you don't do it in time?"

"They die, of course. That's why this job is the most impor-tant, really. And it's why you're so suited for it, see? Nah, they won't waste you much on gathering. This is where you'll be." He doubled over suddenly, and Glim realized he was coughing. A dark stain spread from his mouth and nostrils.

"Are you okay?"

Wert gradually unfolded, then nodded.

"Why do the vapors hurt you like that?"

"Why is water wet? I don't know. But I have to go up soon. Not lasting so long, this time. So let's go see the birthing pool."

As they started back up, Glim glanced back down toward the light, but he didn't see it. Instead he saw a maw full of teeth gaping at him.

"Xhuth!" he gargled, jerking himself to the side and stroking hard to turn.

The fish turned, too, but not before he saw the thing was

fifteen feet long, at least. Its tail was long, whiplike, and it had two great swimming fins set under it, like a whale.

But those teeth would shame a shark to blush.

"Sheartooth!" Wert shouted. "You've made it mad somehow."

Glim swam desperately, but the head kept right toward him, so he slashed at it with his claws. They caught but didn't tear the creature's tough hide. He let go, then struck again, this time at the back, behind the head, and there he dug in. It couldn't bite him there.

It could try, though. It thrashed like a snake in a hot skillet; he saw Wert stab at it with his spear, only to be struck by the tail. The skraw went limp in the water.

Wonderful.

He was starting to get dizzy and his arms and shoulders were aching. He'd have to do something soon.

Here's hoping your belly is softer, he thought. He let go with one set of claws and swung underneath. He was almost thrown clear, but one of the fins actually buffeted him back to the belly, and he slashed with all his might. Again his claws caught. He sank in the other hand.

The sheartooth gyred into a loop, and the force was such that he knew he could only hold on for another few seconds.

But the same force dragged Glim down the belly, opening it up like a gutting knife, and he was engulfed in a cloud of blood.

He kicked hard and swam free of the still-twisting monster, but it had lost interest in him, focusing instead on its own demise.

He realized suddenly that he'd forgotten Wert.

He had drifted down fifty or sixty feet. His eyes were closed and his chest was moving oddly.

Glim slung Wert over his back and kicked straight for the surface. He could feel the man quivering on his back. The light of the sun seemed a long way off.

He burst into air and reversed his hold, keeping Wert's head

out of the sump as he vomited water from his lungs and began
to struggle. His eyes opened, looking wild. He began to make a
horrible sucking sound that wasn't breathing.

"Should I take you back under?" Glim asked.

Wert shook his head violently, but Glim wasn't sure if that
meant yes or no.

But then he seemed to draw a real breath, and then another.
They reached the shallows, where Glim could stand and Wert
could lean against him.

"Shearteeth—usually not so vicious," he said. "Usually don't
attack us. Something about you set it off. Maybe because the sump
was still learning you. Thought you were—intruder."

He glanced at Glim. "Thanks, by the way. I wouldn't have
made it back up."

"I thought you were going to die anyway."

"It's always bad between," Wert explained. "You don't want
to be underwater when you start breathing air again, but then
again, you still can't breathe air."

"That's horrible," Glim said. "There must be some better way
to do this."

"Sometimes a lord or lady will come down for a swim, and
they have other ways, not like the vapors. But the vapors are
cheap, my friend. And so are we—always more of us being born.
You're different—for now."

"For now?"

"Well, the sump knows you now. So does the ingenium. I
wouldn't be surprised to see a few more of your sort, pretty soon.
And when there are enough of you—well, you'll be cheap, too."

THREE

When Attrebus, Gulan, and Radhasa arrived at Ione, dawn was just leaking into the sky. It was cool, and the breeze smelled of dew and green leaves. A rooster gave notice to the hens it was time to face the day. The town was waking, too—smoke from hearths coiled up through the light fog and people were already about in the streets.

"It's not much to look at, this town," Radhasa noticed.

Attrebus nodded. Ione wasn't picturesque; a few of the houses were rickety wooden structures faded gray, but most were of stone or brick and simply built. Even the small chapel of Dibella was rather plain.

"It's not very old," he said. "There wasn't anything here at all fifty years ago. Then—well, do you know what that is?"

They had reached the town square, and he didn't have to point to indicate what he was asking about.

The square was mostly stone, oddly cracked and melted as if from terrible heat or some stranger force. Two bent columns projected up in the middle, each about ten feet high, and together they resembled the truncated horns of an enormous steer.

"Yes, I've seen them before—the ruins of an Oblivion gate."

"Right. Well, when this one opened, it opened right in the

middle of a company of soldiers recalled from the south to fortify
the Imperial City. More than half of them were killed, including
the commander. They would have all died, but a captain named
Tertius Ione managed to pull the survivors together and withdraw.
But rather than retreat all the way to the Imperial City, he instead
recruited farmers and hunters from the countryside and Pell's
Gate. Then he made them into something more than what they
were. They returned and slaughtered the daedra here, and when
they were done with that, he led them through the gate itself."

"Into Oblivion?"

"Yes. He'd heard that the gate at Kvatch had been closed somehow by entering it. So Ione went in with about half of his troops
and left the rest here, to guard against anything else coming out."

"It looks like he closed it."

"It closed, but Captain Ione was never seen again. One of
his men—a Bosmer named Fenton—appeared weeks later, half
dead and half mad. From what little he said that made sense, they
reckoned Ione and the rest sacrificed themselves to give Fenton
the chance to sabotage the portal. The Bosmer died the next day,
raving. Anyway, Ione was gone for a long time before the gate
exploded, and in the meantime his company built some fortifi-
cations and simple buildings. Once the gate was gone, it was a
convenient and relatively safe place, so a lot of people stayed, and
over time the town grew."

He turned about, spreading his arms. "That's why I like this
Ione. Because it's new, because it speaks to the spirit of heroism
that lies at the heart of each of us. Yes, there are no quaint old
buildings or First Era statues, but it's an honest place built by
brave people."

"And you have a house here?" Radhasa asked.

"A hunting lodge, in the hills just across town."

"That's quite a hunting lodge," the Redguard said when they entered the gate.

Something about the tone irked him, made him feel a bit defensive. It wasn't that big. It was built on the plan of an ancient Nord longhouse, each beam and cornice festooned with carvings of dragons, bulls, boars, leering wild men, and dancing, long-tressed women.

"I suppose after the simplicity of Ione, it comes as a bit of a shock," Attrebus admitted. "My uncle built it about fifteen years ago. He used to bring me down here, and left it to me when he died."

"No, I didn't mean to criticize it."

And yet, he somehow felt she had been critical of something. He pushed past it. There were other matters at hand now.

"They're all here, Gulan?" he asked.

"They are."

"And the provisions?"

"You had plenty in your stores. More than we can carry."

"Well, I don't see any reason to dally, then."

He raised his voice and spread his arms.

"It's good to have you with me, my brothers and sisters in arms," he called out. "Give us a shout. The Empire!"

"The Empire!" they erupted enthusiastically.

"Today we ride to the unknown, fellows. Against something I believe to be as deadly and dangerous to our world as that Oblivion gate down there was when it opened—maybe more so. We've never done anything this dangerous; I'll tell you that now."

"What is it, Treb?" That was Joun, an orc of prodigious size even for his race.

He settled his hands on his hips and lifted his chin. Then he laid it out for them.

When he was finished, the silence that followed had an odd, unfamiliar quality to it.

"I know there are only fifty-two of us," he said, "but just below us Captain Ione went into Oblivion with fewer than that and shut down that gate. The Empire expects no less from us—and we are better equipped in every way than he was. Even better, we have someone there, inside this monstrous thing—someone to lead us in, help us find the heart and rip it out. We can do this, friends."

"We're with you, Treb!" Gulan shouted, and the rest of them joined him, but it seemed, somehow, that a note was still missing. Had he finally asked too much of them?

No, they would follow him, and this would knit them all the more tightly as a band.

"An hour, my friends, to settle yourselves for the ride. Then we begin."

But as they dispersed, there seemed to be much furtive whispering.

———

The grass still sparkled with dew when they reached the Red Ring Road, the vast track that circumscribed Lake Rumare. Across the morning gold of the lake stood the Imperial City itself, a god's wagon-wheel laid down on an island in the center of the lake. The outer curve of the white wall was half in shadow, and he could make out three of what would—in any other city—be deemed truly spectacular guard towers. But those were dwarfed by the magnificent spoke of the wheel—the White-Gold Tower, thrusting up toward the unknowable heavens.

He saw Radhasa also staring at the tower.

"It was there before the city," he told her. "Long before. It is very old, and no one is quite sure what it does."

"What do you mean, 'what it does'?"

"Well—understand first I'm not a scholar of the tower."

"Understood. But you must know more than I."

"Well, some think that the White-Gold Tower—and some other towers around Tamriel—help, well, hold the world up, or something like that. Others believe that before the Dragon broke, the tower helped protect us from invasion from Oblivion."

"It holds up the world?"

"I'm not saying it right," he replied, realizing he couldn't actually remember the details of that tutorial. "They help keep Mundus—the World—from dissolving back into Oblivion. Or something like that. Anyway, everyone seems to agree it has power, but no one knows exactly what kind."

"Okay," she replied, and shrugged. "So how do we get to Black Marsh?"

"We'll come to a bridge in a bit and cross the Upper Niben. From there we'll take the Yellow Road southeast until we cross the Silverfish River. Then it's overland—no roads after that except the ones we make." He grinned at the thought of being in wild country again.

"I wish I knew more about Cyrodiil."

"Well, you have an opportunity to learn now."

She was silent for a moment. "This person—the spy on the floating island—how do you speak to them?"

"You don't believe me?"

"Of course I 'believe' you, my Pri—ah, Treb. I'm just curious. Do you have some sort of scrying ball, like in the old tales?"

"Something like that," he replied.

"Very mysterious," she answered.

"Must keep a bit of mystery," he replied.

"We certainly must," she said with a flirty grin.

———

At noon they stopped to water the horses in the springs near the overgrown ruins of Sardarvar Leed, where the ancient

Ayleid elves had once herded his ancestors, bred them for work and pleasure. Attrebus found a quiet spot and took the bird from his haversack.

He saw Annaïg's hands, working at some sort of dough, the cherry red fire pits beyond, and the hellish creatures that swarmed about the place. He dared not say anything now, but something in him needed to see what she saw, to make sure she was alive and well. His father and Hierem were right, in a way; this was in part about Annaïg. She'd picked him to send Coo to because she believed in him, because she knew that he would answer her prayers and do this thing that needed doing, even if that meant opposing his own father.

He had no intention of letting her down, and tonight, when they could whisper to each other across the leagues, he would give her the good news that he was on the way.

He was still thinking about that an hour later when he heard a dull *whump* and half of his men caught fire. For a moment he could only stare, as if watching a theatric. He saw Eres and Klau staggering, beating their hands at the blue flames that engulfed them, their mouths working to produce sounds unrecognizable as human. There was Gulan, not burning but trying to beat the fire off of Pash, but then he suddenly had strange quills growing from his back.

It finally settled through to his brain that they were ambushed, and he drew his sword, looking wildly for the enemy as arrows came whirring from every direction. Radhasa was still next to him, her own weapon drawn and an odd look of joy on her face.

The last thing he saw was her blade swinging toward his head.

———

He clambered up from black depths, but it was a slippery slope. He had little moments when he thought he was awake, but they were full of pain and strange movement, and in the end might have just been a dream within a dream, a little of the Dark Lady's whimsy. A little hope before the nightmares had him again.

Finally, though, he opened his eyes, and bright light filled them. His head throbbed furiously, and there was blood caked in his mouth and nostrils. He was facedown in the dirt and one eye was covered tightly by a cloth of some kind.

He tried to push up, but his hands were behind him, and from the pain in his wrists he knew they must be bound.

He tried to call out, but all that emerged was a croak.

"There you are," a feminine voice said. He flopped his head over and saw Radhasa, sitting against a tree, eating an apple. Her horse was behind her, and so was his, along with a Khajiit and a Bosmer he'd never seen before, speaking in low tones a few yards away.

"You tried to kill me," he said.

"No, I didn't. I hit you with the flat. Could just as easily have been the edge." She smiled. "I was supposed to kill you, though."

"Why?"

"If I told you that, then I *would* have to kill you," she replied. "Don't worry your pretty head about it, *Treb*."

"Where—what happened to the rest?"

"Ah, well, there's the pity. Some pretty good people just died for you."

He tried to understand that. "How many, traitor? How many of my people did you kill?"

"Well, unless you still count me—I'm thinking you don't—I would have to say everyone."

"Everyone?"

"Yep. Even little Dario." She licked juice from her fingers.

"He's just a boy!"

"Not anymore. Graduated with the rest of them."

"Why?" he sobbed. His eyes stung with tears.

"Again, not telling. A little mystery, remember? Like your

bird here." She smiled. "How does it work?"

"I'm going to kill you!" he screamed. "You hear me?"

He lifted his head to direct his shout to the strangers. "Did she tell you who I am? Do you know what you've done?"

Incredibly, they laughed.

"All right," Radhasa said. "Break's over. Get him horsed, fellows, and let's move along."

He tried to fight, but his head was ringing and his limbs were sapped of energy, but most of all he couldn't concentrate, couldn't get his mind to stand still. What was happening? This didn't happen, not to him. How could all of his friends be dead?

The horse started forward, and, slung over its back, he watched the wheel ruts in the road.

She was lying, of course. Gulan and the rest were probably tracking them. Some of them probably were dead, but most of them must have made it. He'd never lost more than three of his personal guard in one battle anywhere, including the Battle of Blinker Creek.

So she was lying, and they were coming. He just had to stay alive until they found him.

How long had he been out? Where were they?

The immediate answer to that last was that they were on a hunting trail of some sort, surrounded by massive oak and ash trees. The land rolled a bit, so it was a good guess they weren't in the Niben Valley anymore, which meant that he must have been unconscious for at least a few days.

His best guess was that they were somewhere in the West Weald, and by the sun, traveling mostly south.

So where were they going?

He looked to Radhasa, riding slightly ahead of him.

"You said you were supposed to kill me," he croaked. "Why didn't you?"

"Because I'm going to sell you," she replied. "I know a certain very eccentric Khajiit who collects people like you. He'll pay more than ten times what I was offered to kill you. So we're off to Elsweyr. Think of it as a holiday. A really, really long holiday that will be no fun at all."

"Radhasa," he said, "that's insane. People know what I look like. Someone between here and there is going to recognize me."

"You haven't seen your face since I whacked it," she replied. "Looks a little different at the moment. And we'll keep the bandages on. Once we get you where you're going, there's going to be a real limited selection of people you're likely to meet, and it won't matter to any of them who you are."

"My father," he said. "He'd pay more yet to get me back. Have you thought of that?"

"He might," she agreed. "But I don't think I would survive that. Too many resources at his disposal, too many ways to trap us."

"Those resources are bent on you already."

"No, not anytime soon, I think."

"When he finds the bodies—"

"Don't worry about that," she said. "It's covered." She chuckled.

"What are you laughing about?"

"Good thing you don't like being addressed as 'Prince,'" she replied. "Because you're never going to hear anyone call you *that* again."

She snapped her reins and broke into a trot. His horse, leaded to hers, followed suit.

FOUR

———

The day after talking with Attrebus, Annaïg felt energized, despite the lack of sleep. She went early to her work archiving the plants, animals, and minerals that appeared on her table every morning. She surveyed what was before her for a moment, then glanced up at the cabinets and drawers that climbed the wall to the ceiling.

"Luc," she said quietly.

The hob peered out of the empty cabinet it habitually slept in.

"Luc," it echoed.

"Luc, you know what's in all of those cabinets up there?"

"Luc knows."

"Do you find them by name?"

"If Luc has name."

"And if you don't have the name?" she pressed.

"Then describe—color, taste, smell."

"I see."

She thought about that for a moment, and then got some of the eucalyptus distillation they had used before.

"Smell this, Luc."

The creature wrinkled its wide nostrils at it.

"I don't know the name of what I'm looking for, but it is black and smells a bit like this. I want you to search the cabinets and bring me anything that fits that description, one container at a time."

"Yes, Luc find."

He bounded off, and Annaïg took a deep breath. She hadn't dared instruct the beast to bring things only when she was alone; it could tell Qijne, and that would raise questions.

Glim had been right about one thing—she needed to re-create the elixir that had allowed them to fly here. Once Attrebus was near, it might be the only way to reach him. In any case, she needed options. Being able to fly would be a big one.

She set to work on what was before her—arrowroot, silk leeches, and cypress needles. Luc brought her a bottle. She sniffed it, and got an intensely stringent, herbal, minty smell.

"Not that one," she said.

Luc bounded back off.

She remembered the sound of the prince's voice. He'd believed her, hadn't he? A prince. And he had talked to her like she was important. She'd always known that was how it would be, if they met, but to have it actually happen . . .

"You're awfully cheerful for a dead woman," Slyr commented from just behind her.

Annaïg jumped about a foot, her heart racing. "It's the lack of sleep," she said. "Makes me giddy." She lifted her pen and scribbled a few notes regarding the willow bark on the table in front of her.

"I need you."

"That's nice to hear," Annaïg replied. "But this is my time for cataloging. Remember?"

"Yes, well that was before we were put in charge if Lord Ghol's victuals," she snapped.

Annaïg shrugged. "If you think you can talk Qijne into releasing me from this duty, I won't argue."

"You're only saying that because you know I wouldn't dare."

"That's true," Annaïg replied. "On the other hand, Lord Ghol is bored, yes? We need something new, and that's likely to come from these things."

"Yes, well, Oorol was using the ingredients you identified, and it didn't help him."

"That's because he didn't understand them," she said. "Any more than you do."

Slyr stiffened, and for a moment Annaïg thought she had gone too far, but then the other woman relaxed. "You're right. That's why I need you. How often are you going to make me repeat it?"

"I'm in this, too."

"She won't kill you," Slyr replied. "She needs you."

"She's insane," Annaïg said. "You can't use logic to predict Qijne."

Slyr chuckled bitterly. "You've a big mouth," she said. "You may be right, but she's not entirely unpredictable—if she hears you said anything like that—"

"She won't," Annaïg said simply.

Slyr stepped back. "Really, you looked beaten and ready for the sump last night. Now you're full of sliwv. What happened last night? Did you cozy up to someone? Pafrex, maybe?"

"Pafrex? The bumpy fellow with quills?"

"Or maybe you've trained your hob . . . unconventionally?"

"Okay, that's disgusting," Annaïg said.

"Disgust," Luc chimed in. "Disgust is what?"

Annaïg felt a sudden flush. The hob was holding out a bottle of something black toward her.

"Just put that down, Luc," she said. "Forget that and fetch me that snake over there," she said.

"Luc!" the hob replied, bounding across the huge table to retrieve the viper she indicated.

Slyr was frowning down at her. Annaïg couldn't tell if it had anything to do with the bottle.

"Look," Annaïg said, "I am helping you. I've an idea."

"And what is that?" Slyr demanded.

Annaïg lifted the serpent carefully, behind the head, even though it was as stiff as a rod. Most of the animals came like this—not dead, but sort of paralyzed, frozen even though they weren't cold. Their hearts didn't beat and they didn't age. They had to be released from that state by a rod Qijne carried. Still, with something this deadly, it was hard for her to trust a spell she didn't understand.

"The Argonians call this a moon-adder," Annaïg explained. "When it bites, it injects venom that—in most beings—is almost instantly fatal. Argonians, however, can survive it, and in fact sometimes seek the venom out."

"Why would they do that?"

"It provides them daril, which means something like 'seeing everything in ecstasy.'"

"Ah. It is a drug, then. We have many of those, but they are not so much in fashion. Besides, we don't want to *poison* Ghol."

"No, no. I'm sure that would be bad. The venom is just a starting point. From what Glim told me, daril unfolds in stages, no stage like the last, and it confuses the senses. You see sounds, hear tastes, smell sights."

"Again, we have such drugs."

"The venom is transformed by a certain agent in Argonian blood—"

"If this is another attempt to find out where your friend is, I can only reiterate that not even Qijne knows where he is—or even has the ability to discover it."

"I know," Annaïg said, swallowing the sudden lump in her throat. "I don't actually need Argonian blood. I'm just explaining. It comes down to this: I think I can make a metagastrologic."

"This is a nonsense word."

"No. It's something I've read about, something the Ayleids— ancient people from my world—once used in their banquets."

"A drug."

"Yes, but the only sense that they affect is taste—nothing else. No general hallucination, no loss of clarity. Look, the essential flavors are sweet, sour, salty, and hot, right?"

"Of course. And with the lower lords like Ghol you can add dead, quick, and ethereat, at the same level."

"Really? How interesting." She wanted to know more about that, but didn't want her idea to lose momentum. "Anyway," she pushed on, "a good dish will still balance those essentials, yes?"

"Yes. Or contrast them."

"So with a metagastrologic, the first taste of the dish will have a certain balance of flavors, but as it lingers on the tongue, they begin to change. Salty is confused for sweet, ah—ethereat for hot, and so forth. And it will keep happening, different each time."

Slyr just looked at her for a long moment.

"You can do this?" she finally asked.

"Yes."

"Such a dish would have to be carefully thought out, so that no matter what inversion of flavors occurred, most would be pleasurable."

"It would require a chef of some skill," Annaïg agreed.

"Well," Slyr sighed, "it will not be boring, at least. I will go work on a foundation."

Annaïg tried not to watch her depart, but she finally stole a glance to make sure she was gone. Then she closed her eyes and thanked the gods, carefully opened the bottle, and smelled its contents.

"That's not it either, Luc," she said. "Keep trying. But—um, I'll ask you to see them, okay? I don't want you interrupting my chain of thought. Just keep them in your cabinet."

"Luc do," the hob said, and started toward the wall.

"First go and find the chef and tell her we need this snake quickened."

"Luc do." He bounded off.

A few moments later he came back following Qijne's hob, which had the baton. Annaïg placed the viper on the table, put the sharp edge of a cleaver on its neck, and touched it with the baton.

When it twitched to life, it jerked back and nearly slipped free, but its head caught and she put all her weight on the cleaver so the edge bit, then followed the skull back to the neck, slicing cleanly through. The body fell away, twitching, which gave the hobs something to hoot about.

She expressed the venom into a glass vial and set to work.

Hours passed, and so absorbed was she in the task that she hadn't realized Qijne was watching her.

"Chef?"

"What's your hob doing going through the cabinets? Everything up there is known to me already."

"But not to me," Annaïg answered. "And if I'm to be a proper cook to Lord Ghol, I need to be familiar with all of it."

Qijne's expression didn't change, but her glaze flickered down to Annaïg's work in progress.

"Not really doing anything you're supposed to do," she observed.

"This is for the meal," she said. "An additive."

"Explain."

Annaïg went back over the general properties of the meta-gastrologic.

The chef tilted her head slowly left, then right. "You're cooking, in other words. When you're supposed to be cataloging."

"I am, Chef."

"Which is not what I told you to do."

"No, Chef. But Slyr is worried—"

"Slyr? Slyr put you up to this?"

"No, Chef. It was my idea. We failed last night. I didn't want us to fail again."

"No, no of course not," Qijne said vaguely. Her eyes lost focus. "Carry on. Only know that if it does not please him, I will kill Slyr and cut off one of your feet, right?"

"Right, Chef."

"That's not a joke, if you think I'm joking."

"I don't think you're joking, Chef," Annaïg said.

———

After the meal went up, Slyr wandered off, her face pinched with fear. Annaïg slipped off, too, and had a look at her locket, but got nothing but darkness. She went back to the dormitory to wait for her meal.

A bit later Slyr rushed into the room.

"Come on," she said. "Come with me."

She followed the chef through the winding corridors and great pantries of the kitchen and into what appeared to be a wine cellar—there were thousands of bottles of something, anyway, racked all around her.

"Through here." Slyr was indicating a sort of hole in the wall just barely wide enough to slip through.

It led into a small chamber illuminated by faint light. Once in it, she could see the light came from the sky—the chamber was at the bottom of a high, narrow shaft.

Slyr handed her a bottle and a basket of something that smelled really good.

"He wasn't bored," she said. "In fact, he sent one of his servants to commend me." She looked up shyly. "Us."

"That's good news."

"News worth celebrating," Slyr said. "Try the wine."

It was dry and delicious, with a fragrance she couldn't quite place but that reminded her of anise. The basket was filled with pastry rolls stuffed with a sort of buttery meat.

"What is it?" she asked, holding up the roll she was eating.

"Orchid shrimp. They live in the sump."

"It's delicious."

"It was supposed to go to the Prixon Palace servants for their night ration. I snatched a few."

"Thank you," Annaïg said.

"Yes, yes," Slyr said. "Eat. Drink."

"What about Qijne?"

"She may be—ah, as you said. But when we succeed, so does she. Lord Ghol was on the verge of becoming the patron of another kitchen. When kitchens lose patrons, people start wondering whether the master chef ought to be replaced. We did well, so she'll look the other way a bit if we take very discreet privileges."

"What sort of privileges?"

"Well . . . this is about it. Having a little of the good stuff and not being watched too closely at night."

Annaïg felt her face burn a bit. "Ah, Slyr—"

"Don't flatter yourself," the chef replied. "I just thought you would enjoy being here, where you can see the sky. And no noisy, smelly dormitory. I love being here, alone—I don't think anyone else knows about it. I just don't dare come here often."

"Well, then," Annaïg said, "I *am* flattered, then."

Slyr became a little sloppy after the first bottle of wine.

"I have heard something about your friend," she confided.

Annaïg nearly choked on her drink. "Really?" she gasped. "About Glim? He's okay?"

"He's in the sump."

It jagged through her like lightning.

"What?" she whispered.

But Slyr smiled.

"No, not like that," she assured her. "He's not dead. He's working in the sump. The guy who brought the shrimp mentioned him. He can breathe underwater, did you know that? All of the sump tenders are talking about him."

"Of course he can breathe underwater," she replied. "He's an Argonian."

"Another of your nonsense words? There are more like him?'

She remembered the slaughter at Lilmoth. "I hope so," she said.

"Oh," Slyr said. "They're down there."

"Don't you ever—" But she stopped herself. She couldn't trust anyone here with thoughts of somehow stopping Umbriel.

But Slyr was waiting for her to finish.

"Have you ever been above?" she asked instead.

"To the palaces? No. But it is my dream to." She looked up and her forehead wrinkled. "What are those?" she asked.

Annaïg followed her regard up to the small patch of night sky.

"Stars," she said. "Haven't you ever seen stars before?"

"No. What are they?"

"Depends on who you ask or what books you read. Some say they are tiny holes in Mundus, the world, and the light we see is Aetherius beyond. Others believe they are fragments of Magnus, who made the world."

"They're beautiful."

"Yes."

And so they ate, and drank, and talked, and for the first time in many, many days Annaïg felt like a real person again.

When Slyr finally curled up to sleep with her blanket, she opened her locket again.

There wasn't anything there, which meant Coo wasn't with Attrebus. She waited, hoping he would answer, but after an hour or so she fell asleep, and her dreams were troubled.

FIVE

———

To Colin, the corpses looked like broken dolls flung down by a child in a tantrum. He couldn't imagine any of them ever having been alive, breathing, talking, feeling. He couldn't find any empathy even for the worst of the lot—those burnt to char—and he knew he ought to. He should at least feel sick or repelled, filled with the fear of such a thing happening to him, but he just couldn't find anything like that in him.

Well, Prince, he thought, congratulations. Well done.

"Stay away from the bodies," he told the royal guardsmen. He didn't have to tell his own people; they were professionals. "Put sentinels on the road and in the woods. Stop any wagons and route foot and horse traffic well around this. Tell them a bunch of ogres have set up camp and we have to clear 'em out.

"Gerring, you start the search for witnesses. Every house, every shack in the area. Hand, you go to Ione and Pell's Gate. Guilliam—you take Sweetwater and Eastbridge. Be discreet. See who's saying what in the taverns. You know what to do."

He nodded at a flurry of "Yes, inspector" but kept his gaze on the scene.

Most had been struck by arrows and had either died of that or of having their throats very professionally slit later. A sizable fraction had been immolated, presumably by sorcery. The attackers, interestingly, either hadn't had any casualties or—if they had—didn't leave them behind.

The arrows he recognized as belonging to an insurgent faction from County Skingrad that called themselves the "Natives." A number of the bodies had been beheaded, a practice also in keeping with that same nasty bunch of thugs.

He stopped in front of one body that was burnt but not incinerated. Bits of clothing and jewelry still clung to it and a notably large ring. The head was missing.

"Too convenient," he murmured as he took a closer look at the ring. As he suspected, it was the signet ring of Crown Prince Attrebus.

Of course, if it had been the Natives, they would certainly have singled out Attrebus's head as the best trophy. But then, why leave the ring?

"Oh, sweet gods," someone gasped. "It's the prince."

Irritated, Colin turned to find Captain Pundus dismounted and standing a few feet away.

"Captain, I asked you to stay clear of the bodies."

Pundus reddened. "See here, I'm the leader of this expedition. Who do you imagine you are, shouting orders at me and my men?"

"You were the leader of this expedition until we found *this*," Colin said, parting his hands. "Now I am in charge."

"On whose authority?"

Colin removed a scroll from his haversack and handed it to the captain.

"You know the Emperor's signature, I assume?"

Pundus's eyes were trying to pop out of his head. He nodded rapidly.

"Good. Then set your men to divert traffic, as I requested, and advise them not to speak of anything they've seen here.

I advise you the same."

"Yes, sir," the captain said.

"After I'm done, we'll need wagons, enough to hold the bodies. We'll want them covered, as well. See if you can locate some in the nearby towns. And again, not a word."

"Sir." The captain nodded, remounted, and rode off.

He looked around a few more moments, then took a deep breath. He found the spark in himself that belonged not to the world, but to Aetherius, to the realm of pure and complete possibility.

He was lucky—this was easy for him. If he'd needed to start a fire or walk on water, it would require training, a mental sequence worked out by someone else to convince him that such things could be done. But for what he was doing, he need only focus and pay attention, look beneath the rock that everyone else didn't notice.

The scene darkened and blurred, and for a moment he thought there was nothing left, but then he saw two spectral forms. One, a woman, was staring down at her body. The other, a man, was crouched into the roots of a large tree.

The man was closer, so he took the few steps necessary. He was already starting to feel himself weakening, the spark fading, so he knew he should hurry.

"You," he said. "Listen to me."

Vacant eyes turned to him. "Help me," the ghost said. "I'm hurt."

"Help is on the way," Colin lied. "You need to tell me what happened here."

"It hurts," the specter said. "Please."

"You came here with Prince Attrebus," Colin pursued.

The man laughed harshly. "Help me up. I just want to go home. If I can get home, I'll be fine."

"Who hurt you? Tell me!"

"Gods!" He breathed raggedly, then stopped. His head dropped against the tree.

A moment later it rose again.

"Help me," he said. "I'm hurt."

Colin felt a sudden surge of anger at the pitiful thing.

"You're dead," he snapped. "Have some dignity about it."

Almost shaking with fury, he went over to the other spirit.

"What about you?" he asked. "Anything left of you?"

"What you see," the woman murmured. "Your accent—you're Colovian, like me."

"Yes," he replied. "Where are you from?"

"I was born near Mortal, down on the river."

"That's a nice place," he said, feeling his anger leave him. "Peaceful, with all of those willows."

"There were willows all around my house," she replied. "I won't see them again."

"No," he said softly. "I'm sorry, you won't."

She nodded.

"Listen," Colin said, "I need your help."

"If I can."

"Do you remember what happened here? Who attacked you? Anything?"

She closed her eyes. "I do," she said. "We were with the prince, off following some half-cocked scheme of his. Headed for Black Marsh, of all places. We were ambushed." She sighed. "Attrebus. I knew he would get me killed someday. Is he dead, too?"

"I don't know. I was hoping you did."

"I didn't see. First there was fire, and then something hit me, hard. I didn't even get to fight."

"Why were you going to Black Marsh?"

"Something about a flying city and an army of undead. I didn't listen that closely. His quests were usually pretty safe, well in hand before we even arrived, if you know what I mean."

"The Emperor forbade him to go. He disobeyed."

"We weren't sure what to believe," she said. "Might've been

part of the game. There were other times like that." She shook her head. "I wish I could help you more."

"I think you've helped me quite a lot," Colin said. He looked around at the carnage. "Are you staying here, do you think?"

"I don't know much about being dead," she said, "but it doesn't feel that way. I feel something tugging at me, and it's stronger all the time." She smiled. "Maybe I only stayed to talk to you."

"Are you afraid?"

"No," she said. "It doesn't feel bad." She cocked her head. "You, though—something wrong with you, countryman."

"I'm fine."

"You're far from fine," she said. "You take care of yourself. Maybe next time you see a willow, think of me."

"I will."

She smiled again.

He pulled back into himself and the sun returned. They were all just broken dolls again. He thought his head was ringing, but then he understood that it was just birds singing.

He was starving. Unsteadily, he went to find something to eat, and to hear the reports.

SIX

———————

"Draeg's late," Tsani told Radhasa, her golden tail twitching in agitation. "Really late."

Attrebus, nearly asleep in the saddle, tried to appear actually asleep, in hopes they might let something useful drop if they thought he couldn't hear them.

It had taken him two days to figure out there were eight of them, because no more than four were riding guard on him at any given time. The others, he guessed, were scouts—one in front, one in back, one on each flank, and probably pretty far out. Radhasa was a constant, but he was just too out of it at first to realize the other faces were rotating. Now, after a week, he knew all of their names. Tsani, one of four Khajiit in the group, the others being Ma-fwath, J'yas, and Sharwa. Besides Radhasa, there was a flaxen-haired Breton woman named Amelia, a one-handed orc named—not too surprisingly—Urmuk One Hand. He'd had an iron ball fixed to his stump. The missing Draeg was the Bosmer he'd seen earlier, on awakening.

Radhasa didn't say anything, just tugged at her mount's reins to guide him down the steep path through increasingly more arid country. In the last few days the land had risen, and the thick forest and lush meadows of the West Weald had devolved into scrubby oaks and tall grass. Now, on the southern side of the hills, trees were more like big bushes, except when they came to a stream or pool, and tall grass prevailed in clearings.

His spirits had been sinking with the altitude, because he was certain they were already in Elsweyr. It would be more difficult for his friends to find him here; few of them had ever been south of the border, and the cats were less than friendly with the Empire they had once been a part of. Any force that tried to retrieve him might be seen as an invasion.

But then he saw a glimmer of hope in the situation.

By the time they were camping for the night, it was clear to everyone Draeg was probably more than delayed. The glimmer brightened.

"Trolls, probably," Radhasa opined. "The hills stink with them."

"I can't imagine Draeg having trouble with a troll—or much else for that matter," Sharwa said. "More likely he just decided this deal was too dangerous."

"We *were* supposed to kill him," Tsani said. "That's what we were paid to do. Now we potentially have two powerful enemies—the Emperor and our employer."

"He will be thought dead," Radhasa replied. "There's nothing to worry about."

"I'm not—at least not enough to scratch at the money. But Draeg—he's a worrier."

"Well, more for us, then," Radhasa said. "Tsani, you go back and take his position."

"Fine. Are we going into Riverhold?"

"Are you crazy? It's swarming with Imperial agents. We'd have to keep his highness gagged, and that might attract attention. No, there's a little market town a few miles west of there, Sheeraln. Ma-fwath and J'yas will go in and trade our horses for slarjei and water."

They came to the crest of the last of the hills before sundown, and the plains of Anequina stretched out to the horizon. He'd always imagined Elsweyr as an unrelieved desert, but here it was green. The tall grass of the upland prairies had been replaced by a short stubble, but that still seemed a far cry from the naked sand he'd been expecting. Streams were visible by the swaying palms, light-skinned cottonwood, and delicate tamarisk that lined them. A herd of red cattle grazed in the near distance.

Riverhold was visible a bit east, sprung up at the convergence of three dusty-looking roads. The walls were saffron, irregular, and not particularly high. Behind them, domes and towers of faded azure and cream, vermilion and chocolate, gold and jet, crowded together like a gaggle of overdressed courtiers waiting in the foyer of the throne room. It was a city that seemed at once tired and exuberant.

He wished they were going there.

But instead they did as Radhasa planned—they followed a goat trail into a copse of trees along a meandering stream, where he was forced to dismount. Then Ma-fwath and J'yas took the horses.

"Bathe," Radhasa told him. "You're starting to smell."

"Hard to do with these bands on."

"You promise to be good?"

His heart sped a bit. "Yes," he said.

"Swear it on your honor that you won't try to run."

"On my honor," he replied.

She shrugged, came up behind him, and untied the ropes.

"There," she said. "Go, then, bathe."

He stripped off his stinking clothes, feeling watched and somehow ashamed. Radhasa had seen him undressed before— had helped undress him, in fact. He hadn't felt in the least un-comfortable then. Now he hurried into the water and submerged himself as quickly as possible.

The water was cool, and felt unbelievably good. He let it

wash over him, closing his eyes and trying to concentrate only on the sensation.

It might have been a half an hour before he opened them. When he did, he saw that Radhasa was the only one besides himself in the camp. She was sitting with her back to a tree, not quite facing him. She seemed deep in thought.

Between him and her lay a pile of gear, and protruding from it was the hilt of his sword, Flashing.

He didn't hesitate, but launched himself out of the water toward the weapon. Radhasa saw him, but even then didn't seem to understand the situation until he actually had the weapon in his hand. Then she came slowly to her feet.

"You promised," she accused. "On your honor."

"I promised not to *run*," he corrected.

She drew her sword. "Ah," she said. "I see."

He circled her, waiting. She wasn't in armor, so there was no advantage there. And he'd fought her before, knew her signals.

He feinted, but she didn't twitch. He cut deeper, and she evaded with a quick sidestep. Then she did what he knew she would; her whole body sagged, the tell that she was about to make a hard attack.

She started forward; he threw up his parry and stepped to meet her . . .

Except that her attack was suddenly short, and he was blocking nothing but air. Then she was in motion again, cutting at his exposed legs. He tried to jump back, but he had too much momentum, and so dropped his blade to parry.

But that was also a feint, and in an instant she was inside, right on him, and her off-weapon hand wrenched at his grip in a strange, painful manner, and then he was facedown on the ground. Flashing thumped to earth a few feet away.

Radhasa stepped back.

"Want to try again?"

Growling, he once more took up the blade and came at her with his famous six-edge attack, but halfway through it her point was at his throat.

"Again?" she asked.

Enraged, he flew at her with everything, but almost without seeming to work at it she had him disarmed and on the ground once more.

"You—You lost on purpose, when you were applying," he said.

"You think?"

He climbed back to his feet. "You'll have to kill me," he said.

"No I won't. I'll just knock you out again."

"Why did you do this? For entertainment?"

Her usually beautiful face twisted into something rather ugly.

"I wanted you to *know*," she said. "I hate losing, and I hate pretending to lose."

"Then why did you? Back at my villa?"

"Orders, Prince."

"From your employer? To get me to let my guard down?"

She rolled her eyes. "From Gulan, you idiot. Don't you understand yet? You're a worse than mediocre fighter. You've never fought a fair fight in your life. You've never been in a battle that wasn't a rigged, foregone conclusion. Until now."

Attrebus suddenly realized he'd missed something about Radhasa; she wasn't merely deceptive, treacherous, and greedy—she was completely insane.

"Sure," he said. "Whatever you say. Clearly you hate me, although I don't know why. I was nice to you, took you into my guard."

"I don't hate you as such," she said, "I just hate what you are. It's not your fault really—this was done to you. Yet I can't help feeling that if you'd ever used your brain just once, if you had the slightest ability to step outside of your narcissistic little world—"

"You've been with me two days. What do you know about me?"

"Everyone interviewed for your guard is told, Attrebus. And they all talk, don't they? How could they not? The way you blustered about as if they were your friends, the casual, everyday condescension—I don't see how any of them stood it for more than two days. I mean, yes, the pay is good, and in general you're assured fairly safe situations, but Boethiah's ass, it's annoying."

A slow, gentle cold was working its way up from his belly.

"This isn't true," he said. "My men loved me."

"They mocked you behind your back. The least of them was worth three of you. Did you really think you're the hero in the songs, in the books? Were the odds really ten-to-one at Dogtrot Ford?"

"Some authors tend to exaggerate, but it's all basically true. I can't help the mistakes some bard in Cheydinhal makes. But I *did* those things."

"At Dogtrot Ford you faced half your number, and they weren't insurgents, they were condemned criminals told that if they survived, they would be freed."

"That's a lie."

He felt dizzy, very dizzy. He leaned against a tree.

"You're starting to see it, aren't you? Because somewhere in that skull of yours you have at least half of your father's brain."

"Just shut up," he said. "I've no idea why you're saying this, but I won't listen to it anymore. Kill me, tie me back up, but just shut up, for the love of the Divines."

She wrinkled her brow and leaned on her sword. "Are you really that dense?"

He charged at her, howling. A moment later he was on the ground again.

"If it's any consolation," she said, placing her foot on his throat, "even if by some fluke you managed to kill me, Urmuk and Sharwa have been watching the whole time."

As she said it, he saw the orc and the Khajiit appear from behind a copse of bamboo.

The boot came off of his neck. He turned his head and saw someone else—a lean, hawk-nosed man with charcoal skin and molten red eyes striding purposefully into the clearing. Had he missed someone?

"You there!" Sharwa shouted. "What do you—"

The man kept coming, but he thrust out his arm, and his hand flashed white-hot. Sharwa's hideous yowl was like nothing Attrebus had ever heard before.

Radhasa kicked him in the head, and he rolled, groaning, sparks flashing behind his eyes. Sobbing in pain, he came to his feet and rubbed the tears from his eyes.

He was just in time to see the orc lose his other hand, making him—presumably—Urmuk the Handless. The newcomer's long, copper-colored blade pulled right through his wrist, then angled up to deflect a murderous head blow from Radhasa. Urmuk stumbled back and tripped over Sharwa, who seemed to be trying to stand, despite the smoke rising from her chest.

Radhasa jumped back and continued to retreat. Attrebus didn't blame her. This wasn't a man—this was some daedra summoned from the darkness beyond the world, a fiend.

"What do you want?" Radhasa screamed. "You've no business with us."

The fiend didn't say anything. He just picked up the pace, half running toward Radhasa, and then suddenly bounding forward. She planted herself and then danced nimbly aside as his blade soughed by her, and her own weapon came down two-handed toward the juncture of his neck and shoulder.

He caught her blade with his off-weapon hand. Attrebus saw Radhasa close her eyes, and then his blade went in through the pit of her left arm so deeply the point came out through her ribs on the other side.

He withdrew the weapon and stalked toward Urmuk, who was holding the bleeding stump of his wrist. Whatever Urmuk was, he wasn't a coward, and he hurled the massive weight of his body at his attacker, clubbing at him with the iron ball he had fixed to his left hand. Sharwa was crawling away on her belly.

Urmuk fell and the fiend turned on Sharwa.

"You can't," Attrebus managed. "She's injured—"

But her head was off by then.

And now the fiend turned on him.

Attrebus snapped out of his paralysis and ran toward his sword, but when he had it, he saw the killer was merely watching him.

Attrebus brought his weapon to guard.

"I killed a Bosmer back in the hills and a Breton on the ridge back there," the man said. His voice was hard and scratchy. "I make there are two more—Khajiit. Where are they?"

"They went to some village," he replied. "To change the horses for slarjei, whatever they are."

"Slarjei are better in the desert than horses," the man said. "How long have they been gone?"

"An hour, maybe."

"Well, Prince Attrebus, we ought to be going, then."

"Who are you? How do you know who I am?"

"My name is Sul."

"Did my father send you?"

"He did not," Sul replied.

Now that he was closer and not in constant motion, Attrebus had a better look at him. He was old, his dark skin pulled in tightly against his bones. His hair was black and gray and cropped nearly to his skull.

"Who, then?"

"My reasons are my own," he replied. "Would you rather I hadn't come?"

"I don't know the answer to that yet, do I?" Attrebus said.

"I'm not here to kill you," Sul assured him. "I'm not here to hurt you. We have a common destiny, you and I. We both seek the island that flies."

Attrebus blinked. He felt as if the earth kept shifting beneath his feet. "You know of it?"

"I just said so."

"And what is your concern with it?"

"I will destroy it or send it back to Oblivion. Isn't that what you want?"

"I . . . yes." What was happening?

"Then we are together, yes?" Sul said. "Now, should we go or wait around so that I have to fight the other two as well?"

"You didn't have much trouble with these," Attrebus noticed.

"Most men die surprised," Sul said. "One of those two might have a surprise for me. I don't fight anyone without a reason. I have you, and I don't want slarjei unless we need to go south into the desert. Do we need to go south?"

"No."

"Well, pick the direction, and let's be off."

Attrebus stared at him, teasing that out. Then he understood. "You don't know where Umbriel is."

Sul barked out something that might have been a laugh. "Umbriel. Of course. Vuhon . . ." He trailed off. "No, I don't know where it is."

"How do I know you won't kill me as soon as I tell you?"

"Because I need you," Sul said.

"Why?"

"I'm not sure. But I know I do."

Attrebus considered his reply for a long moment. But really, what did he have to lose?

"East," he said. "It's over Black Marsh now, heading north."

"North toward Morrowind," Sul sighed. "Of course."

"Does that mean something to you?"

"Nothing that matters right now. Very well. East we go, then."

"Let me get my things," Attrebus said.

"Hurry, then."

———

Attrebus was glad Coo was in Radhasa's haversack and not on her body. The idea of approaching her, seeing what Sul made of her, made him sick. True, she was a lying traitor, but she had been warm in the bed with him not long ago. Alive and beautiful, sweaty, enthusiastic—or so she had seemed. Of all of the women he'd been with, she was the first to be—well, dead. At least so far as he knew. It was upsetting.

Sul gathered a few things from the bodies, then led him upstream among the trees for some distance until they finally came to three horses—two roan geldings that looked as though they were from the same mother and a brown mare. One of the roans was packed up, the other two horses were saddled.

"Ride the gelding," Sul said.

Attrebus sighed, feeling that was somehow fitting. A few moments later he was riding east with the man who had saved his life, wondering what would happen if he tried to run north, to Cyrodiil, to home.

And he had to admit that at the moment he didn't have the courage or the confidence to find out.

SEVEN

————————

Colin curbed the impulse to pace, but although he had walked into the room of his own free will—and there was no evidence that he couldn't leave it—he felt caged somehow. But his mind had been spinning for two days now, and the thread it turned out was beginning to look more like a garrote.

The vanishment of Prince Attrebus wasn't his first case—it was his third. The first had been simple enough; he'd planted spurious intelligence in the minister of war's office and waited for it to come out somewhere. When one of their agents in a local Thalmor nest reported it, he easily backtracked the leak to a mid-level official who was apparently hemorrhaging information to a mistress who was—as it turned out—a Thalmor sympathizer. It was simple, clean. No arrests and no bodies. Once the leak was known, it was more useful to leave it in place.

His second assignment had been to discover the whereabouts of a certain sorcerer named Laeva Cuontus. He'd found her without ever knowing why he was looking for her. He didn't know what happened to her after he reported her location, and he didn't want to know.

When he'd been sent out with the patrol to locate Prince Attrebus, it hadn't seemed that odd. Apparently the prince often had to be shadowed, and it didn't require a particularly senior member of the organization to do the job of what amounted to a bit of tracking, questioning, and bribing.

But now he was in the middle of something pretty bad, and a sensation between his sternum and his pelvis told him that it hadn't been an accident that such a junior inspector had been sent to discover such nasty business.

He didn't have any proof of that, of course. Just that feeling, and the certainty that he was missing some piece of the puzzle. And now he was in a well-furnished room on the second floor of the ministry, which was apparently the office of no one.

He turned as Intendant Marall entered the room, followed by two other men. One was Remar Vel, administrator of the Penitus Oculatus. The other . . .

"Your majesty," he blurted, taking a knee. He felt suddenly in awe, an emotion he hadn't experience in a while. As a child he'd worshipped this man. Apparently some part of him still did.

"Rise up," the Emperor said.

"Yes, highness."

The Emperor just stood there for a moment, hands clasped behind his back.

"You were there," he finally said. "Is my son dead?"

Colin considered his answer for a moment. If anyone else had asked him . . . But this wasn't anyone else.

"Sire," he said, "I do not believe so."

Titus Mede's eyes widened slightly and his brow relaxed, but that was his only reaction.

"And yet his body was recovered," Administrator Vel said drily.

"A body, sir," Colin said. "A headless body."

"It's said that the rebels in that area take heads," the Emperor said. "Other heads were taken."

"I don't believe the Natives were responsible, majesty."

"Why not? They're vicious enough, and we have information, do we not, that they are supplied and funded by our 'quiet enemies'?"

"You mean the Thalmor, majesty."

"They are in everything, these days."

"And yet I don't see how killing your son advances their aims."

"Who are you to say what their aims are?" Vel snapped. "You've only been an inspector for a month."

"Yes, sir, that's true. But my training focus was the Thalmor."

"Which does not include—by any means—everything we know about them. Their aims are obscure."

"I respectfully disagree, sir. I may well not be privy to many details, but their goal is clear—the pacification and purification of all of Tamriel—to bring about a new Merithic era."

"We have an inkling of their long-term goals, Inspector, but their intermediate plans are less scrutable."

"Begging your pardon, sir, but not always. When they took Valenwood, that was pretty straightforward, and quite logical— they put the old Aldmeri Dominion back together, which makes perfect sense in terms of their ideology. Their harassment of refugees from the Summerset Isles and Valenwood also fits their broader pattern, as does what little we know of their activities in Elsweyr. But the murder of a prince—I've tried many ways of looking at that, and it doesn't make sense."

Vel started to retort to that, but the Emperor shook his head and held up his hand. Then he spoke again to Colin.

"What is your opinion? If my son is not dead, do you believe him kidnapped? And if so, by whom, and for what purpose? And why leave this trail that seems to lead to the Thalmor?"

Colin took a another deep breath, and began to lie.

"If we assume that much of the 'evidence' left for us was false," he began, "then I might suggest it's someone interested in drawing our attention to the Thalmor. A distraction to keep our eyes turned, perhaps even coax us into a fight."

"Leyawiin?" the Emperor muttered. "They are still restless under our rule."

"Maybe it's not someone restless under your rule, majesty. Maybe it's someone who would prefer someone else inherit the throne."

"My brother?" He massaged his head. "It's not impossible. I do not like to think it."

"Sire," Vel said, "your brother did not hatch this plot. He is more than adequately surveiled."

"He is perhaps more clever than you think," Mede replied. "But lay that aside. If we find my son, we find our enemy. So I want him found." He frowned and stroked his upper lip. "Captain Gulan was among the dead?"

"He was," Vel replied.

"Is there any question regarding his identity?"

"No, sire," Vel said. "He was killed by arrowshot, and his head was not taken. Sire, I know it isn't easy to accept, but we must consider the possibility that the body we have is that of the prince, the inspector's opinion notwithstanding. It is the right size and shape—"

"My son had a birthmark on his right side, just where the ribs end. I have seen the corpse; that portion of it is charred while other parts are not. Like the inspector, I find that too convenient. And it does not *feel* like Attrebus. So—I believe him alive. Someone has him. I want him found. Inspector, is there any indication of where the attackers went?"

"They broke into smaller parties and left in different directions. But I would look south for Attrebus, your highness."

"And why is that, Inspector?"

"Because it is the only direction in which there were no tracks whatsoever, sire."

The Emperor grunted and nodded. "Inspector, Intendant, Administrator," he said, addressing the three, and left.

Vel waited a moment and followed him, shooting Colin an unpleasant look.

"That wasn't the brightest thing you could have done," Marall said.

"The Emperor asked my opinion," Colin said. "Isn't it my duty to give it?"

Marall sighed. "The Emperor doesn't care if you get assigned to sewer cases for the rest of your life—or worse, sent to spy on Nords. It's better if these things go up the chain of command. Now, Vel appears to be less well-informed than his most junior inspector."

"I fully intended to follow that chain," Colin said. "I came here believing Administrator Vel was going to hear my report. It isn't my fault that the Emperor was present."

Marall nodded. "You're right, of course. It's just your inexperience showing. You shouldn't have so bluntly disagreed with a superior. There are more subtle ways to go about things."

How subtle is a knife? Colin angrily thought, but then pushed that away.

"I'm still learning, sir."

"If Attrebus is alive, and they find him on your counsel, you will gain the Emperor's favor, and that will be a good thing for you. But if they do not find him, or if that body is him, then the Emperor will not think of you again. I advise you to keep as quiet as possible now, and find some way to come to Vel's attention in a more positive way."

"In that case," Colin said, "I wonder if I could be reassigned?"

"Oh, I can guarantee that," the intendant said. "Vel will put you under a rock. The only question is for how long."

———

When he emerged from the palace, night had fallen and the sky blazed down upon the Imperial City. He was tired, but he wanted a walk and a pint. He needed to think.

He *was* missing something. He had an idea what it might be, and that went well with the stroll and the ale.

In Anvil, where he was born, darkness brought quiet to the city; people went home or to the pubs and taverns, but the streets were pretty empty.

Not so here, at least not in the Market District, which was his destination. The streets were crowded with trinket vendors and soothsayers, self-styled prophets of any daedra or Divine imaginable. Women, mostly comely ones, stood outside of alehouses, flirting to attract business, and there were others of both genders and all races flirting to sell somewhat different wares. Beggars choked the edges of walkways, and little stalls were turning out the enticing smell of roasted oysters, fried cheese, bread, skewered meats, and burnt sugarcane.

People wandered in crowds, as if afraid the city would swallow them up if they found themselves alone for long.

The Crown's Hammer was off the main thoroughfare, around a corner and almost hidden in an alley. It was a half-timbered building, very old. He pushed his way in the front door.

The barkeep was a withered old fellow who favored Colin with a nod.

"You're having?" he asked as he cleaned a mug with a rag that looked slightly dirtier than the container it was wiping out.

"Ale," Colin said.

The man nodded, held the glass under the tap of a wooden keg and filled it with a rich, dark red liquid.

Colin paid for the drink and then found a table in a corner. He took a seat where he could see the door, and sipped at the ale. It was strong, sweet, and had just a taste of juniper, a Colovian Highland style now popular throughout western Cyrodiil, but hard to find here in the East.

The place was nearly empty when he came in, but it was starting to fill up now, because the patrol and the soldiers were changing shifts. The Hammer catered to Colovians, and Colovians in this part of the world were mostly military.

So he wasn't surprised when Nial Sextius walked in, noticed him, and grinned.

"Colin, lad," he said. "It's been an age."

"It's good to see you, Nial," he replied. "I was hoping you would be in tonight. Have a seat—let me buy you a drink."

"Well, fine, if I can have the next round."

When they were both looking over foam, Nial cracked his knuckles and settled his elbows on the table. He was a big man, thick in every dimension, with a ruddy, wind-worn complexion that made him look older, although he and Colin were of an age.

"Where've you been?" he asked. "It's almost two years. I thought you'd left town."

"No, just very busy," Colin said.

Nial wagged a finger at him. "Come to think of it, you were a little thin on why you're all the way over here last time we talked. Distracted me with that story about my sister."

"Yah," Colin said, taking a drink. "I—ah, work in the palace."

Nial's eyes widened. "And don't I, too?" he asked. "So why haven't I seen trace of you?"

"I'm in a different part of the palace, I guess. In the tower."

"Doing what? Making ladies' dresses?"

"Studying," he said. "In school, as it were."

"In school? But that—" He stopped, rolled his eyes and took a drink. Then he lowered his voice. "Ah, Colin, you're one of them—you're a specter, aren't you?"

"I serve the Empire, same as you," Colin said.

"Not the same as me," Nial disagreed. "Col, why?"

"They offered me a way up, Nial. A way so my mam doesn't

have to work herself to death. I'm sorry if that doesn't make sense to you."

"Now, don't get your back up, scruff," Nial said. "I'm just surprised, is all. I don't fancy most of your fellows, but I'll make an exception for you."

"*I* don't fancy some of my fellows," Colin said. "But I don't fancy being judged either. If the Emperor didn't think we mattered, we wouldn't exist."

"Fine, like I said," Nial said. His voice dropped even lower. "So, see here," he said. "Maybe you'd know, then. Is all this true about Prince Attrebus?"

"I don't know what you've heard."

"Heard he finally got himself—and all of his guard—murdered."

"It looks like that," Colin said. "Did you know any of them?"

"Yeah, a few. I thought about applying a few years back, but I didn't think I could handle it, you know?"

"The danger, you mean?"

Nial grunted out a laugh. "That's funny," he said.

"What do you mean?"

"You mean you're a specter, and you don't know about the prince?"

"Not my field of expertise," Colin said.

"Well, he was just for show, you know. Only he didn't know it."

Colin nodded. That fit with the picture forming in his head. So why hadn't he been briefed about that before being sent to fetch the prince back?

"Well, he walked into a bit of danger this time," Colin said.

"Yeah."

"I wonder how? I mean, he must have been watched, if what you say is true."

Nial thumped his glass on the table. "You're prying me, aren't you? *In*specting."

Colin sighed. "It's this, Nial," he said. "I'm new to all of this. I think there's something strange going on, and I'm not sure who to trust. Except you. I believe I can trust you."

Nial stared at him for several long moments, then took his mug back up.

"What, then?"

"The Emperor asked about a man named Gulan, specifically. He wanted to know if his body was found."

"Was it?"

"Yeah."

Nial nodded. "Gulan was Attrebus's right hand. He kept him out of trouble. Whenever the prince would try and go be a hero in the wrong place, Gulan would bring it to the attention of the Emperor, and something would happen to stop it."

"Well, he didn't this time, it seems. He didn't report directly to the Emperor, did he?"

"No, he'd go through the prime minister's office."

Colin nodded. Now he was sure about what he was missing.

"Thanks, Nial," he said.

"You look tired, boy," Nial said. "Are you all right?"

"I'm fine. I have some trouble sleeping, that's all."

"You used to sleep so sound thunder wouldn't wake you," Nial said.

"Things change," Colin said. He studied the table for a moment, before looking back up at his friend. "Look, try to forget we had this conversation. Don't ask any questions, just leave it be."

"I might be able to help," Nial said.

"You've helped me more than enough. Now, come on. Let's talk about something else."

"Yeah, like what?"

"Like what a slut your sister is, for instance."

"If it weren't true, I'd thwack you for that. Maybe I should thwack you anyway. Let's have another round while I think it over."

"That's good for me," Colin replied.

He finished the ale and watched Nial walk off to fetch two more. There wasn't anything else to do tonight, and it felt good to talk to a friend. It had been a long time since he'd done that.

And it might well be the last.

EIGHT

———————◄►———————

Qijne glared down at the trays and the food they contained.

"Explain," she snapped. "Start with the fish."

"Annaïg calls it 'catfish,'" Slyr said. "The taskers bring us quite a lot of them."

"I'm aware of that," Qijne said. "We've burned hundreds for the Oroy mansion workers. What I want to know is, why are you sending a complete fish to Lord Ghol? It's far too coarse for his palate."

Why question us? Annaïg wondered. *Except for that first time, we've done nothing but succeed. Can't you just trust us?*

She could not, of course, say that out loud.

"That's true, Chef," she said instead. "He will be surprised by it, I believe."

"Not pleasantly, I should imagine by looking at it."

"Ah, yes, but when he touches or breathes on it, it will deliquesce. That will release a series of odors viandic; the fish will liquefy and mingle with the void and fire salts there around the fish, which will then release their essences. That will lead nicely into the second course, here, a cold broth of tadpole bones garnished with live frog eggs. Finally, the white froth of Terriswort will cause his palate to vividly recall each aroma and taste—but in reverse order."

"Another of your metagastrologics?"

"Yes, Chef."

"These are tricks, stunts," Qijne complained. "You hazard boring him."

"I think he will be pleased," Slyr said. "But if you have any suggestions, I would be most happy to hear them, Chef."

Qijne narrowed her eyes, clearly trying to decide if she should feel insulted. Annaïg had to stop herself from holding her breath.

The moment passed, ending when Qijne simply walked off.

"That's it, then," Slyr said. "Let's send it up."

———

The news from above was good that evening. She and Slyr hadn't been back to the little room with its view of the night sky in days, but that night they celebrated there again. Slyr brought baubles as well as food this time—little coils of glass that glowed like small suns.

And after Slyr was asleep, Annaïg felt her amulet wake.

"Thank Dibella," she murmured. She lifted a coil, rose and tiptoed out of the room into the cellar, and only then did she open the locket.

And there was Prince Attrebus, looking back at her. The light seemed to be firelight, for shadows flickered about him, but his face was bruised and battered. His eyes were full of concern, but now his features relaxed in relief.

"There you are," he said. "I was worried about you."

"And I about you, your highness. It's been days. I've tried to contact you—"

He nodded. "I've been unable to respond," he said. "I . . ." He trailed off. He seemed different—not the assertive, confident man she remembered from their earlier conversation.

"I understand, Prince Attrebus," she said. "You're a busy man."

He nodded. "I want you to know," he said, "that I am coming, as I promised. But it may be that . . ."

Again he didn't finish. He seemed very vulnerable.

But then something seemed to strengthen him and his tone became firmer, more familiar.

"Have you discovered anything new?"

"Yes. I've found a place where I can see the sky—a way in and out. And I'm trying to re-create the tonic that Glim and I used to reach this place."

"That's good," he said. "Perhaps I can find something like that on my way there. We should pass through Rimmen in a few days, and then Leyawiin."

That sounded a little odd, as if he didn't have his mages with him, but maybe he preferred to handle certain things himself.

"I've always wanted to see Rimmen," she told him. "They say the Akaviri built a magnificent shrine there, the Tonenaka. They say it houses ten thousand statues. And the canals are said to be amazing."

"Well, I've never been there either," Attrebus said. "But I'll tell you about it next time we speak."

"That would be wonderful, Prince."

"I shan't be dawdling there, though," he went on. "Time is of the essence. But I'm sure I'll see something worth mentioning." He paused. "I find titles cumbersome in conversation. I would prefer you did not use them."

"What should I call you, your highness?"

"Attrebus will do, or 'Treb.' It will save time when we talk."

"I'll try," she said. "It seems strange to be so familiar with you."

"Try it, for my sake."

There was that troubled look again.

"Are you—well, Attrebus? Is something wrong?"

"There have been some setbacks here," he said. "I won't bore you with the details."

"It wouldn't be boring," she said.

"Well, then I'd rather not talk about it," he modified.

She realized then that his eyes were glistening a bit.

"I must go now," he said. "Keep yourself safe, above all. Will you do that?"

"I will," she said.

He nodded, and then his image vanished behind Coo's door.

She stood there for a moment, a bit breathless, then snuck back into the shaft-room. Slyr didn't look as if she had stirred.

Annaïg sat with her back against the wall.

Something was wrong with the prince. That didn't bode well, did it?

But at the moment there wasn't much she could do but continue to stay alive, try to get in touch with Glim, rediscover the secret of flying . . .

Actually, that was quite a lot, wasn't it? Her hands were full.

So she needed her rest. No use to worry about things that were, at the moment, beyond her.

But she hoped Attrebus—he'd asked her to call him Attrebus!—she hoped he was all right.

———

Attrebus closed the little door on the bird. This was the first time he'd seen her face; her green eyes and generous, sensual lips, a nose that some might consider a bit large, but belonged perfectly on her face. Hair like dark twists of black silk.

The face of the woman he'd failed.

"Well, she, at least, is alive," he told Sul, who sat on the other side of the small fire they'd built.

"So I gather," Sul said. "Interesting, that bird. The dwemer used to make similar toys, before the world swallowed them up. Do you know where it's from?"

"She said it came from her mother, and I gather her mother was middling nobility from Highrock."

"Well, things move around," Sul grunted. "Let me see it."

"See here—" Attrebus began, but the look in the Dunmer's eyes stopped him. He stood and extended Coo. Sul took her, examined her a bit. The little door wouldn't unclasp for him.

"Smart," Sul said. "Only opens for who it was sent to."

"I believe so," Attrebus replied. "Radhasa couldn't make it work."

"Why didn't you tell her?" Sul asked, prodding the fire, snapping a swarm of sparks toward the sky. "This Annaïg. Why didn't you tell her you've lost all of your guard?"

"I don't want to discourage her."

"You'd rather give her false hope?"

"I don't intend to give up."

"That's good," Sul said. "It's better that way."

"As opposed to what?"

Sul didn't answer right away, but instead drew his sword and examined the edge a bit before resheathing it. Finally he looked up at Attrebus.

"Here's my worry," Sul said. "I'll make it plain right away, so it's not between us from here on out. Let's start with this: I'm going to find Umbriel. When I do, there's going to be slaughter, pure and simple. I'm going to bring it down. It's been suggested to me that you can help me, and that's why I followed you, that's why I killed your captors. But I saw your fight with the Redguard—I was waiting to be sure of where the others were before I made my move, and it was clear she had no intention of killing you. I heard the conversation."

"She was lying," Attrebus said.

"She wasn't," Sul replied. "You're telling yourself that now because you're too weak to face it. But like she said, you're not fundamentally stupid. The branch already has too much weight on it—it's starting to creak. You barely managed to get through your talk with the Breton girl without getting weepy—"

"My friends have just been killed!" Attrebus heard himself shout. "Friends, lovers, companions, all dead. Of course I'm not myself!"

Sul waited for him to finish, then started again.

"In days or weeks that branch will crack, and down you'll come. You'll realize how right she was, and the world will turn over, and my worry is, will you be any use to me then? Will any of these principles you think you adhere to—honor, courage, honesty—survive it? Or are you just a child, playing at these things, as you played at being a warrior and commander?"

"You're wrong about this," Attrebus snapped. "Based on one conversation you overheard, you conclude she was right? Granted, she could outfight me—"

"A child with palsy could outfight you."

"I'd been wounded, tied to a horse for days—"

"This isn't an argument, Prince Attrebus."

"Look, I'll swear it even now. I will stop Umbriel, or I will die trying."

"You're not listening to me," Sul said. "I'm trying to help you."

"By telling me that everything I believe about myself is a lie?"

Sul's eyes were fragments of the fire, lifting up to burn him.

And yet when he spoke, it wasn't to Attrebus, and it wasn't in Tamrielic. The only part of it the prince caught was the name "Azura"—one of the daedric princes. Then the Dunmer sighed harshly.

"Everyone faces that, you spoiled child. Most simply turn away and continue with their delusions—only a few are forced to accept the truth."

"Not everyone, not like this," Attrebus said. "I'm a prince—

I'm supposed to be Emperor one day. If what Radhasa says is true, I've been mocked my whole life without ever knowing it."

"Your 'whole life' is a heartbeat," Sul said.

"Maybe to you. But if people have been laughing at me—"

"Enough," Sul snarled. "Enough. I've done far more for you than I should. I've tried to warn you, but instead I'm just going to have to wait and see what the baby does. How's this, then? With or without you, I'll do what I've set out to do. If it comes to it, I'll cut off your head and revive it now and then to talk to the bird. Would that be a fair price for you breaking that vow you pledged so earnestly just now?"

Attrebus couldn't meet those eyes anymore, and turned instead to the living heart of the fire, which was certainly cooler.

"Yes," he mumbled. But now he was afraid. What did this man really want? What did Sul really need from him? Was it even true they had the same goal?

But then he suddenly understood that didn't matter. Every single thing Sul had told him could be true, but that still wouldn't put Sul on the right side of things. Maybe he was planning something even worse than whatever the master of Umbriel was up to.

In the end, they might be enemies—that would certainly explain this attempt to undermine him even more than Radhasa had. Maybe he and Radhasa had been working together and then had a falling-out.

Maybe Sul was the man she had been planning to sell him to, and this was all part of some elaborate game of his, breaking the will of a prince, reducing him to believing he was nothing . . .

He felt like screaming. He wanted to be alone, to think, to be free of fear long enough to sort through the confusion. He had a horse now . . .

But then again, running might be exactly what Sul wanted. Sure, he could keep his vow and go after Annaïg and Umbriel himself, but Sul would be at his back the whole time. Hadn't his father always said it was better to have your enemies where you could see them?

For now, that was probably his only choice. He had to keep his wits about him, think for himself, and not let Sul toy with him. He would work with the Dunmer as long as their goals appeared to be the same, and be ready the moment they weren't. He was a Mede, after all. A Mede.

———

Annaïg thought that the first explosion was a vat shattering; it had happened before, especially at the Oroy station.

But the second was much louder, while sounding somehow farther away.

And then the screaming began. Some of it sounded like war-like howls, some like shrieks of terror and pain, but everything in Umbriel was still frightfully strange, and none of it gave her any purchase on what was happening.

Luc hopped down from the shelves and crouched behind her. For her part, Annaïg climbed up onto the table to get a better view, but the wavering air above the fire pits obscured the far end of the kitchens. Still, the scamps were all swarming in that direction, leaping through the wires, grills, and racks above the pits. Beyond, a black curtain of flame and smoke occluded what the shimmering air did not. Only in the central aisle could she see anyone, and there the cooks and their helpers were black silhouettes, crowded shoulder-to-shoulder.

"You," Qijne snapped, from off to her left. "What are you standing about for?"

"What's happening?"

Slyr was with her, and the rest of the staff from Ghol's station, along with a motley collection of the largest and most dangerous-looking cooks in the kitchen, including Dest, a hulking ogrelike fellow with black and yellow fur. They were all armed to the teeth with butchering knives and cleavers.

"Don't ask stupid questions," Qijne snapped. "Come, now."

The closed around her, moving at a trot, through the huge boilers, parsers, and stills, the pulsing soul-cable, and into territory Annaïg had never seen—high-chambered rooms filled with long, watery trenches in which she caught glimpses of serpentine movement. As they went along, chefs darted out and made adjustments to the equipment, until at last they came to a stair leading up.

"All of it, now," Qijne said.

"But they're coming," Slyr protested. "Look, you can see them."

She pointed back the way they had come, and Annaïg made out, darting in and amidst the strange machinery, a handful of chefs, cooks, and tenders.

"They let them live, in hopes we would delay," Qijne said. "We won't. Do it. Send your hob."

"Yes, Chef."

They continued up the stairs, but a moment later a vast rumble began.

Annaïg found herself pushed up against Slyr.

"What's happening?" she asked.

"Qijne's purging the kitchens," she said.

"Purging them?"

"We're invaded, Annaïg."

"Invaded?" She had a surge of sudden wild hope.

"By another kitchen. It hasn't happened in years."

They had reached the top of the stairs now, and emerged through a massive iron valve into a cavernous room. Dest closed and sealed it. Then the chefs began laying various odd-looking packages about in front of it.

Slyr was still hustling her back, toward the far end of the cavern.

"What now?" Annaïg asked.

"We wait. The kitchens are full of fire and thirty kinds of toxins. If anyone survives that, we'll fight them here."

"I don't understand. Why would another kitchen invade?"

Slyr blinked and looked at her as if she were stupid. "To get you," she said.

"How—How do you know that?"

"From what I saw, it has to be one of the upper kitchens, the ones that serve the greater lords. They could have attacked as we defended, with venomous gases. Instead they sent cooks. That tells me they want someone alive, and that must be you."

"So everyone we left down there—"

"Not just dead, dissolved," Slyr replied.

"Then—"

But a hollow boom filled the chamber, and another. Then a silence settled.

"Be ready," Qijne said. "They were prepared."

"Ah, sumpslurry," Slyr moaned. "How could anything survive all that?"

"That's a rhetorical question, I take it," Annaïg said, trying hard not to shake.

The door glowed white-hot for an instant, then turned into a drifting vapor.

"Ready!" Qijne repeated.

For a few heartbeats nothing happened. Then a monster leapt through the door. Annaïg's first impression was of a bull-sized lion with a thousand eyes set on squirming stalks. She had no second impression, for the packages Qijne's people had scattered in front of the door suddenly revealed their natures and became variously fire, force, cold, and vitriol. The monster, whatever it was, was disintegrated.

But behind it, through the newly formed fog, poured hordes of cooks.

In appearance they were the same mixture of physical types that Annaïg was becoming used to in the kitchens. They wore gold and black.

Qijne screamed like some sort of bird of prey and ran at the attackers, her staff behind her.

In only seconds they were enveloped, and although Slyr kept trying to push Annaïg back, after a moment the fighting was all around her. Blood spurted up her chest and face as a cleaver chopped someone's arm off; she slipped and fell, blinded by the blood in her eyes. When she managed to wipe it out, she saw Minn staggering by, clutching her bleeding gut, her face dissolving into yellow worms. She tried to scream, and might have, but if so, her voice was lost in the din.

All of a sudden Qijne was there, pulling her up from another fall. One of her ears was missing and much of her left arm had turned a strange gray color.

Qijne pulled her close.

"He won't have you," she shouted in Annaïg's ear.

Then she pulled back, and Annaïg saw her arm come up, and as blood sprayed from nearby, she saw it outline a long, wickedly curved *nothing* protruding from the chef's finger. She stared at it, unable to move, knowing what came next.

But then Slyr buried her cleaver in Qijne's neck, and the chef's eyes fluttered. Annaïg felt something tug at her neck and thought her throat had been cut before realizing the invisible blade had sliced through her locket chain. Slyr hacked again, and then Qijne staggered back, swiping her hand at Slyr, but the slate-skinned woman, trying to step back, slipped over a body. Then Qijne toppled, knocking Annaïg over yet once again.

They landed face-to-face. Qijne still wasn't dead. She was trying to get her hand back up. Annaïg grabbed her wrist. The blade was invisible again, but Annaïg felt something at her forehead, and a lock of hair fell past her nose.

She shrieked and pushed the hand back. For a long moment Qijne resisted, but then the spurting from her neck slowed to a trickle and her eyes went dull.

Annaïg lay there, panting, oblivious to the chaos still reigning around her. She kept hold of the hand and saw—inside the sleeve—a sort of tightness on Qijne's arm, as if it were constricted by an unseen band. She tugged at it, but couldn't find any sort of catch, buckle, or tie. She was just in the process of carefully laying the arm aside when something brushed her wrist and then, to her horror, cinched around it. Reflexively she grabbed at it with her other hand, but all she could feel was a sort of gummy torus, encircling her wrist. There was no blade.

She realized that it was almost silent now. She began to turn, but someone grabbed her up by the back of her jacket, and a moment later she was standing unsteadily on her feet again. Corpses were sprawled all around her. Slyr was a few feet away, held by two unfamiliar men. Everyone else she knew from the kitchen was dead.

From the press of black and gold before her, a man emerged. He might have been a Breton, with his high, delicate cheekbones and sensuous lips. He put a finger to his chin, and she saw it was long, slim, manicured. He wore the clothing of a chef, but it was as black as his hair.

He turned sky blue eyes first on Slyr, then on Annaïg.

"So," he murmured in a silky voice. "You two are responsible for Lord Ghol's last several meals?"

Slyr lifted her chin. "We are," she said.

"Very well, then. You have nothing to fear. I am Chef Toel. You belong to me now."

He touched his finger to her lips, and everything faded to black.

NINE

"Something's moving up there," Attrebus said.

Sul nodded. "I know," he replied.

Of course you do, Attrebus thought sullenly.

Earlier that day the short-grass prairie had abruptly dropped off into one of the strangest landscapes Attrebus had ever seen. It looked as if a massive flood had stripped everything away but the dirt, and then cut that up into a labyrinth of arroyos and gullies. It was beautiful, in a way, because the vibrant rust, umber, olive, and yellow strata of the soil were exposed, like one of those thirty-layer cakes that Cheydinhal was famous for.

From above, it was fine to look on. But once in the maze, Attrebus felt mostly claustrophobic. And now someone or something was stalking them, up on those crumbly ridges.

"What if they attack us?"

"If they wanted to do that, we'd already have arrows in us," Sul grated. "They'll let us know what they want soon enough."

That didn't make Attrebus feel any more comfortable. Not that he'd been at ease before—not just because of the terrain, but because he found himself obsessively combing back through the events of his life. It wasn't that he fully believed Radhasa and Sul—but he conceded that there might be some element of truth to their rantings, an element they were exaggerating.

Sul, annoyingly enough, proved correct about those spying on them. The trail they were following bottled tighter, until it was only a few yards wide, and as they turned a corner, they found themselves facing four Khajiit.

Attrebus had known many Khajiit, of course. Some of his guard had been of the cat-people, and they were common enough in the Empire. But he had never seen any quite like this.

What struck his eye first were their mounts—monstrous cats that stood as high as a large horse at the shoulder. Their forelimbs were as thick as columns and half again as long as their rears, giving them an apelike appearance. Their coats were tawny, rib-boned with stripes the color of dried blood, and their feral yellow eyes seemed to promise evisceration—and that was only to start with.

Two of the riders seemed hardly less bestial, although they wore shirts that covered their torsos, and cravats around their necks. Where their fur was visible, it was pale yellowish-green spotted with black. Their faces were altogether more catlike than any Khajiit he'd ever met, and they slouched forward on their mounts.

The third rider was more like what Attrebus was used to, with features that were more manlike, although still unmistakably feline. And the final rider had such fine, delicate features, she might easily have been of merish blood, had her face not been splotched with irregular black rings.

"Well, there," the woman said in a beautiful, lilting voice. "Who do we have here traveling on our road?"

Attrebus cleared his throat, but Sul spoke more quickly.

"No one of consequence," he said. "Just two wayfarers going east."

Attrebus realized that—out of sheer habit—he'd been about to tell them exactly who he was. Sul had known that, too, hadn't he?

"East, you say?" the woman said. "East is good. The moons come from there. We're in favor of east. We're going there. But east for you—not so good, I think. East is not so friendly to men and mer, except, you know, in Rimmen. But how could you get there? And on our road?"

Attrebus heard a shuffle behind him, and a glance showed him what he should have known—there were two more riders behind him.

"We've no need to go to Rimmen," Sul replied.

"Rude," the woman said. "Where are my manners? Would you ride with us? Accept our protection?"

"We would be honored," Sul replied.

"Now wait a moment—" Attrebus began.

"The whelp is speaking out of turn," Sul cut in. "We would be honored. I had no idea the East was so fretful. And of course, we offer Je'm'ath in return for your kindness."

"Ah," the woman said. "You also have manners, outlander. Very well. Travel with my brothers and cousins and me. We are happy to share what we have."

And with that, they turned their mounts and rode east.

The trail soon debouched into a broad wash, a stream only inches deep but several yards across. Olive, tamarisk, and palm traced its outline, and beyond it three large tents had been pitched.

The air buzzed with metallic-looking dragonflies.

They've been waiting here, Attrebus thought. For us, or someone like us.

To him, that didn't bode well, but Sul seemed pretty relaxed about the whole situation. Did he imagine he could kill all of the Khajiit, if it came down to it?

It seemed possible. He remembered Sul's philosophy about fighting. Maybe he was just biding his time.

"Come," the woman said. "Let's have cake."

The tents were set up facing a small circle of stones within which ashes faintly smoked. They were ushered to sit, and when they complied, all of the Khajiit that accompanied them joined them. Even the tigerlike mounts folded themselves down next to their riders.

From the tents, Attrebus heard excited mewing and talking, and several very small kittenish faces poked out of one of the flaps and were just as quickly drawn back in.

After a moment what seemed to Attrebus to be a very old female came out, bearing a tray of small, round cakes, a bowl, and a narrow-necked bottle of rose-colored glass.

She knelt in front of Sul, placed a small cloth on the ground, then a cake on the cloth. With a precise movement of her hand, she pinched some sort of powder from a small bowl in the tray and sprinkled it on the cake. Then she took the bottle and let exactly four drops of golden liquid drip on it.

She moved to him, and then each of the Khajiit in turn, repeating the ritual gesture for gesture.

"Now we'll tell our names," the merish-looking woman said.

This near, she seemed even more beautiful and exotic than she had at a distance, and he noticed with a bit of surprise that the marks on her face were tattoos, rather than natural. Maybe she wasn't a cat after all.

"I am Lesspa," she said. "Our clan is F'aashe." She motioned with her knuckles toward the Khajiit to her left. "She is M'kai, my sister. There is Taaj, my maternal cousin. There is Sha'jal, my brother . . ."

Attrebus blinked. She seemed to be indicating one of the mounts.

He remembered something now, from his lessons as a boy— or was it the story his nurse had told him, about the four Khajiit and the riding kite?

He didn't know anything about these people at all, did he?

She finished naming everyone. Then he and Sul gave their

names—he called himself simply "Treb"—and they all lifted the cakes.

"Touch it to your mouth, but do not eat," Sul said as Attrebus opened his mouth. "That will satisfy the spirit of the ceremony. Khajiit food can be dangerous for us."

Lesspa nodded knowingly, but did not add anything.

So Attrebus watched the Khajiit first lick and then devour the sweets, while his belly growled.

After that, the rest of the camp turned out—another eight adults and about twelve children of various ages. They quickened the fire and set about making a stew of some sort.

"Can I eat that?" he asked Sul.

"If you want. I'm pretty sure it's honey and date soup. The cakes had moon-sugar in them. It's a drug, the same stuff they make skooma out of."

"They don't seem to be feeling any ill effects," Attrebus said.

"Because they're Khajiit—they eat the stuff every day, in one form or the other—and they're more naturally tolerant of it. Built different from you. Doesn't help them with skooma, though—there are plenty of Khajiit addicts."

"Lesspa doesn't look like she's all that different from us."

Sul snorted. "Some used to think that the Khajiit were another variety of mer. But it's the moons—the phases they're in when the kits are born determines how they turn out."

"So the mount—that really is her brother? They had the same parents?"

"Yes. But I'd stay away from that subject, if I were you. It's too easy to say the wrong thing."

Attrebus nodded, feeling stupid. Sul seemed to know everything, and he was starting to feel as if he knew very little. Whenever he went someplace he hadn't been, he always received a briefing about it. That had always been enough—it hadn't occurred to him to learn much about any place he had no business with. It made him wonder what important things he didn't know about Black Marsh.

But what really nagged him was that he had *known* Khajiit, been practically brothers with them. And yet he hadn't been aware of the most fundamental facts of their existence.

He tried to remember conversations he might have had with the cats in his guard, and realized he couldn't remember any that went on for more than a few sentences.

So maybe they hadn't been his friends. Maybe he really hadn't known most of his guard that well.

Which led him back to the festering question: Was Sul right about everything?

This depressing train of thought was interrupted by Lesspa returning her attention to them. She folded lithely down into a squat that looked as if it ought to hurt but clearly didn't.

"Now," she said, "we discuss Je'm'ath."

"Very well," Sul replied. "How can we help you?"

"Moon-sugar is scarce here, but plentiful in Rimmen. But the new potentate there forbids our clans inside the walls, and will not sell us sugar. You're not Khajiit. You go into Rimmen, get the sugar."

"Why won't he sell you sugar?"

"Doesn't like the free clans. He's outlawed us on our own land. Khajiit that work in the walls have all they want, but we won't live like that, yes? We won't."

"That sounds reasonable," Sul said. "But our path takes us beyond Rimmen, to the border."

"Ours turns back from here."

Sul nodded thoughtfully. "Very well."

"Wait a minute," Attrebus said.

"No," Sul said. "You don't understand this."

"I'm starting to. You promise not to kill us if we help you get moon-sugar?"

"We *protect* you," Lesspa said.

"Yes, you protect us from you."

"You meet us first," Lesspa said. "That's good for you. There is no order in the North. Bandits, killers, prey even on weak Khajiit, and your kind is very unpopular on these plains. Miles to Rimmen. Many more to the border. We help you survive, you help us."

"What if we say no? You'll kill us?"

"No. We ate cake with you. Maybe kill you next time, but not now. Still, you'll die soon enough without us."

Attrebus looked at Sul. "Is she right?"

"Probably. The last time I was here, this was all still in the Empire and pacified. Things have changed."

"Pacified," Lesspa said. "Yes. Not now. All is wild. The mane was assassinated, you know? There is war in the South. Here, just chaos and potentate."

"Look," Attrebus said, trying to force a little gravity into his voice. "What Sul and I are doing is very important. Something very, very bad is happening in Black Marsh, something that could destroy us all. You should be proud to help us. There would be much honor in that."

"We will help you. And you will give us Je'm'ath. Then you will go find this bad thing, and we will go west."

"Agreed," Sul snapped before Attrebus could say anything else.

———

Annaïg didn't reply that night, but he didn't let it concern him. Likely she was just asleep or busy. He went to sleep still sour over the bargain Sul had made and annoyed that Lesspa naturally assumed the Dunmer was the leader.

The next day he had to grudgingly admit things might have worked out for the best. Twice before noon they met other bands of Khajiit who plainly wanted to kill Sul and him. The first bunch offered to buy them, and the second actually had to be backed down by a show of force.

They left the badlands and entered a ragged steppe of thorn-scrub. It lifted and rolled in long undulations. Two days on that and finally, over a distant hill they could see a golden gleam.

"Rimmen," Lesspa said. "We dare go no nearer."

"That's still a long way," Sul said. "What's between here and there?"

"Rimmen's patrols. Traders. Not so dangerous for you in there, but dangerous for us." She handed him a plain leather bag. "Get a good deal."

And so they left Lesspa and her clan and continued on toward Rimmen.

"This is a waste of time," Attrebus complained. "We're going to lose a day."

"No we aren't," Sul said. "We're just going to ride on to the border. We've no business in Rimmen."

At first Attrebus wasn't sure he'd heard right.

"But you took their oath," he protested when it sank in. "Bound us to do it. We have their money!"

"Which I'm sure will be of use to us."

"But they kept their end of the bargain," Attrebus said. "We can't—"

"We can," Sul replied. "I've broken much deeper oaths than this. I survived it. This is not only a waste of time, it's dangerous. We'll be breaking the law, supplying them with contraband."

"The law doesn't sound fair," Attrebus said.

"Fair? What do you even mean by that? No law is fair to everyone. A law against stealing is unfair to thieves. The thing to think about is whether you'll be able to save your precious Annaïg if you're clapped in a dungeon or beheaded."

And something burst in Attrebus.

"What can I do anyway?" he shouted. "You say I'm not a tenth the man I think I am, right? So what are we going to do, the two of us, against this *thing*? With me being so useless and all?"

To his horror, he heard his voice crack and realized he was starting to cry.

"Here we go," Sul said.

"What do you care anyway? I can't imagine you care if Umbriel kills everyone."

"That's right, I don't," Sul admitted.

"But—then *why*? Why are you bothering, if you don't care?"

Sul glared at him, and Attrebus suddenly saw something in those terrible eyes he hadn't seen before: pain.

"I loved someone," Sul snarled. "She was murdered. My homeland was destroyed, my people decimated and scattered to the winds. I lost everything. Those responsible for that must pay, and one of them is on Umbriel. Is that simple enough for you?"

His speech struck Attrebus dumb for a moment. Not so much the words as the tone, the sheer tortured flatness of Sul's voice.

"I'm sorry," he finally said.

"Just ride," Sul snapped.

But he couldn't let it go. "You mean to say that you were there when the Red Mountain exploded? You know what happened?"

Sul didn't answer.

"It must be terrible. I can't imagine—"

"Please, for the favor of Mephala don't tell me what you can and can't imagine. Just do what I say."

His tone was still odd, and Attrebus still didn't exactly trust the man. But he was starting to believe him, at least as far as Umbriel was concerned. And in other things.

He took a deep breath. "It's true, isn't it? What Radhasa said about me?"

"Oh, thank the gods," Sul intoned, "we're back to you again.

Are you still worried about the shame? About everyone knowing but you?"

"Wouldn't you be?"

"But they don't," Sul said, his voice softening a bit. "Most people in the world *don't* know you're a fraud."

"My father, my mother, most of the court—they all must have been sniggering behind my back."

"So what? More people believe in you than don't."

"They believe in a lie. You just said it."

"Then become the truth, you idiot. Become what they *think* you are."

Attrebus let that sink in for a moment.

"You think that's possible?"

"I don't know. But we can find out."

"You'll help me?"

"I suppose I must," Sul sighed.

"Why?"

"You said it yourself—it's just the two of us. We have to get to Morrowind, and we have to get there before Umbriel."

"Why? What's in Morrowind? How do you know Umbriel is going there?"

"It is, just trust me. And we'll never beat it on foot or horse-back. I think I might know the way, but we'll need to make it to the Niben Valley first. And it would be helpful to have allies. The legendary Prince Attrebus ought to be able to drum up a few."

Attrebus thought that over and found that it made some sense. "Thank you," he finally said.

Sul nodded reluctantly.

"But here's the thing . . ." Attrebus continued.

"What now?"

"Prince Attrebus wouldn't take Lesspa's money and betray his oath. He'd get the moon-sugar and bring it back to her."

For a long moment Sul didn't say anything, but then his shoulders seemed to relax slightly.

"Right," he said.

———

Rimmen had elegant bones of ivory-colored stone with few towers but many domes. Soldiers—human soldiers—met them at the gate, searched them, questioned them, and eventually passed them through. For another hundred yards they snaked through the twists and turns of an entry overlooked by platforms for archers, mages, and siege weapons. That brought them to the market, a bustling, colorful plaza empty in the middle but girdled by tents and stalls and bounded by canals. A broad avenue flanked by even more expansive waterways continued on to what was clearly the palace, an ancient-looking structure raised up on a high, tiered stone substructure. The tiers held some buildings, and apparently earth, because he could see trees growing there. Surmounting that was a cylindrical building with a large golden dome. Water cascaded down the sides of the palace, feeding the pool that encircled it.

Attrebus wondered where all of the water came from.

Off to the eastern side of the palace, he could see the odd curly-edged roof of what had to be the Akaviri temple Annaïg had mentioned. The only place he'd ever seen with similar architecture was Cloud Ruler Temple, which he had viewed from a distance when he was ten, hunting with his father's traveling court in the mountains north of Bruma. He remembered that trip with fondness—he'd killed his first bear.

Or maybe he hadn't, now that he thought of it. It had been moving a little strangely when he saw it, hadn't it? Had it already been wounded? Poisoned? Ensorcelled?

Why would his father have done that? Why all of this?

He pushed that down, trying to focus. He'd promised Annaïg a description of Rimmen.

He was surprised that fewer than half of the people he saw were Khajiit, and many of those lolled about with wild or vacant eyes, skooma pipes clutched in their hands. It was a strange sight to see in an open, public square. He began to understand Lesspa and her people better.

They left the plaza, crossing a canal on a footbridge and thence down a narrow street where gently chiming bells were depended between the flat roofs of the buildings and viridian moths flittered in the shadows. The addicts were even thicker here, a few watching them and holding out their hands for money; but most were shivering, lost in their visions.

They arrived at their destination, a smaller square with a fortified building surrounded by guards in purple surcoats and red sashes. A sign proclaimed the place to be kingdom of rimmen state store.

Once again they were searched, questioned, and then passed into a low-ceilinged room where twenty or so people stood on line at a counter. Only one person, an Altmer, seemed to be dealing with the customers, but others worked behind him, wrapping paper packages into even larger paper packages.

"This was your idea," Sul pointed out. He handed him the bag of coins.

"What do I do?" Attrebus asked.

"You've never stood on line, have you?"

"No."

"Well, embrace the experience. I'm going to sit down. When you get to the man at the counter, I'll come back."

As bored as the man at the counter seemed from a distance, he somehow seemed even less enthusiastic when Attrebus and Sul reached him an hour later.

He took the gold, looked it over, and then weighed it.

"What do you want? He asked.

"Moon-sugar."

"Forty pounds, then," he said.

"Sixty," Attrebus challenged. He'd bargained before, for fun.

"There's no negotiation," the mer said wearily. "Outlanders! Look, the price is fixed by the office of the potentate. Take it or leave it, I really don't care."

"We'll take it," Sul said.

"It is my mandatory duty to warn you that if you sell or attempt to sell moon-sugar in the Kingdom of Rimmen," the man said, "you will be subject to a fine of triple the worth of the sugar. If you sell or attempt to sell more than two pounds, you will be subject to execution. Do you understand these terms?"

"Yes," Sul said. Attrebus just nodded, feeling his face warm.

"Very well. Your name here, please." He shoved a ledger at Attrebus.

He hesitated, then signed it *Uriel Tripitus*.

The rest was easy. They packed the stuff on their horses, rode out of Rimmen, and headed west.

They reached Lesspa's camp near sundown. She was there, along with the others, crouched around the fire. She watched them come, her expression odd but unreadable. Her mouth moved, though, as if she was trying to say something.

Sul stopped.

"This isn't right," he said. "Something isn't right."

"Dismount!" someone shouted. "This is Captain Evernal of the Kingdom of Rimmen regulators. Remove your weapons and make your beasts available for search."

Beyond the fire, Attrebus could now make out figures, moving from cover.

A lot of them.

PART III

BETRAYALS

ONE

———————

Mere-Glim swam through a forest of sessile crabs. Their squat, thorny bodies attached to the floor of the sump were barely noticeable, but their tiny, venomous claws were set on the ends of twenty-foot-long yellow and viridian tentacles that groped lazily after him.

The quick silver blades of nickfish whipped about him, dodging among the crabs. He saw one that didn't dodge fast enough; it struggled only an instant before the toxin killed it and it was dragged slowly downward.

Glim missed Annaïg. He missed Black Marsh, and hoped desperately that something was left of it.

But he liked the sump. It was strange and beautiful and mostly quiet. And since he did his jobs well—or at least they thought he did—he was mostly left alone. When he was with the other skraws, he took care not to show exactly how fast he could swim. That way—on days like this—he had a little time to explore.

He moved into deeper water, searching for the opening he'd seen a few days before. So far none of the passages he'd found went anywhere interesting, but he continued to hope. This one he'd noticed because of the efflorescence of life around it, as if the water coming down was more nourishing somehow.

He found it, a rather low-ceilinged passage, and began swimming up it. It wasn't long before he emerged from the water, but as he'd hoped, the tunnel continued at a steepening angle, so he began to climb.

Not much later he began to hear a peculiar sound, an inconstant musical note, a very low whistle, and as he ascended, it grew louder.

He could see light before he recognized it as the wind blowing over the hole he now saw above. Excited, he quickened his pace.

When he got there, he knew it had been worth the climb.

He stood between forest and void.

Below the ledge he stood on was a fall of a few thousand feet to the verdant green canopy and meandering black rivers of his homeland. That took his breath, but the trees nearly kept it.

At his back a massive trunk as big around as a gate tower sprouted from the stone, its roots dug into the cliff over hundreds of feet like the tentacles of some huge octopus. It split into four enormous limbs, one of which passed just over his head and out, like a ceiling above him, twisting gradually left as it did so, and dropping down to eventually obscure some of the landscape below. This was the lowest limb visible; but above him they were so thick he couldn't see the sky.

He stood there for a long moment, letting language leave him, letting it all fill him as shapes, colors, smells. He had a profound feeling of familiarity and peace.

And sound—the musical piping of thirty kinds of strange birds, a distant voice singing in words he couldn't make out—and the wind, soughing through the branches as Umbriel slowly rotated.

And very faintly, the screams from below.

In that long moment, he felt something. A sort of hum in the air, or beneath it. Or in his head.

And after a moment he realized it was coming from the trees. He walked over and put his hand against the bark, and it grew louder, a sort of murmuring. The bark, the leaves . . .

And then he understood; they resembled the Hist.

They weren't; the leaves were too oblate, the bark less fretted, the smell a bit off. But it could be a cousin to them, as red oaks and white oaks were cousins.

Intrigued, he climbed up the leaning back of the tree and out onto one of the branches, following along its very gentle upward and outward slope. A troop of monkeylike creatures went by on another branch, each of them bearing a net-sack held on by a tumpline across their foreheads. The sacks were full of fruit, the kind the skraws called bloodball. A little later he saw some bloodball himself, growing on vines that wound in and out of the branches. More curiously, as the branch got higher and he could see the sun, he found fruit and peculiar masses of grass heavy with seed growing directly out of the trunk tree itself, as if planted there. He was examining it when he heard a little gasp.

He turned to find a young woman with the coloring of a Dunmer staring at him in apparent horror. She wore a broad-brimmed hat, knee-length pants, and a loose shirt. Her feet were bare.

She took a step back.

"I mean you no harm," Mere-Glim said in his softest voice. "I was just exploring the tree."

"You surprised me," the woman said. "I've never seen anyone who looks like you."

"I work in the sump," he said.

"Oh. That explains it. I've never met anyone from there." She paused. "Do you like it, the sump?"

"I do," Glim replied. "I like the water and the things that live in it. And it's interesting, helping people be born." He glanced around. "But this—this is beautiful, too. You must like it here."

"It's funny you should ask that," she said. "Because I never thought about that until—well, until all of that appeared below us." She gestured toward Black Marsh.

"What was there before?"

"Well—nothing. The elder tree-tenders say that there was a time before when there was a sky, and land beneath—some even say that long ago Umbriel didn't fly, that it was planted like those moss-oats there. Isn't that a funny notion? To live planted?"

"It's how I've always lived until lately," Glim told her.

"What do you mean?"

"I'm from down there," he said, gesturing at Black Marsh.

As the words left his mouth, he wished he could suck them back in. If she told anyone, word would get around that he'd been here. He hadn't exactly been forbidden to come here, but lack of explicit permission to do something usually amounted to forbiddance on Umbriel.

"Down there?" she said. "That's amazing. What's it like? How did you get here?"

"I flew here," he said. "I thought everyone on Umbriel must know about that. Everyone in the kitchens seemed to."

"You were in the kitchens?" A little tremor ran through her.

"Yes. Why?"

"Was it horrible? I've heard terrible things. My friend Kalmo takes grain to five of them, and he said—"

"Do you know how to reach the kitchens from here?" he interrupted.

"No, but I can always ask Kalmo."

"Could you do that?"

"Now? I'm not sure where he is."

"No, just ask him next time you see him. I have a friend that works there I'd like to talk to."

"But then how will I tell you?"

"I'll come back," he said. "You can tell me when you're usually here, and I'll meet you."

"Okay," she said. "But—you have to do something for me."

"What's that?"

"Orchid shrimp. We almost never get to have them—our kitchen doesn't use them much. Please?"

"I can do that," he assured her.

"And you have to tell me about down there."

"Next time," he promised. "Right now I need to go."

"Next time, then," she said. "You can find me here every day about this time."

"Good." He paused uncomfortably. "And would you mind, ah, not mentioning me to anyone? I'm not sure I'm supposed to be up here."

"Who would I mention? You haven't told me your name."

"Mere-Glim."

"That's a strange name. But then it would be, wouldn't it? My name is Fhena."

Glim nodded, not knowing what else to say, so he turned and reluctantly retraced his steps back down the tree, through the tunnel, and into the sump again.

But now he had a way out. If he could find Annaïg, if she had reproduced her flying potion.

There were still many ifs.

He went back down the Drop, but none of the sacs had changed color in the few hours he'd been gone, so he went quickly back to the shallows, because Wert had asked him to collect a few singe anemones—Wert was really supposed to do it, but the stingers couldn't get through Glim's scales, so the skraw had asked him to do it.

He went to the place in the shallows where they grew thickest, and found that area particularly messy with bodies. He tried to ignore them, as he usually did, but a familiar face caught his eye.

It was the woman from the kitchen, the one who had Annaïg. Qijne. Even in death her gaze was terrifying.

Suddenly frantic, he began searching through the corpses. They all wore the tattered remnants of the same uniform. What happened to kill them all? Some sort of accident? A mass execution?

He continued, each time fearing the next lifeless face would be Annaïg's, but even after he went over them twice, she wasn't there. But that didn't mean anything. A carrion scorp or any of several large bottom feeders could have dragged her off.

He was about to begin a third search when a gleam caught his eyes, something in the sand.

He reached down and pulled it up—Annaïg's magic locket.

He felt like something hot was vibrating in him when he got back to the skraw warrens. When he took Wert the anemones, he found him with Eryob, their overseer.

"You're late," Eryob said. His gaze moved to the anemones. Then to Wert. "Did you send him to do your work?"

"Wert does his job, and more," Mere-Glim bristled. "I was just helping him out. Everything got done."

Eryob's bushy red eyebrows sank so low they nearly covered his eyes. "That's not the point, skraw."

"Well, enlighten me," Glim snapped. "What is the point? And who are you to make it? You don't inhale the vapors. You don't pick around corpses or bring anyone up to be born. What does the sump need with you? Just leave us alone and everything will get done. In fact—"

He didn't get to finish. Eryob lifted his fist and uncurled it, and black pain exploded in Glim's head. His limbs spasmed and he toppled to the floor. It went on for a long time.

TWO

———

Heat woke her, suffocating heat wrapped around her body, burned into her lungs. She gasped and flailed; the air seemed incredibly heavy and murky. She wrapped her arms around herself, feeling only slick, wet skin.

She heard a whimper and then a strangled shriek. She made out a silhouette a few feet from her, revealed in the dim illumination from four fuzzy-looking globes of a dark amber color, one in each direction, all above her.

"Slyr?"

"Yes," the frantic voice answered. "What's happening? We're being burned alive!"

Annaïg swung her feet down and found the floor, wincing at the heat of the stone against her soles. The air hurt to move through, too, especially when she found the vent in the floor it was coming out of. She jumped back with a shriek.

"It's steam," she said.

"Why? What are they doing to us?"

Annaïg recalled the battle, and Toel's blue eyes. Then he had touched her lips. That was all she remembered.

She found a wall and began working down it and soon discovered a seam that might be a door.

Slyr had joined her in exploring now, panting hoarsely.

"I don't know what's going on," Annaïg said. "But I . . . I think this isn't meant to kill us. It's hot, but not that hot. And I don't think it's getting worse."

"Right," Slyr said. "You must be right. Why would he go through the trouble of capturing us only to kill us? He wouldn't do that, would he?" She sounded as if she were trying to convince herself.

"I don't know Toel," Annaïg said. "I don't know anything about him."

"Why do you think I do?" Slyr snapped.

There was something strange about her tone.

"I didn't say you did," Annaïg replied.

Slyr was silent for a moment.

"Well, I do know a bit," she finally offered. "He—" She stopped, then laughed softly. She folded back down on her bench.

"What?"

"I think they're cleaning us," she replied. "I've heard they use steam to draw the impurities from the body."

"I've heard of that," Annaïg remembered. "In Skyrim they do it, and it's come and gone as a fashion in Cyrodiil. Black Marsh is already a steaming jungle and Argonians don't sweat, so it never caught on there."

Her breathing slowed as panic faded. Now that the surprise and fear were gone, the pervasive heat actually felt pretty nice.

"What else do you know about Toel?"

"Everyone has heard of Toel," Slyr said. "Most master chefs of the higher kitchens are born to it, but Toel started down with us. When he wants something, he will do whatever is necessary to get it."

"Clearly," Annaïg replied.

"More than you know. Qijne and her kitchen served three lords. Toel serves a much greater one, but that is still a dangerous thing. Bargains must have been struck, and probably a few assassinations accomplished."

"A few?"

"Other than the rest of our kitchen, I mean."

"They're all dead, aren't they?"

"I didn't see anyone moving."

Annaïg was starting to feel a little dizzy. It wasn't getting any hotter, but the heat was beginning to sit more heavily on her.

"I'm sorry," she said. "I didn't know many of them very well, but you . . ."

"I hated most of them," Slyr said. "And I was indifferent to most of the rest."

"But you saved my life. Qijne was trying to kill me."

"You're—ah—different," Slyr said.

"Well—thank you."

Slyr crossed her arms. "Besides, he came for you. If you were dead, what use would I be to him?"

"Don't sell yourself short."

"I don't," Slyr said softly.

An awkward pause followed.

"I hope they let us out of here soon," Annaïg ventured, to try to lighten things.

"Yes."

But it was too hot to talk after that. Annaïg sat with her head on her knees, closed her eyes and pretended she was on the levee at Yor-Tiq, back in Black Marsh, lazing in the sun while Glim went diving for trogfish. It was a difficult fantasy to maintain; images of the slaughter kept coming back to her, especially Qijne's dying gaze.

Remembering that, she felt at her wrist. It was still there, the torus. They hadn't noticed it when they took her clothes. If she could figure out how to use it, she would at least have one small advantage.

She squeezed it, tried to *think* the blade out, but nothing worked, and the heat made her so tired she finally stopped trying.

Just as she thought she couldn't take any more, light came flooding through what she had earlier guessed was a door, and behind it the sweet kiss of cool air.

"Out, and into the pool with you," a voice said. Annaïg hesitated, embarrassed at her lack of clothing but anxious to get out of the heat. She saw the mentioned pool ahead. It looked cool, lovely.

Slyr was already on her way, so she followed. To her surprise, she didn't see anyone, although the voice had sounded near.

The water was so shockingly cold that for an instant she thought she might lose consciousness. Her yelp literally got closed in her throat.

"Kaoc'!" she finally managed.

"Sumpslurry!" Slyr gasped.

Their gazes met, held for an instant—and then together they began laughing. It just exploded out of Annaïg, as if it had been bottled and pent up for a thousand years. The feeling wasn't happiness; it was more like being crazy.

But it was a lot better than crying.

"You should have seen your expression," Slyr giggled when she finally got control of herself.

"I'm sure it was no more ridiculous than yours," she replied.

"Lords, this is cold."

Annaïg took in the new chamber then; it had low ceilings of cloth woven in complicated, curvilinear patterns of gold, hyacinth, lime, and sanguine. It draped down the walls, giving the appearance that they were in a large, very oddly shaped tent. Globes like those in the sweat-room, but brighter, depended here and there, filling the chamber with a pleasant golden light. On the near wall, two golden robes hung.

"I hope those are ours," she said.

"Not yet they aren't," the voice from earlier said. "Back in the heat with you."

This time her gaze found the speaker—a froglike creature about two feet high, mottled orange, yellow, and green. It was crouched above the doorway.

"We have to go back in there?" Annaïg said.

"You're both extremely polluted," the thing said. "This could take a while. But at least you seem to be enjoying it."

———

She wasn't enjoying it an hour later, when the alternating heat and cold had rendered all the strength out of her. She was also starving. But finally the frog-thing gave a little nod and sent them across the room to the robes.

The fabric was like nothing she had ever touched before, utterly smooth, almost like a liquid. She thought she had never felt anything better.

"Come along," the creature said, hopping down from its perch and landing, to stand on its hind limbs. It waddled off, through a slit in the cloth that draped the walls and into a smooth, polished corridor.

After a few turns he led them into a room appointed much as the pool-room had been, except the drapery was of more muted, autumn shades. Her heart struck up a bit when she saw a small, low table set with a pitcher of some sort of liquid and bowls of fruits, fern fronds, and small condiment bowls.

"Eat," the creature said. "Rest. Be ready to speak with Lord Toel."

Annaïg didn't have to be told twice.

The pitcher contained an effervescent beverage that had almost no taste, but reminded her of honeysuckle and plum, though it wasn't sweet. The fruits were all unknown to her: a small orange berry with a tough rind but sweet, lemony pulp inside; a black, lozenge-shaped thing with no skin that was a bit chewy and was a lot like soft cheese; tiny berries no larger than the head of a needle, but clustered in the thousands, which exploded into vapor on touching her tongue. The ferns were the least pleasant, but the various jellies in the small bowls clung viscously to them, and those were delightfully strange.

She couldn't taste alcohol in the drink, but by the time she felt sated, things were getting pleasantly spinny.

"This is nice," Annaïg said, looking around. There were two beds, also on the floor. "Do you think this is our room? One room just for the two of us?"

"Like our little hideaway in Qijne's kitchen."

"But bigger. And with beds. And—ah—interesting food."

Slyr closed her eyes. "I've dreamed of this," she said. "I knew it would be better."

"Congratulations," Annaïg said.

Slyr shook her head. "It's because of you. These things you come up with . . . when Toel figures that out, I'll be out of his kitchen, just as your lizard-friend was out of Qijne's."

"That won't happen," Annaïg said. "Without you, I wouldn't have known where to start, and now I don't know where to start again. I need you."

"Toel will have cooks of more use to you."

"He won't," Annaïg said. "It's both of us or neither."

Slyr shook her head. "You're a strange one," she said. "But I—" She put her head down.

"What?"

"I said I didn't care about anyone in Qijne's kitchen. But if you had died, I think I might be sad."

Annaïg smiled. "Thanks," she said.

"Okay," Slyr said, rising unsteadily. "Do you care which bed?"

"No. You choose."

Annaïg soon found her own bed. Like the robe, it was a delight, especially after weeks of hard pallets and stone floor.

She was dropping off to sleep, feeling content for the moment, at least in a creature sort of way.

She thought maybe she should open her locket, contact

Attrebus, let him know how things had changed.

But then it struck her: Her amulet was gone.

———

Even with worry as her bedmate, when she woke the next morning she was more rested and felt better than she had in a long time, even before coming to Umbriel. Slyr was still dead to the world, but the frog-creature had returned and was waiting patiently near the table.

"You'll break your fast with Lord Toel," he said.

"Let me wake Slyr," she said.

"Not her," it said. "Only you."

Slyr's fears from the night before were still fresh in her mind. "I'd rather—" She began.

"You'd rather not protest Lord Toel's wishes," the thing interrupted.

She nodded, reminding herself that she had a greater mission. Besides, she could never put in a good word for the other woman if she never got to talk to Toel.

"What's your name?" she asked the creature.

"Dulgiijbiddiggungudingu," it sputtered. "Gluuip."

She starred at the froth the name had formed on the creature's mouth.

"Dulbig—" she started.

"Dulg will do," he added.

"Lead the way, Dulg."

"You don't imagine you're going in that?" Dulg asked. He gestured toward a curtained area.

She followed his gesture, and in the enclosure discovered a gold and black gown. Like everything else here, it might have been spun of spider silk, or something far finer.

She never wore things like this. It clung embarrassingly to her contours and was uselessly ornamented with fine beaded webs at the cuffs and collars. She felt clunky and far more out of her element than she had in Qijne's fire pits. Although her father held a noble title in High Rock that had once had currency in Black Marsh, since before she was born there had been no balls, no cotillions, no evenings at the theater. All of that—and the frippery that went with it—was swept away when the Argonians retook control of their land.

And good riddance to that, at least. Or so she had always thought.

But she felt herself wondering if Attrebus would think she looked passable in this outfit.

"Come, come," Dulg called impatiently. "Your hair and face must be tended to."

An hour later, after the services of a silent, slight, blondish man, Dulg finally led her through a suite of richly furnished rooms and into a chamber with fresh air pouring through a large door and beyond . . .

Toel was there, but she could not make her gaze focus on him. There was too much else to wonder at.

She was outside, and Umbriel rose and fell all around her.

She stood on an outjut in a cliff face that was steep but not vertical, and that looked out on a vast, conical basin. Below her spread an emerald green lake and, above, the city grew from the stone itself, twisting spires and latticed buildings that might have been built with colored wire, whole castles hanging like bird cages from immensely thick cables. Higher still, the rocky rim of the island supported gossamer towers in every hue imaginable, and what appeared to be an enormous spiderweb of spun glass that broke the sunlight into hundreds of tiny rainbows.

"You like my little window?" Toel asked.

She stiffened, afraid to say anything for fear it might be the wrong thing, but just as fearful of saying nothing.

"It's beautiful," she said. "I didn't know."

"Didn't know that anything in Umbriel could be beautiful, you mean?"

She opened her mouth to try and correct her mistake, but he shook his head.

"How could you, laboring down in the pits? How could you have imagined this?"

She nodded.

"Do you fear me, child?" he asked.

"I do," she admitted.

He smiled slightly at that, and then walked closer to the rail, putting his back to her. If she were quick and strong, she might send him toppling over.

But of course he knew that. She could tell by the easy confidence with which he moved. He knew she couldn't—or wouldn't—do any such thing.

"Do you like your quarters?" he asked.

"Very much," she replied. "You are very generous."

"I've elevated you," he said. "Things are better here. I think you will find your work more enjoyable, more stimulating."

He turned and walked to a small table furnished with two chairs.

"Sit," he said. "Join me."

She complied, and a slight man in a vest with many buttons brought them a drink that hissed and fizzed and was mostly vapor. It tasted like mint, sage, and orange peel and was nearly intolerably cold.

"Now," Toel said. "Tell me about this place you are from."

"Lord?"

"What is it like, how was your life there? What did you do? That sort of thing."

She wondered at first why she felt so surprised, but then it occurred to her that no one—not even Slyr—had ever asked her about her life before coming to Umbriel—not unless it concerned her knowledge of plants and minerals.

"There's not much left of it, I think," she said.

"No, I imagine not. And yet some of it lives in you yet, yes? And in Umbriel."

"You mean because their souls were consumed here?"

"Not merely consumed," he replied. "Mostly, yes, Umbriel must use living energy to remain aloft and functioning. But some of it is cycled, transformed, reborn—it's not all lost. Take solace in that, if you can. If you cannot, it's no matter to me, really, but a waste of your time and energy."

"You think grieving a waste?"

"What else could it be? Anger, fear, ecstasy—these states of mind might produce something useful. Grief and regret produce nothing except bad poetry, which is actually worse than nothing. Now. Speak of what I asked you."

She closed her eyes, trying to decide where to start, what to say. She didn't want to tell him anything that might help Umbriel and its masters.

"My home was in a city called Lilmoth," she said. "In the Kingdom of Black Marsh. I lived with my father. He was—"

Toel held up a finger. "Pardon me," he said. "What is a father?"

"Maybe I used the wrong word," she said. "I'm still learning this dialect."

"Yes. I know of no such word."

"My father is the man who sired me."

Again the blank stare.

She shifted and held her hand up, palms facing each other.

"Ah, a man and woman, they, ahh . . . procreate—"

"Yes," Toel said. "That can be very entertaining."

She felt her face warm and nodded.

"You think so, too, I see. Very interesting. So a father is the man you used to procreate with?"

"No. Oh, no. That would be—no. I mean I've never—" She shook her head and started again. "A man and woman—my father and mother—they procreated and had me."

"'Had you'?"

"I was born to them."

"You're not making sense, dear."

"After they procreated, I was conceived, and I grew in my mother until I was born."

He sat back, and for the first time she saw his eyes flash with real astonishment. It looked very strange on him, as if he had never been surprised at anything.

"Do you mean to say that you were inside of a woman? And came out of her?"

"Yes."

"Like a parasite—like a Zilh worm or chest borer?"

"No, it's normal, it's—weren't you . . . ?"

"That's revolting!" he said, and laughed. "Absolutely revolting. Did you eat her corpse after you came out?"

"Well, it didn't kill her."

"How big were you?"

She shaped her hands to indicate the size of a newborn.

"Well, I have to say, this is already one of the most interesting—and disturbing—conversations I've ever had."

"Then you people aren't born?"

"Of course we are. Properly, from the Marrow Sump."

"So when you use the word 'procreate'—"

"It simply means sex. Copulation. It has no other sense, that I know of."

Annaïg suddenly felt the world rearranging itself around her. She had been assuming that all the talk about coming from the sump and returning to it was a metaphor, a way of talking about life and death.

But Toel wasn't kidding, she was sure of that.

"Please, go on. Tell me more such disgusting things."

And so they talked on. After his initial outburst, however, he did not interrupt her much; he listened, with only the occasional question, usually concerning terms he didn't know. She talked mostly about her life in Black Marsh, about history, about the secession of Black Marsh from the Empire and the subsequent collapse of the Empire. She did not say anything about the revival of the Empire, about the Emperor or Attrebus—but it was a challenge, because the way he listened, the way he hung on her every word, made her want to keep talking, to not let it stop, to keep that attention on her forever.

When she finally forced herself to stop, he steepled his fingers under his lip. Then he nodded out at his world.

"You speak of vast forests and deserts, of countries whose size almost surpasses my imagination. I have never walked such lands—I never will. This, Umbriel, is the only world I can ever know. This, Umbriel, is your home now, and the only place you will ever know again. The sooner you understand that, the better. Waste no time on what you have lost, for you will never have it again."

"But my world is all around you," she said. "I could take you there, show it to you . . ."

He shook his head. "It is not so simple. The outside of Umbriel, in a sense, is in your world. But here, where you find yourself now—surely you observed the larvae, saw how they lose corporeal form when they move fully into your plane. The same would be true of me, were I to leave. My body would dissolve, and Umbriel would reclaim the stuff of my soul. There is no leaving for me. Or you."

"But I am not from Umbriel," she said. "I am not a part of it."

"Not yet," Toel said. "But in time you will be as much a part of Umbriel as I am."

THREE

The man who had named himself Captain Evernal stepped from behind the tent. He was fortyish, with tanned skin, blond hair, and an impressive mustache.

Attrebus could see twenty men, but he suspected there were more.

"What's this?" Sul asked.

Evernal shrugged. "That depends on your business here."

"We have no business here," Sul replied.

"You're a mile off the main road."

"Is that a crime?"

"It isn't," Evernal said. "But it suggests you were coming to this camp, since there isn't anything else in this direction."

"Happenstance. We were sightseeing. Hoping to run across a flock of greems. The lad here has never seen one."

"Well, then," the captain said. "You won't mind us searching your packs."

Sul gestured at their mounts. Four of the regulators strode over. It didn't take them long to find the moon-sugar.

"Well, this is interesting," the captain said.

Attrebus saw Sul's shoulders relax, slightly.

Oh, Divines, he's going to try it, Attrebus thought.

"Why is it interesting?" Attrebus blurted. "I paid a fair price for that."

"Then surely you were warned about the penalties of trafficking with the wild cats."

"There's no trafficking here," Attrebus said. "I've not offered to sell anything."

Evernal rolled his eyes. "Oh, come now."

Attrebus drew himself straighter. "No, *you* come now, Captain Evernal. Do you have a charge to make? Based on what evidence?"

"Evidence? I don't need evidence," Evernal said. "I know very well that you bought that sugar for these cats. Look around you—there's no court involved. No witnesses."

"I see. Then you're bandits, plain and simple."

"We're regulators. We uphold the law."

Attrebus snorted. "Do you even know what a contradiction is? You just as much as said you could murder us with impunity, and you specifically bragged there are no courts involved. You're a common brigand, sir."

Evernal reddened, but some of his men had uneasy expressions, which suggested he'd hit a nerve.

"Go," Evernal finally said. "Leave the sugar."

Attrebus felt his stomach unclench a bit. But then he saw the expression on Lesspa's face.

"What about them?" he asked.

"I told you to go. Count your blessings and do it."

"Come on," Sul said.

But then Attrebus noticed something. He pushed away his uncertainties, pulled his center tight.

"No," he said.

"No?" the captain repeated incredulously.

"Who do you think I am?" Attrebus thundered. "I know you by your Nibenese accent, Evernal. You may work for the thug who runs Rimmen, but your body and soul belong to the Empire.

Who do you think I am?"

He saw Evernal waver and his eyes widen.

"Milord . . ."

"Wrong title," Attrebus snapped. "Try again. My likeness is common enough, even here, I'm sure."

The captain swallowed audibly. "My Prince," he managed. "Your face is a bit bruised, and . . ."

"Is it?" Attrebus said. "I suppose that it is. And so you are to be forgiven for that. For *that*. But I do not care to have my business questioned or my escort detained."

Evernal looked around at the Khajiit.

"Escort?"

"It is my business, Captain. We'll be out of your territory in a day, and you'll never see any of us here again."

"It's not that simple, highness—"

"It is," Attrebus said. "Look around you. There are no courts here."

Evernal sighed and stepped near. "I fought for your father," he said. "I've heard much of you. But work has been scarce in Cyrodiil."

Attrebus softened his tone. "Then you know in your heart what's right. And you know my reputation. I'm on a mission of greatest gravity, and already I am too much delayed. Will you really let it be said that you hindered Prince Attrebus Mede?"

"No, Prince," Evernal replied. "I would not."

Attrebus clapped him on the shoulder. "Good man," he said.

Evernal bowed, then beckoned to his men. In a few moments they were alone with the Khajiit.

"That was quite a gamble," Sul said when they were gone. "Telling them who you were. What if they had decided to ransom you?"

Attrebus smiled, suddenly feeling a bit shaky.

"I saw he was wearing the badge of the eighteenth legion,"

he said. "Just under his cloak, pinned next to a lock of some girl's hair. I knew he'd not only fought for my father, but that he was still proud of it."

Sul's glare lessened a bit.

"You're trembling," he said.

Attrebus sat down on the ground. "Right," he said, running his hands through his hair. "I didn't really think. I've made so many speeches—and people cheered and followed my orders. But if all of that was a lie—"

"You sounded like a prince," Sul assured him. "Confident, in command, imperious."

"Yes, but if I had given it any thought . . ."

"It's a good thing you didn't," Sul replied. "For Evernal, the tales about you are true. You acted the part, and where we might have died, we live."

"Become who they think I am," Attrebus muttered.

Lesspa was approaching, so he stood.

She regarded him silently for a moment, then scratched herself on the chin and reached over to scratch his.

"You brought it," she said. "Another might have taken our money. And what you did just now—we are grateful."

"You protected us," Attrebus said. "I couldn't do any less."

She nodded. "Your words ring like music. You are really the prince?"

"I am."

One of the tents was down, and the Khajiit were already folding it.

"We will be ready in less than an hour. I pray you wait."

"You said you were going back west. I must go east."

"They would have taken our kits and slain the old ones," she said, "imprisoned the rest of us until we became city-ghosts, sniveling in the dust, begging for skooma. It was not your concern. You reached out from your interests to embrace ours. That is Sei'dar, an important thing to us." She smiled. "Besides—you survive, you are Emperor, yes? That's not a bad friend to have."

———

East of Rimmen the land rose from the dust in a series of rolling ridges covered in brush and scrub oak, and eventually—as they ascended higher—timber.

The hills were swarming with Khajiit renegades organized around rough hill forts, but they kept their distance, which they certainly had Lesspa and her companions to thank for.

By noon the next day they were descending into the lower Niben Valley, and he was back in the Empire. It was like walking down into a cloud, so much wetter was the air of County Bravil than the Elsweyr steppes. Thick mats of fern and moss muffled their footsteps and a canopy of ash, oak, and cypress kept the sun from them.

It seemed to make Lesspa's people nervous.

They reached the Green Road near sundown and made camp there.

"What now?" Sul asked.

Attrebus considered the road. Dusk was settling and the frogs in the marshes below were singing to Masser as it rose above the trees. Willows rustled in the evening breeze, and the jars and whills tested their voice against a forlorn owl. Fireflies winked up from the ferns.

"North takes me back home," he said. "My father might listen to me now, give me troops."

"Do you really think so?"

"No. The only thing that's changed is that I lost the men and women he *did* trust me with. He'll still think Umbriel is no immediate threat. He'll put me in an extremely comfortable prison to make sure I don't run off again, at least not until I've supplied an heir."

"What then? You said Umbriel was traveling north, toward Morrowind. I think it's going to Vivec City, or what's left of it. If that's true, we need to beat Vuhon there."

"You said that before. You didn't explain it."

He saw the muscles clench in Sul's jaw. "Where is it now?" the Dunmer demanded. "How fast is it moving?"

"I'm not sure of either of those things. It's moving slowly, or it was. It took the better part of a day to cover the distance from the south coast of Black Marsh to Lilmoth, which Annaïg said is around fifteen miles."

"Thirty miles in a day and a night, then. That only gives us a few days."

"To get to Vivec City? Through the Valus Mountains? We can't do that in *twenty* days. What if we went to Leyawiin, got a ship there—"

"No, not unless you know someone with a flying ship. We'd have to sail all the way up to the top of the world and come back down, or else land and go overland through wasteland."

"Walk back, then. Why do we have to beat it to Vivec City?"

"Because I believe there is a thing there, something the master of Umbriel needs. Something he fears."

"You seem to know everything about Umbriel except where to find it—and now I've told you that. I think it's time you told me what *you* know."

Sul snorted. "Don't let your success with the regulators go to your head. You're not my prince, boy."

"I never said I was. But I've told you everything I know. You can return the favor."

Sul's eyes flamed silently for a moment, then he scratched his chin.

"I don't know much about this flying city of yours—not specifically. I believe its master is a man named Vuhon. He vanished into Oblivion forty-three years ago, and now I think he's come back."

"This is the man who killed your woman."

Sul went rigid. "We will not speak of her," he said in a low, dangerous tone. "There was once a place in Vivec City—the Ministry of Truth."

"I've heard of it," Attrebus said. "It was considered a wonder of the world. A moon from Oblivion, floating above the Temple District."

"Yes. Held there by the power of our god, Vivec. But Vivec left, or was destroyed, and his power began to fade, and with it the spells that kept the velocity of the ministry in check."

"What do you mean?"

"It fell from the sky, you understand? It was traveling quickly, more quickly than you can imagine. Vivec stopped it with the power of his will. But the velocity was still there, ready to be unleashed. Do you see what that meant?"

"You're saying it would complete its fall as if it had never been interrupted."

"That's what our best feared, yes. And one of our best was Vuhon. Along with others, he built an ingenium, a machine that continued to hold the ministry aloft. But there was a . . . cost."

"What cost?"

"The ingenium required souls to function."

Attrebus felt pinpricks along his spine.

"Umbriel—Annaïg says it takes the souls of the living . . ."

"You see?"

"But what happened?"

Sul was silent for so long this time that Attrebus thought he wouldn't speak again, but he finally sighed.

"The ingenium exploded. It hurled Vuhon into Oblivion. Then the ministry crashed into the city, and Vvardenfell exploded."

"The Red Year," Attrebus gasped. "He caused that?"

"He was responsible. He and others. And now he has returned."

"For what?"

"I don't know what designs he has on Tamriel, but I'm sure he has them, and I'm sure they aren't pleasant ones," Sul responded. "But I think his immediate objective is a sword, an ancient and dangerous weapon. It's tied somehow to Umbriel and Vuhon."

"You've been hunting Vuhon all of these years?"

"I spent many of them merely surviving."

"You were in Morrowind when all of this happened?"

Sul made an ugly sound that Attrebus later would realize was the man's bitterest chuckle.

"I was in the ministry," he answered, "I was also thrown into Oblivion. For thirty-eight years."

"With Vuhon?"

Sul rubbed his forehead. "The ingenium used souls to keep a sort of vent into Oblivion open, specifically into the realm of the daedra prince, Clavicus Vile. You know of him, I assume?"

"Of course. He has a shrine not far from the Imperial City. They say you can make a pact with him, given the right cantations."

"That's true," Sul agreed. "Although a pact with Vile is one you're likely to regret. He's not the most amiable of Oblivion princes."

"And yet he allowed Vuhon to draw energies from his realm?"

Sul cracked his neck. "Vile has a thing for souls," he said, "and if he noticed the rift at all, he probably enjoyed what was coming through more than he missed the energies going out. It's even possible that Vuhon made a formal bargain with the prince. I just don't know." He gestured at a log and sat on it. Attrebus followed suit.

"When we arrived, there was someone—or something— waiting for us. But it wasn't Vile. It was shaped like a man, but dark, with eyes like holes into nothing. He had a sword, and as we lay there, it laughed and tossed it through the rift we'd come through. I tried to follow it, but it was too late."

"Waiting for you? How did it know you were coming?"

"He called himself Umbra, and like Vile, he had a thing for souls. He'd been attracted to the rift by the ingenium and had even tried to enlarge it, with no success. So he'd cast a fortune and learned that a day was coming when it would briefly widen, and so there he was."

"Just to throw a sword through it?"

"Apparently. Umbra took us captive—he *was* powerful, almost as powerful as a daedra prince. In fact, it was the power of a daedra prince—he'd somehow managed to cut a piece from Clavicus Vile himself."

"Cut a piece? Of a daedra prince?"

"Not a physical piece, like an arm or a heart," Sul clarified. "Daedra aren't physical beings like you and me. But the effect was similar—Vile was, in a sense, injured. Badly so. And Umbra became stronger, though still not so strong as Vile. Not strong enough to escape his realm once Vile circumscribed it against him.

"Circumscribed?"

"Changed the nature of the 'walls' of his realm, made them absolutely impermeable to Umbra and the power he had stolen. Understand, at all costs the prince didn't want Umbra to escape. The circumscription was so strong he couldn't even go through the rift himself—but the sword could."

"Again, why the sword?" Attrebus wondered.

"Umbra claimed to have once been captive *in* the weapon. He feared that if Vile got his hands on it, he would return him to it."

"This is making me dizzy," Attrebus said.

"But you wanted to hear everything, remember?" Sul snapped. "Well, let's keep it simple then, shall we? Clavicus Vile was nursing his wounds and hunting for Umbra. Umbra used his stolen power to conceal himself in one of the cities at the fringe of Vile's realm. But he still couldn't escape. Vuhon promised him that if Umbra spared his life, he would build a new ingenium, capable of escaping even Vile's circumscription. Umbra agreed, and I suppose that's what they did."

"They brought the city with them?"

Sul shrugged. "I don't know about that part. I never saw much of the city. Vuhon wasn't very happy with me. He only kept me alive to torture. After a few years he forgot about me and I escaped. I had some arts, and since the forbidding wasn't on me, I managed to leave Vile's realm, albeit into another part of Oblivion."

"So it's Umbra that wants the sword, not Vuhon?"

"It might be either. Maybe Vuhon has turned against Umbra and seeks to imprison him. Whatever the case, we can't let them have it."

Attrebus opened his mouth, but Sul jerked his head from side to side. "Enough. You know what you need to know for now."

"I— So I allow all this—we still can't get there in time."

"No," Sul said. "As I said, there is a way. If we survive it."

"What way would that be?"

"We'll take a shortcut. Through Oblivion."

And he left Attrebus there with the willows and soft, gliding voices of the night birds.

FOUR

"Perfect," Toel opined, his mysterious little grin turning into something a bit larger. He dipped his finger in the little bowl of viscous mist and brought the bit that clung to it up to his lips for another taste. With his other hand he stroked the back of her neck lightly, familiarly, and she felt her cheeks warm.

"I've come to expect the very best from you," he said. "Come around this afternoon so we can discuss your progress here."

He gave a perfunctory nod to the rest of the staff and then left.

Still embarrassed, Annaïg studied her vapor another moment. When she looked up, the rest of the cooks had returned silently to their jobs. All except Slyr.

"Another evening with Toel," she said softly. "How he must enjoy your conversation."

Annaïg felt a bit of sting from that. "I hope you don't think anything else is going on."

"What would I know?" she replied. "I've never been invited to Lord Toel's quarters. How can I imagine what might go on there?"

"It sounds like you've been imagining it quite a lot," Annaïg returned. "But if you're fantasizing about anything improper, that's nothing to do with me."

"Him having you there at all is improper," Slyr countered. "It's bad for morale."

"Well, maybe you ought to tell *him* that."

Slyr looked back down at the powders she was sifting.

"I'm sorry," she said after a moment. "You know I worry."

"You're still here, aren't you?"

"It's only been a few days," she said. "He never even speaks to me."

Annaïg snorted a little laugh. "Now you're talking like he's *your* lover."

Slyr looked back up. "I just worry, that's all."

"Well, worry over this for a bit, then," she replied, rising to her feet. "I need to go check on the root wine vats."

————

Toel's kitchen was very different from Qijne's inferno. There was only one pit of hot stone and one oven, and neither was of particular size. In their place were long tables of polished red granite. Some supported brass steaming chambers, centrifuges, a hundred kinds of alchemical apparatuses. Others were entirely for the preparation of raw ingredients. While the production of distillations, infusions, and precipitations of soul-stuff had been a minor part of Qijne's kitchen, here more than half the cooking space was dedicated to the *coquinaria spiritualia*. The rest of the cavernous kitchen was devoted to one thing—feeding trees.

She remembered the strange collar of the vegetation that depended from the edge and rocky sides of Umbriel. She didn't know much about trees, so it hadn't occurred to her to wonder how they survived. As it turned out, plants—like people and animals—needed more than sunlight and water to live. They also needed food of a sort, and Toel's kitchen made that food. Huge siphons drew water and detritus from the bottom of the sump and brought it into holding vats, where it was redirected into parsers that separated out the matter most useful to the trees. What wasn't used was returned to the sump. What remained was fortified by the addition of certain formulae before being pumped to the roots through a vast ring beneath Umbriel's rim. Toel wanted her to learn all of the processes in his kitchen, so she spent an hour or so each day with the vats, and ostensibly she was experimenting with some of the formulae to try and improve upon them.

In fact, the vats were very far from everything else, and very quiet. And, in a large cabinet in the work area, was the most complete collection of materials she had ever seen.

Dimple, her new hob, was already there when she arrived, and had found four substances for her to examine. None of them smelled right, so she sent him away and went back to her experiment with the tree-wine. She wondered if trees tasted anything, if they knew one "flavor" of tree-wine from another. She stirred a reagent of calprine into her flask wand and watched it turn yellow.

After a moment she saw Dimple return with more containers.

Absorbed in what she was doing, she didn't actually look at what he'd brought, but when she took a break, she rubbed her eyes and turned her attention there.

One of the jars was half filled with a black liquid. She blinked and hesitated, not wanting to get her hopes up too high, not wanting to be disappointed again.

She knew it by its smell.

"That's it, then," she whispered. "Everything I need."

But she felt oddly empty, because that wasn't really true.

She didn't have Mere-Glim and the knowledge she needed to destroy Umbriel. Or her locket, so Attrebus would know where she was.

If Attrebus was still alive. The last time they'd spoken, there was something about him, vulnerability. And the way he talked to her, as if he cared, as if he was risking his life just for her . . .

She shook that thought off and read the label on the jar.

ICHOR OF WINGED TWILIGHT.

Well, that made sense. She put it in the little cabinet that was for her private use, along with the other ingredients she needed, and a great many she did not. Then she finished out the hour and went back to help with dinner.

————

Slyr watched her dress in yet another new outfit that Dulg had appeared with, a simple green gossamer slip of a gown. The other woman was halfway through a bottle of wine already.

"Don't forget me," she said as Annaïg left.

As usual, she met him on his balcony. They sipped a red slurry that—despite being cold—burned her throat gently as it went down.

"Lord Irrel sent his compliments," Toel said.

"He enjoyed your meal, then."

Toel nodded. "The meal was not uninspired," he said. "I am an artist. But you have added so much to my palette, and the special touches you invent—Lord Irrel is usually pleased with what I make him, but lately his compliments have come more frequently and sincerely."

"I'm happy to have helped, then."

She felt a little giddy, and realized that whatever was in her drink was already having an effect.

"With me you will become great," he said. "But there is more to being great than being an artist. You must also have vision, and the strength to do the thing that must be done. Do you understand?"

"I think so, Chef."

"And you must learn to make choices uncolored by any sort of passion."

Annaïg took another drink, not liking the direction the conversation was going.

"When I took you from Qijne, I spared Slyr as well. But since she has been here, I haven't felt justified in that decision. I rather think she should go."

"Without her, I would never have come to your attention," Annaïg said. "Without her, I would never have learned so much in so little time."

"And yet how far you have outstripped her, and how slowly she is learning the ways of my kitchen. Do you really believe she has any business being here?"

"She saved my life," Annaïg said. "Qijne would have killed me."

"Yes, I know that," he replied. "In that moment she was very useful to me, and to you. But that moment is gone."

"I pray you," she said.

"Don't pray to me," he said. "I give this decision to you. You could have Sarha or Loy for assistants—with them you would learn quickly, rise quickly. You could work directly for me, as my understudy. But so long as Slyr is here, she will be your only assistant. But if you ask me to rid you of her, I will do it in an instant."

"Let her stay, please."

"As I said," he went on, disappointment evident in his voice, "it's your choice, and remains your choice. I hope you will try to consider that decision without passion or sympathy. I hope you will be great."

"I will try to be great," Annaïg said. "But I hope to do it without betraying my friends."

"Does this work, where you are from?"

"I . . . I don't know. Sometimes, I hope."

He nodded and his gaze found hers, and in his eyes she saw something both frightening and compelling. She felt again the caress on the back of her neck, and her belly tingled.

"There is another decision I give you to make," he said, very softly. "Like the first, you are free to make it on any evening I have you here."

She couldn't find any words, or even think straight. She had flirted with a few boys, kissed a few, but it had always seemed clumsy and ridiculous, and she'd certainly never been swept away by the sort of passion she had read of.

But this wasn't a boy. This was a man, a man who wanted her, wanted her very badly, who could probably take her if he desired it.

She realized she was breathing hard.

"I—ah . . ." she started. "I wonder if I can have some water."

He smiled, and leaned back, and signed for water to be brought, and she sat there the rest of the evening feeling drunk and foolish and very much a little girl. He could see right through it all, through any manner and bearing she tried to fabricate.

But beneath all of that there was this other, little voice, the one that reminded her that it should always be her choice, that it shouldn't be something someone could condescend to give you. And that voice didn't go away, and when dinner was over she returned to her room, where Slyr had passed out, alone.

FIVE

———

A short morning's ride brought them to a hill overlooking Water's Edge, a bustling market town that—like Ione—had done most of its growing in the last few decades. During the years when the old Empire was collapsing, it had served as a free port when Bravil and Leyawiin were independent and often at odds with each other, and Water's Edge had been protected by both and by what remained of the Imperial navy. Even enemies needed some neutral ground for trade, a place where conflict was set aside.

And now that the Empire was reunited, it was growing still, attracting entrepreneurs and tradesmen from crime-ridden Bravil especially.

"I don't understand why we didn't just go to Bravil," Attrebus complained to Sul. "That's at least in the right direction."

"This was closer," Sul replied. "Distance doesn't matter so much as time. We're short of time as it is. If I can get the things I need here, we have a far better chance of succeeding."

"And if you can't get what you need?"

"The College of Whispers has a cynosure here," the Dunmer replied. "The things I'm after aren't terribly uncommon."

"I should think opening a portal into oblivion would require something rather extraordinary."

"It does," Sul said. "But I already have that." He tapped his head, then swung himself up on his horse.

Attrebus began saddling his own mount.

"What are you doing?" the Dunmer asked.

"You said you wanted allies. I'm going to see what I can do."

Sul looked as if he tasted something bad. "Let me check things out first," he said. He switched his reins and rode off.

Attrebus watched him go, then resumed making his horse ready.

"You're going into town, too?" Lesspa asked.

Attrebus nodded. "Yes. There's a garrison there, and I know the commander. I need to send word to my father I'm still alive. I might even be able to recruit a few more men."

"We aren't enough for you, Prince?"

"Yes," Attrebus said. "About that. I appreciate your help up to this point, but you deserve to know what we're up against. When you've heard me out, if you still want to go, that's great. But if you don't, I'll understand."

"My ears are twitching," she replied.

And so he told her about Umbriel—or at least everything he knew about it—and about Sul's plan to reach Morrowind. When he finished, she just regarded him for a moment. Then she made a little bow.

"Thank you," she said. Then she walked back over to her people.

He finished saddling, then splashed a bit of cold water from the stream on his face and shaved. By the time he was done with that, he noticed one of the Khajiit tents was already down.

He sighed, but part of him was relieved. He needed them, yes, but the thought of leading more people to be slaughtered was a hard one.

His mood lifted a little as he entered the town and felt—for the first time since crossing the border—that he was really back in the Empire, in his element. The shops—many with freshly painted signs—cheered him, as did the children laughing and playing in the streets. A question merrily answered by a girl drawing water from the well at the town center sent him toward the Imperial garrison, a couple of wooden barracks flanking an older building of dark stone. A guard stood outside the door, wearing his father's colors.

"Good day," the guard said as he drew near.

"Good day to you," Attrebus replied, watching for the glimmer of recognition, but either the man did not know his face or was good at concealing his reactions. "Can you tell me who is on post here?"

"That would be Captain Larsus," the fellow said.

"Florius Larsus?" Attrebus asked.

"The same," the guard replied.

"I should like to see him," Attrebus said.

"Very good. And whom shall I say is calling?"

"Just tell him it's Treb," he replied.

The guard's eyes did widen a bit, and he went into the building. A moment later the door swung open and Florius appeared. He looked irritated at first, but when his gaze settled on Attrebus, his jaw hung open.

"By the Divines," he said. "You're supposed to be dead!"

"I hope I get to have my own opinion about that," he answered.

Larsus bounded over to him and clapped him on the shoulders. "Great gods, man, get in here. Do you even know how many men your father has out looking for you?"

Attrebus followed him into a simple but ample room with a desk, a few bookshelves, and a cabinet from which Larsus produced a bottle of brandy and two cups.

"If everyone thinks I'm dead, then why does my father have men out searching for me?"

"Well, he doesn't believe it. But the rumor is they found your body."

"Some rumors are better than others."

Larsus poured the brandy and passed the cup to Attrebus.

"Well, it's good to see you alive," the captain said. "But don't keep me in suspense. Tell me what happened."

"My companions were all slain, and I was taken captive. They took me to Elsweyr with the intention of selling me, but they ended up dying instead. And so here I am."

"That's—I don't know what to say. Are you alone?"

"Yes," Attrebus lied.

"Well, you look well enough. A little battered—listen, I'll arrange for your transport home immediately, and send a courier ahead to let your father know the good news."

"Send the courier," Attrebus said. "But I won't be returning to the Imperial City."

Larsus frowned, but at that moment another fellow entered the room—a man with sallow Breton features and curly black hair. He looked familiar—Attrebus was sure he had seen him at court, or at least in the palace.

"Riente," Larsus said. "See who it is!"

Riente cocked his head to the side, and then bowed. "Your highness," he said. "It's wondrous to see you alive."

"Captain Larsus and I were just discussing that," Attrebus said.

"Well, I shouldn't intrude, then," Riente said. "I only came to report that the matter at the Little Orsinium Tavern is cleared up."

"Thank you, Riente."

"Captain, majesty," he said, bowing again before vanishing through the door whence he'd come.

Larsus turned back to Attrebus. "Now, Treb, what are you talking about? My orders are to return you to the Imperial City without delay."

"I'm giving you different orders," Attrebus said.

"You can't countermand your father." He paused and looked

a bit sheepish. "My orders include permission to restrain you if necessary."

"But you won't do that."

Larsus hesitated again. "I will."

Attrebus leaned forward. "Listen, Florius. I always thought we were friends, but recent events make me wonder. I know now that my life, up until now, has been something of a fantasy. Perhaps you, like so many, only pretended to like me. But I remember those days after we first met, when we were six? Did it really all go back so far?"

Larsus colored. "No," he said. "We were friends, Treb. We are. But the Emperor . . ."

"I can't go back, not yet. There are things I must do. And I need your help."

Larsus sighed. "What things?"

And so for the second time that day, Attrebus recounted what he knew of Umbriel.

"I've heard of it," Larsus acknowledged. "But this doesn't change anything. When the Emperor learns I've let you go, it's my head."

"I won't let that happen."

"How can you prevent it, if you're in Morrowind, probably dead?"

"I'm asking you to go with me, Florius. It's the real thing this time, not the playacting of before. But this needs doing, and I'd like you at my side."

"Just the two of us?"

"I lied. There is one other."

"I—even if you can keep me out of the dungeons, this will end my career, Treb."

"If we succeed, all will be forgiven. My father could never punish a savior of Cyrodiil—the people would never have it, and you know how quickly stories about me get around. I'll write letters to my biographers—the story of our quest will be circulating in days." He raised his voice, like a bard. "'The prince, all thought him dead, but he rose up from defeat and went to find the foe . . .'" He returned to normal speech. "My father will have to embrace the story. And your part in it."

Florius squinted, as if Attrebus's words were still there in the air to be examined.

Then he nodded. "Very well," he said. He rustled through the desk. "Write your letters and post them at the Gaping Frog— it's just off the town square. I'll send your father a message by Imperial courier, informing him of your safety—and my resignation. I'll meet you at the Frog in, say, three hours."

"I knew I could count on you, Florius."

"I'm a fool," Florius said.

"But you're my fool now."

"Go on. I'll see you in three hours."

————

The Gaping Frog was almost empty when Attrebus made his way in and took a seat at the smoothest table he saw, which still had its share of nicks, scratches, and knife-scribed autographs. The place was mostly empty, rather sunny for a tavern, smelling pleasantly of ale and some sort of stew. He had an ale and wrote two more or less identical letters to his best-known biographers and posted them with the barkeep, a female orc with two broken teeth. Then—it being about midday—he had a bowl of what turned out to be mutton daube and two more ales, and sat there, feeling full and civilized, wondering how Sul had made out.

The few people who had come in for lunch wandered out, until it was just Attrebus and the barkeep. But less than a minute after the last of the other patrons left, the door opened again. He looked up, thinking it might be Florius come a bit early, but instead it was a group of people. At first he didn't understand what was wrong with their faces, but then he understood; they were wearing masks. And all of them had naked blades.

He bolted up, drawing his own sword, Flashing. The barkeep made an odd sound, and he saw her stagger and then drop heavily behind the counter.

"Who are you?" he shouted. "Show your faces." He made a wild cut at the one nearest, but stepped back as his companions moved to circle him.

The door burst open again, and the man on his left jerked his head to look. Attrebus thrust with Flashing, catching him in the ribs. The man cursed and fell back, clutching his side, even as one of his companions cut at Treb's head. Attrebus dropped, feeling the wake of the blade on his scalp.

He was struggling to get his blade back up when something big hit his only remaining attacker. The other three were busy defending their own lives against Lesspa and her cousins, and he now saw that it was Lesspa's brother, Sha'jal, savaging the man at his feet.

By the time he got around them, the rest of the fray was over.

Attrebus rushed to the bar, but the barkeep was dead with a knife in her right eye.

"Are you all right?" Lesspa asked.

"I am, thanks to you," he replied. "I thought you were leaving."

"No, no. We sent the kits and the old ones back with a few warriors, but the rest of us stay with you. We've been watching out for you. These fellows with their masks, they didn't seem to have the best of intentions."

"Take their masks off," Attrebus said, bending toward the corpse nearest him.

Four of them were unfamiliar, but the fourth was Riente, the fellow from Florius's office.

"Florius!" he swore.

He ran the two hundred yards back to the garrison, not caring if the cats were with him or not. He shoved the door open, blade in hand.

Florius was in his chair, with his head on the table. There wasn't much blood; he'd been stabbed at the base of the skull.

———

"It told you to *wait*," Sul said. "I should have tied you up before I left."

"He was going with us," Attrebus said. "I talked him into it. I killed him."

"You killed him the moment he knew who you were. There was a guard dead, too—did you talk to a guard?"

"Yes," he said, feeling sick.

"The massacre of your men, and now this? You need to ask yourself—who wants you dead?"

Attrebus closed his eyes, trying to concentrate. "I've seen Riente before. In the Imperial City. And some of the things Radhasa said made it sound like someone there had hired her. I assumed it was some criminal faction, but . . . I don't know who could want me murdered."

"It's not just anyone," Sul said. "It's someone with a lot of connections. They may have scried you were coming here, but from your description it sounds more likely that they put someone here, in Bravil, Leyawiin—anyplace they thought you might turn up."

"One of the dukes, my uncle maybe. Maybe someone who doesn't want me to be Emperor."

"Yes, but why now? Why not a year ago, in your sleep with venom from some woman's lips? Why not a year from now?"

"You think it has something to do with Umbriel?"

"What else could it be?" Sul demanded. "Track back. Who knew what you were up to?"

"Gulan. My father. Annaïg. Hierem, my father's minister. But we weren't in private—others surely heard."

Sul's eyes went a bit strange for a moment, as if something Attrebus had said registered with him, but then it was gone.

"Ah, well," he said. "It's moot for the moment."

"Florius is dead. It's not moot."

"For the moment, I said. I found the things we needed. When both moons are in the sky tonight, we'll go where no one will follow—that, you can be sure of. Now, I'm going back to town to sell the horses, because we can't take them with us, and to pick up more supplies for the trip. This time, stay put. I'll take some of the cats to help."

————

Sul returned a few hours before sundown, and under his direction they began to hike north, first on the trail, then through the bottomlands. At dusk they reached their destination—the ruins of an Oblivion gate, not notably different from the one at Ione, except there wasn't a town built around it. They gathered on the glassy, fused earth, and Attrebus and the cats knelt in a circle around Sul, who walked among them dabbing a red ointment from a small jar and marking each of their foreheads, and finally his own.

When he was finished, he stoppered the jar and put it in his haversack.

"Get what you need," he said. "We'll be traveling light. When we start, stay close to me, as close as you can. We'll be moving fast."

Attrebus shouldered his pack and put his hand on Flashing's hilt. He faced the Khajiit. There were four of the massive Senche-tigers and four riders. Lesspa with Sha'jal, Taaj with S'enjara, M'kai with Ahapa, and J'lasha riding M'qar.

"You're sure about this, all of you?" Attrebus asked them.

"Our lances are with you," Lesspa said.

"Only our lances," M'kai added. "I hope you know how to use them."

His accent was so thick and his tone so solemn that it took a snicker from Taaj before he realized M'kai was joking.

"We're ready, Prince," Lesspa said.

"Okay," he told Sul. "I'm ready, too. You can start whenever." He looked up at the moons.

Sul nodded and the sky shattered.

SIX

———————————

The landscape beneath Mere-Glim had changed considerably since he'd last been in the Fringe Gyre. Gone the dense forest, winding rivers, and oxbow lakes, all replaced by ash-colored desert and jagged peaks. That meant they were out of Black Marsh at last, and well over Morrowind.

He'd never been out of his homeland before.

Not that it mattered anymore. He was dead to the Hist, and almost everyone he knew was dead. For all intents and purposes, he hadn't been in Black Marsh since he and Annaïg had come upon Umbriel. Crossing a border was just a formality.

Of course, he could jump. Why shouldn't he? His body would be too broken to become one of the living dead he could see massed in every direction now that the concealing canopy was gone.

He hissed. Maybe later. Annaïg was probably dead, but until he was sure, he would go through the motions as if they mattered.

So back up the tree he went, retracing his path to where he'd met Fhena.

True to her word, she appeared within half an hour, smiling. Her grin broadened when he handed her a sack full of orchid shrimp.

"I thought you might not be coming back," she said.

"I . . . got in trouble last time," he said.

Her smile vanished. "I didn't tell anyone," she said. "I promise."

"It wasn't that," he said. "I got distracted on the way back. I was late. Since then I've had to be a little more careful."

"Well, I'm glad you came back. Everyone else I meet—they're all pretty much the same. You're very strange."

"A . . . thanks."

"I mean it as a compliment."

"I'll take it that way, then."

She perched on one of the smaller branches and crossed her legs. "Where you come from—is everyone strange, like you?" she asked, plucking one shrimp from her sack and biting its head off.

"Well, of course where I'm from doesn't exist anymore, thanks to Umbriel." At least the place that I grew up doesn't. Everyone I know there is probably dead."

"I know. I'm sorry. But what I meant—"

"I know what you meant," he replied. "Where I *was* from—is called Black Marsh. That's where my people are from. But there are other sorts of people, just as there are here."

"What do you mean, 'other sorts of people'?"

Right, he remembered. They're really all just worms. Their appearance is superficial.

"Well, there is a whole race of people, for instance, who look a lot like you. We call them the Dunmer, and they used to live in Morrowind, which is what's below us now. Now most of them are gone."

"Used to live?"

"There was an explosion," he said. "A volcano erupted and destroyed most of their cites. Then my people came in and killed or drove out more."

"Why? To claim their souls?"

"No, because—it's a long story. The Dunmer have preyed on my people for centuries. We paid them back for that. The few that remain are scattered. Most are on Soulstheim, an island far north of here."

She clapped her hands in delight. "I don't understand half of what you're saying. More than half."

"That makes you happy?"

"Yes! Because it gives me questions. I love questions. Like—what's a volcano?"

"It's a mountain that has fire inside of it."

"See? So what's a mountain?"

It went on like that for a while, and he actually found himself enjoying it, but finally he knew it was best he go, so he said so.

"Can we meet again?" she asked.

"I'll try to come back." He gathered his courage to ask his question, but she swam ahead of him.

"I found your friend!" she said. "I should have told you to start with, but I was afraid you would leave without talking to me if I did."

"You know where Annaïg is? She's alive?"

"I'm sorry—were you hoping she was dead?"

"No, I—where is she?"

"I didn't mention you, when I was asking," she assured him. "She's very famous in the kitchens, especially after the slaughter."

"Slaughter?"

"She was in one kitchen, but then another kitchen invaded it to capture her. Like your story about your people invading Morrowind, I guess. And now she's in a much higher kitchen."

"Do you know which one?"

She concentrated for a moment. Then her face brightened again. "Toel," she said. "Toel Kitchen."

"And do you know where it is?"

Her face fell. "I don't. I don't know my way around outside of the Fringe Gyre. I could ask Kalmo or someone else who makes deliveries, but then they might want to know why I'm asking."

"It's okay," he said. "Don't ask, for now. I don't want to get you in trouble. It's enough to know she's alive."

"I'm glad I was helpful," Fhena said.

"You've no idea," Mere-Glim told her. He hesitated, and then touched his muzzle to her cheek. She jerked away in surprise.

"Why did you do that?" she asked.

"It's called a kiss," he said, feeling stupid. "Humans and mer do it to express—"

"I know what a kiss is," she replied. "We do it during procreation. Not like that, though. Are you asking me to procreate?"

"No," Mere-Glim said. "No. That was a different kind of kiss—it just expresses thanks. I'm not trying . . . No."

"I wonder if we even could?" she wondered.

"I'm going now," Glim said, and hurried away.

———

Mere-Glim woke from nightmares of emptiness and pain and it was a moment before he understood someone was whispering his name. He sat up, grunting, and made out Wert's features in the dim light.

"What is it?" he asked.

"Come with me," Wert replied. "We want to talk to you."

He groggily followed Wert through the skraw passages and then out of them, into a place that had a stale sort of smell to it, as if it wasn't used very often. Light wands had been placed in a little pile, and around it stood eight other skraws.

"What is this?" Glim asked.

Wert cleared his voice. "You stood up to the overseer," he said.

"I was angry," Glim replied. "And I'm not used to being treated like that."

"He'd never felt the pain before," another of the skraws said.

"I'll bet he wouldn't do it again."

"Well?" Wert said.

"Well, what?"

"Would you stand up to him again?"

"I don't know. If I had reason to. It's only pain."

"He might have killed you. Probably the only reason he didn't is that there's only one of you, and you're so valuable. But that'll change soon."

"Why are you asking me this?" Glim snapped. "Why do you care?"

"You said it yourself," Wert said. "Why should we have to take the vapors? I didn't really understand you when you started talking that way. It's hard to think like that. But you've been most of your life without overseers. Things occur to you that don't to us."

"It's never occurred to you that your lives could be better?"

"No. But now you've brought it up, see? Now it's hard to make the thought go away."

"And you've spread it around."

"Right."

"So what do you want with me?"

"Let's say we want free of the vapors—just that one thing. How do we go about that?"

Glim almost felt like laughing. Here was Annaïg's resistance, such as it was.

"Well," he said slowly, "I haven't thought about it. I'm not sure I want to."

"What do you mean?"

"I mean this isn't my sort of thing," Glim replied. "I'm not interested in leading a revolution."

"But that's not right," Wert blurted. "If it weren't for you, we wouldn't be in this situation."

"Situation? You haven't done anything yet, have you?"

"Situation," Wert repeated, tapping his head.

"Look—" Glim began, but then stopped. He could use this, couldn't he? If they thought he was leading them in some sort of insurrection, he could use them to get to Annaïg.

He saw they were all watching him expectantly.

"Look," he said again, "without the sump, no one is born. Probably more than half of the food supply comes from here, and I'll bet the Fringe Gyre needs water from here to produce the rest. And we control the sump."

"But the overseers control us."

"But they can't—or won't—do what we do. What if things started going wrong? Mysteriously? We don't tell anyone that we're behind it, and they punish us, but if things keep going wrong—if water doesn't go where it's supposed to, if the orchid shrimp die because we forget to scatter the nutrients, well, we'll make a point. They can't kill us all, because then who would see that new skraws are born? And then we let them know that all we ask for everything to go back to normal is something better than the vapors, something that doesn't hurt you so much."

He saw they were all just staring at him, dumbstruck.

"That's crazy," one of them finally said.

"No," Wert breathed. "It's genius. Glim, how do we start?"

"Quietly," he said. "For now, the only thing I want you to do is make maps."

"Maps?"

"Maps of any place we deliver to—food, nutrients, sediment—anything. I want to know where the siphons at the bottom of the Drop go and why. Do we have access to the ingenium through any of them?"

"I mean, what's a map?" Wert asked.

Glim hissed out a long sigh, and then began to explain.

SEVEN

———

Attrebus screeched involuntarily and the Khajiit howled; the sensation was like falling—not down, but in all directions at once. The moons were gone, and in their place a ceiling of smoke and ash. Stifling heat surrounded them and the air stank of sulfur and hot iron. They stood on black lava, and lakes of fire stretched off before them.

"Stay together!" Sul shouted. He took a step, and again the unimaginable sensation, and now they were in utter darkness—but not silence, for all around them were chittering sounds and the staccato scurrying of hundreds of feet.

They were in an infinite palace of colored glass.

They were on an icy plane with a burning sky.

They were standing by a dark red river, and the smell of blood was nearly suffocating.

They were in the deepest forest Attrebus had ever seen.

He was braced for the next transition, but Sul was suddenly swearing.

"What?" Attrebus said. "Where are we? Is this still Oblivion?"

"Yes," he said "We've been interrupted. He must have sniffed out my spoor and laid a trap."

"What do you mean?"

"This is part of a trail I made to escape Oblivion," he said. "It took me years to make it. It starts in Azura's realm and ends in Morrowind. I used the sympathy of Dagon's gate to enter his realm at the point my trail crossed it, so we really started in the middle. A few more turns and we would have been there. Now . . ."

He scratched the stubble on his chin and glanced at the leaves overhead.

"We're lucky," he murmured. "We have some time before dark. We might have a chance."

"A chance against whom?" Attrebus asked

"The Hunter," Sul answered. "The Father of the Manbeasts—Prince Hircine."

In the distance Attrebus heard the sound of a horn, then another behind him.

"We're being hunted by a daedra prince?"

"The Hungry Cat, we call him," Lesspa said. She actually sounded excited. "I knew coming with you was the thing to do. There could be no worthier opponent than Prince Hircine."

"That may be," Attrebus said, "but I don't intend to die here, no matter how honorable a death it might be."

"He won't necessarily kill us," Sul said absently, turning slowly, looking out through the curiously clear forest and its enormous trees. "He didn't kill me, the time he caught me. He just kept me here for a few years."

"How did you escape?"

"That's a very long story, and I didn't do it without help."

"Well, being held here won't do either."

"He'll probably kill us," Sul said. He pointed. "It's that way—another door that will put us back on track. It's in a more difficult place, which is why I prefer this one—but it will do."

"And if it's trapped, too?"

"Hircine always gives a chance," Lesspa said. "That's his way."

"She's right," Sul agreed. "It's not sport if the prey can't escape."

The horns sounded again, and a third joined them, in the direction Sul had just pointed.

"That's bad," Attrebus remarked.

"Those are Hircine's drivers," Sul said, "not the prince himself. We haven't heard his horn—you'll know it when you do, believe me. If we can get past the driver, we might have a chance."

"We'll get past him," Lesspa said. "Mount behind me, Prince Attrebus. Sul, you ride S'enjara with Taaj."

Attrebus climbed up behind Lesspa. There was no saddle, or anything to hold onto but her, so he reached around her waist.

The tigers began at an easy lope that was still far faster than Attrebus could have run. Lesspa had a lance in her left hand, and so did Taaj. The other two Khajiit had small but efficient-looking bows.

The horns sounded again, the loudest now being the one they were headed toward.

Because of the lack of understory, and because the huge trees were spaced so far apart, they caught glimpses of Hircine's driver from a fair distance, but it wasn't until the last thirty yards that Attrebus saw what they faced.

The driver himself might have been a massive albino Nord with long, sinewy arms. He was bare to the waist and covered in blue tattoos. His mount was the largest bear Attrebus had ever seen, and four only slightly smaller bears ran along with him.

"Bears," Lesspa sighed. It sounded as if she were happy. She shouted a few orders in her native dialect.

The archers wheeled and began firing, but Sha'jal was suddenly moving so fast that Attrebus nearly fell off. Everything to the sides blurred; only their destination was clear, and getting larger with terrifying speed.

Sha'jal bellowed out a deafening roar and bounded up on one of the bears, using it as a step to kick himself even higher, and all of the weight went out of Attrebus as they soared straight at the driver. He brought up a spear with a leaf-shaped blade bigger than some short swords, but not quick enough to hit the huge cat. Lesspa's lance went true into the driver's chest, but the resulting impact spun them half around, and Attrebus finally lost his grip. He hit the ground on his shoulder, felt pain jar through his skeleton, but all he could think of were the bears all around him, so he scrambled back up despite the pain.

A good thing, too, because one was coming right for him. He drew Flashing, made a wild stroke, and staggered aside as the bear lunged for his throat. Flashing bounced off the beast's skull, leaving a cut that appeared to only make it madder. Then it reared up over him, giving him the opportunity to thrust his blade into its belly. It bawled and threw its weight on him, wrenching his weapon from his hand. He threw up his arms to protect his head and tried to roll aside.

He was only partly successful; the beast came down on his lower body, claws ripping into his byrnie. He kicked at the crushing weight, but it was only the bear rolling off to lick at its wounded belly that freed him. Heaving for breath, he took Flashing back up and chopped though its neck.

A flash like lightning lit the trees; he turned and saw another of the bears topple, smoking, as Sul leapt over it and toward the heart of the fray. The white giant was gone, and in its place something between a man and a bear was fighting the Sench-tigers. It hurled two away, but even as it did, Sha'jal leapt on the driver's back and closed his viselike jaws behind his neck. The other Khajiit were finishing off the mount. The other bears lay in brown heaps.

The were-bear bawled and tried to shake free. Sul strode up almost casually and cut him from crotch to sternum.

The tigers plunged into the were-beasts' steaming entrails. They were quick about it, and before Attrebus had taken another twenty breaths, they were mounted again, riding hard as the other horns drew nearer. By the sound of it, one of the drivers was behind them and the other was coming from their left flank.

"Hold on!" Lesspa yelled. He was just wondering why when they were suddenly moving downhill in what amounted to a controlled fall. They burst into open sunlight and bounded over a stream as they left the forest behind and plunged downslope to a grassy savanna. A red sun was just touching the horizon, painting bloody the river that meandered across the flatland. Of course, this was Oblivion, so it might *be* blood. Off to what he presumed was the south, he saw a herd of some large beasts, but before he could figure out what they were, they were on the plain and he couldn't make them out anymore. They were in the same general direction as one of the drivers who was approaching and blowing, so he hoped that whatever they were, they might slow him down.

"More our element, grassland," Lesspa told him.

It was only then that he noticed that M'qar was riderless.

"Where's J'lasha?" he asked Lesspa.

"On Khenarthi's path," she replied.

"I'm sorry."

"He died well. There's no sorrow in that."

A herd of antelopes with twisting horns scattered at their approach.

Lesspa slowed Sha'jal to a walk and dismounted. Taaj and Sul followed her lead.

"The other drivers are still coming," Attrebus pointed out.

"The Sench are sprinters, not distance runners," Lesspa replied. "They need to get their wind back if we're to run again."

They were parallel to the river now, which had dug itself a respectable ditch here, at least a hundred feet deep. It made Attrebus nervous to have a sheer drop on one side and riders coming from every other direction. He told Sul so.

"A tributary comes in up ahead," Sul told him. "It makes a gentler slope going in, and we can get down into the canyon there. The door we're looking for is up the canyon another mile or so."

"You really think we'll make it?"

"Hircine himself won't show up until after it's dark. He hunts with a pack of werewolves. Until then all we have to do is avoid the drivers."

"Ground is shaking," Lesspa observed.

Attrebus felt it, too. At first he wondered if it wasn't some characteristic of Hircine's plane; he'd heard that Oblivion realms were often unstable. But then he saw the cloud of dust off to the south and understood the truth; what he felt was the thunder of thousands of hooves.

"We probably want to avoid that, too," he pointed out.

"The driver," Sul growled.

"To mount!" Lesspa called, then sang out in Khajiit.

Once again the tigers dug in and flew along the edge of the precipice. He could see the stampede now, but could only tell that the herd was brown.

"Up ahead!" Sul shouted. "You see, there? That's where we go down."

Attrebus could see it, all right, and could see that they were never going to make it, not at the speed that herd was moving. In less than a minute they were close enough for him to see they were some sort of wild cattle, albeit cattle that probably stood six feet high at the shoulders and had horn-spans almost that wide.

Impossibly, the tigers increased their speed, and the tributary grew nearer, but now he could hear the beasts snorting and bellowing, closer and closer, a wall falling on him . . .

And suddenly he saw the tiger Sul was riding make a peculiar leap that took it over the edge of the cliff.

Then Sha'jal was in the air, too.

The fall opened below him as if in a dream. Everything seemed to be moving quite slowly. They were nearly parallel to the cliff, and Sha'jal was lashing out at something—a tree, growing up from below them. He caught it and then all of the blood rushed from his head as they swung down and in toward the cliff face.

When his senses returned, he was fetched up hard against some sort of recess in the rock wall; he could see the trunk of the tree rising from somewhere lower, but even as he watched, it was smashed from view by the rain of cattle that began pouring down a few yards in front of them. He looked right and left, and incredibly, all of the Khajiit and Sul were there, pressed against the back of the shallow rock shelter. Flakes of shale rained on their heads, and he could only hope that the weight of the wild cattle didn't break it.

They kept coming, bleating, eyes rolling, legs flailing.

Lesspa started laughing, and the other Khajiit quickly joined her. After a moment, Attrebus found himself chuckling, too, not even certain why.

And, finally—as the last of the light was fading—the beasts stopped falling.

"Quickly, now," Sul said. "I think we can work our way down on this side. We don't have much time."

Sul proved right—their hideaway was part of a larger erosional gully, probably an earlier channel of the tributary. They were able to step and slide their way down it.

The river was choked with dead and dying cattle, and the water stank of their blood, urine, and feces.

They continued downstream, crossing the tributary a few moments later. Attrebus could barely see now, but the Khajiit and Sul seemed to be having little trouble, and the strand along the river was sandy and relatively flat. And then a new, silvery light shone as a moon rose into the sky.

Above, two horns blared, quite near.

Upstream, another answered in a voice so incredibly deep and primal that Attrebus suddenly felt like a rabbit in the open, surrounded by wolves. It chased all thought from him, and before he knew it he was dashing forward in mindless terror.

Something caught him from behind, and he swung violently, trying to break the grip before realizing it was Sul . . .

"Easy," he said. "Snap out of it."

"That's Hircine," Attrebus said. "It's over."

"Not yet," Sul said. "Not yet."

The horn sounded again, and now he heard wolves baying.

"Keep together," Sul warned them. "When we get there, we'll have to be quick."

Dark figures watched them from both rims of the canyon, and strange bestial sounds drifted down, but apparently the other drivers were content just to keep them bottled in and let their master have the kill.

They rushed on, breathless, limping. Sul shouted something, but Attrebus couldn't make it out because of the wolves. He glanced behind him, and in the moonlight saw an enormous silhouette shaped like a man, but with the branching horns of a stag.

"He's here!"

"So are we!" Sul shouted. "Ahead there, you see, where the canyon narrows. It's just through there."

It was all running then, following Sul. The howls grew closer, so near that he could already feel the teeth in his back. The canyon narrowed until it was only about twenty feet wide.

"Another fifty yards!" Sul shouted.

"That's too far," Lesspa said. She stopped and shouted something in Khajiit. They all turned to face the hunt.

"We'll catch up after we've killed him," she said.

"Lesspa—"

But Sul grabbed his arm and yanked him along.

"Don't spit on their sacrifice," he said. "The only way to make it worthwhile is to survive."

Behind them he heard Lesspa's warrior shriek, and a wolf howled in pain.

He tried to concentrate on keeping his feet working beneath

him and off the fire in his chest. He was terrified, but he wanted to stand with Lesspa, to stop running.

And yet he knew he couldn't.

The walls of the canyon narrowed further, until they were only about ten feet apart. The shingle vanished, and they were running in swiftly moving water. And something was splashing behind them.

Then he took a step, and nothing was under it—the river dropped away into empty space. He didn't see any bottom.

EIGHT

———————

Annaïg passed a bit of what had once been a soul along a wire drawn through a glass globe full of greenish vapor. As she watched, droplets formed on the wire and then quickly condensed into beadlike crystals. She waited for them to set properly, then carefully unsealed the two hemispheres of the globe and slid the wire out, so the tiny formations tinged and settled in the hollow glass and shone little tiny opals.

"There's that down," she murmured. "Forty-eight more courses to go."

Lord Irrel's tastes tended toward the inane. No meal of less than thirty courses ever pleased him, and fifty or more was safest.

Almost everything he ate was the product of some process involving stolen souls. She'd been squeamish about that at first, but like a butcher getting used to blood, she had become less focused on what it was and more on what to do with it. At times she still wondered if she was destroying the last bit of a person, the final part of them that made them *them*. Toel assured her that wasn't how it worked, that the energy that came to the kitchens came from the ingenium, which had already processed it to purity.

In the end she felt sure she would have been more bothered by dismembering human corpses, even though there was nothing there to feel or know what was happening.

A soft clearing of the throat behind her caused her to turn. A young woman with red skin and horns stood there, looking a little worried. Annaïg did not know her, but she was dressed as a pantry worker.

"Pardon me, Chef," the woman said. "Do not think I presume, and I'm certain what your answer will be, but a skraw is here with a delivery, and he says he will only give it to you."

"A skraw?"

"That's what they call them that work in the sump."

Annaïg's spirit lifted in a sudden rush. Mere-Glim worked in the sump, or at least so Slyr had said.

"Well," she said, trying to keep her composure, "I suppose I have a moment. Take me to this fellow."

She followed the woman through the pantries and beyond, to the receiving dock, where she had never been. It wasn't particularly imposing, merely a room with various tunnels leading away. There were also two large square holes in the walls that didn't seem to go anywhere until she realized they were shafts going up and down. In fact, as she watched, a large crate came into one of them from above. Several workers sitting on the top of it got down and began unfastening the latches on the front.

She did not see Mere-Glim. Instead, there was a dirty-looking fellow in a sort of loincloth holding a large bucket.

"This is him, Chef."

"Very good—you may go," Annaïg told her.

She bowed and hurried off.

"Well," Annaïg asked. "What's this?"

"Nothing, lady," the man croaked. He looked unhealthy, jaundiced. "Only I was told to deliver this just to you."

She peered into the bucket, which seemed to be filled with phosphor worms, annalines, and dash clams.

"That's it?"

"That's it, lady."

"Very good, then. I'll take them."

She took the bucket and went back up, hoping no one would see her, torn between hope that the bucket contained something from Glim and worry that it was all some weird practical joke.

She stopped in the pantry and put the seafoods in their various holding tanks, and was leaning toward the practical joke end of things when her hand found something smooth and familiar.

Her locket.

She clutched it tight, realizing dizzily that this was one of the best moments of her young life. To have Glim back. And her mother's amulet. And hope—she hadn't realized just how resigned she had become to Umbriel. With no way to contact Treb, she'd tried not to think about him, which was to say not to think of escape. Yes, she'd found what she needed in order to leave, but hadn't even put them together yet.

She realized she must be grinning as if mad, so she took a moment to compose herself, slipped the amulet in her pocket, and went back to work. She went by the tree-wine vats first, however, and, making certain no one was in the area, flipped open the amulet.

Inside was a little piece of some sort of hide or vellum, and although it was damp, the letters hadn't run. It was in the private hand that she and Glim had invented as children.

Annaïg: I found you and I've found the sky. I know more than I did. Let me know what and when and where. You can send a note by any of the skraws.

She placed the locket in one of her drawers. The note she dipped in vitriol and watched it dissolve. Then she returned to her cooking station.

She was putting a film on the soup when Slyr came over from her station.

"Could you try this?" she asked. "I've been experimenting

with condensations of those black, bumpy fruit. I forget what you call them."

"Blackberries?"

"That's right. Only they're not black, are they? Their juice is almost the color of blood."

"Sure," Annaïg said. She took the spoon, which had little droplets like perspiration on it, and carefully licked them off. They tasted a little like blackberries, but more like lemon and turpentine.

"That's pretty good," she said, "at least by the lord's standards. I should think it would go nicely on white silk noodles."

"That was my thought," Slyr said. "Thanks for your advice." She tilted her head. "I was looking for you earlier. I couldn't find you anywhere."

"I went down to the pantry to check on a few things," she said.

"Ah," Slyr said. "That explains it."

But her tone hinted that it didn't.

Annaïg sighed as the woman walked off. Slyr grew more jealous by the day, even though she had learned to hide it pretty well. Slyr seemed convinced that she was trysting with Toel at every possible moment. Sometimes she felt like telling her about Toel's offer and conditions, but worried that might actually make things worse.

She finished filming the soup, then went back to her work with the tree-wine, thinking she might find the privacy there to open her locket.

She had just reached the vats when she felt a funny scratch in the back of her throat. Her nose was numb, her head was ringing, and suddenly her heart was beating strangely.

"Slyr!" she gasped, stumbling forward. Her lungs felt like they were closing. She shut her eyes, focusing on the taste, the scent, the feel of the stuff Slyr had given her, then leaned against her cabinet, rifling for ingredients. The ringing was growing louder, and all her extremities were cold.

She built a picture of the poison in her mind, tried to think what would settle it, pacify it, break it apart, but everything was happening too fast. She fell onto the table, spilling jars and shattering vials. She let her instincts take over, just operating by smell, drinking some of this, a finger dab of that . . .

The ringing crescendoed, and she went away.

———

She came back on Toel's balcony on a white couch draped with sheets. Toel himself sat a few feet away, looking over a scroll. She must have made a noise, because he turned, smiling.

"Well, there you are," he said. "That was very near."

"What happened?"

"You were poisoned, of course. She used ampher venin. Its effects are delayed, but once symptoms develop, it works very quickly. Sound familiar?"

She nodded, realizing to her dismay that under the sheets she didn't have any clothes on.

"You should have died, but you didn't," he continued. "You somehow concocted a stabilizer. That kept you alive the half an hour before someone noticed you lying there. Without me, of course, you would have died anyway, but it is . . . remarkable."

"I didn't know what I was doing," she replied.

"On some level you did," he replied. He put his hands on his knees. "Well," he said. "How shall I have her executed?"

"Slyr?" She felt a stab of anger, bordering on hatred. What had she ever done to Slyr to deserve murder? It was quite the opposite, wasn't it? She had protected her.

And yet, execution . . .

He must have seen it in her face, because he sighed, crossed his legs, and sat back in his chair.

"Don't tell me," he said.

"She's just afraid," Annaïg said.

"You mean jealous," Toel replied. "Envious."

"It's all the same thing, really," Annaïg said. "She—I think she is not only afraid for her position here, she also desires your, ah . . . affections."

He smiled. "Well, once my 'affections' are bestowed, they are not easily forgotten."

"What do you mean?"

He rolled his eyes. "Are you really so naive? You don't know?"

"I'm not sure what you're talking about."

"How do you suppose you came to my attention? How do you think I so easily bypassed Qijne's outer security? Why do you think Slyr fought so hard to save your life?"

"She betrayed Qijne?"

"She saw a chance to rise. I admire that in her—I came from a lowlier position than hers, and my desire to better myself brought me here. She has the ambition but not the talent—you have the talent but not the ambition."

Oh, I have ambition all right, Annaïg thought. The ambition to bring all of you down.

But did she? If she could find some way to destroy Umbriel, could she do it, and doom all of these people?

But she thought of Lilmoth and knew that she could.

Why, then, couldn't she bring herself to let Toel kill Slyr, who, after all, had just tried to murder her? Who had betrayed her comrades in Qijne's kitchen to violent death? Surely this was someone who deserved to die.

But she couldn't say it, and she knew it. It was too personal, too close.

"Let her live," Annaïg said. "Please."

"The terms remain the same," he said. "She remains your

assistant. What makes you think she won't try again?"

Because I won't be here, she thought.

"She won't," she told him.

He made a tushing noise. "You really don't have it, do you? I thought you might be great, perhaps even greater than me one day, but you can't do what must be done."

He signed, and one of Toel's guards pushed Slyr from just beyond the door. The woman's red eyes brimmed with misery.

"What's wrong with you?" Slyr asked. "I don't understand you at all."

"I thought we were friends," Annaïg replied.

"We were," Slyr said. "I think we were."

"That's beautiful," Toel said. "Touching. Now listen to me, both of you. Annaïg may have no drive, but she is more than a curiosity. She gives this kitchen the edge over the others, and I will brook no threat to her. Slyr, if she slips in the kitchen and cracks her head, you will die in the most horrible manner I can conceive, and I'm sure you've heard the rumors. I don't care if Umbriel himself walks down here and strikes her down by his own hand, you will still suffer and perish. Only her breathing body keeps you alive. Do you understand?"

Slyr bowed her head. "I do, Chef," she murmured.

"Very well." He lifted his chin toward a servant in the corner. "When Annaïg is steady enough, bring her her clothes and return her to her rooms."

"And this one?" the guard said, indicating Slyr.

"She's shown initiative," he said, "misguided, but there it is. Clean her up and bring her to my quarters."

Slyr's eyes registered disbelief, but then her lips curled in triumph.

Molag Bal take them all, Annaïg thought. I'm getting off this damned rock.

NINE

———

Annaïg was still weak from the effects of the poison, but she insisted on sleeping in her own quarters that night, and Toel's servants allowed her her wish. Slyr did not return—a fact for which she was extremely grateful.

That night she wrote Glim a note, in the same argot he'd written hers in. It was very simple.

Glim. I'm glad you're alive. I've got what we need. I'm ready to go. How soon, and where? Love.

The next day, still pale and tending to tremble, she went early to the pantry. She found a skraw—not the same one—a woman this time.

"What do you have here?" she asked her.

"Thendow frills," the skraw wheezed. "Sheartooth loin. Glands from duster stalks . . ."

After a few moments, the pantry workers stopped their curious stares and went back to their business. They probably figured if one of the chefs wanted to come down and do their jobs, who were they to argue?

When she was pretty sure no one was looking, she slipped the skraw the note. "I want the pearl-colored ones next time," she said. "Do you understand?"

"Yes, lady," the skraw replied.

"Good," she said, and left the dock.

She returned to the kitchens, did her portion of the dinner—Lord Irrel only ate one meal a day—and then went back to the tree-wine vats. With no hesitation at all she made eight vials of tonic. She put four in her pocket and the rest in the cabinet, and it was all very much like moving in a dream, detached, without fear, as if the poisoning had somehow made her invulnerable.

It had certainly made her less visible. Toel didn't speak to her at all, and Slyr kept her distance, although she did occasionally catch the other woman looking at her with what was probably disdain.

But it didn't matter. It just didn't matter.

She slept alone again that night, and the next morning she had a reply from Glim.

Midnight tonight. Meet me at the dock.

———

Something struck his feet, and Treb's knees buckled, taking him straight down on his face in a bed of yellow wildflowers that smelled like skunk. He and Sul were on a hillside covered in various colorful blossoms and odd, twisting trees with caps like mushrooms.

They were on a jagged island in a furious sea beneath a sky half-filled with a jade moon.

They were on an island of ash and shattered stone, still surrounded by water, but this water appeared to be boiling. The steaming air stank of hard minerals, and the sky was bleak and gray.

Sul just stood there, studying the ground, kicking at what looked like a shallow excavation, but he didn't appear surprised.

"Are we trapped again?" Attrebus asked.

"No," Sul grated. "We've arrived. Welcome to Vivec City."

He spat into the ash.

"I thought we were still in Oblivion."

"This doesn't look homey to you?"

"I—" He took in the scene again.

The island stood in the center of a bay that was close to perfectly circular, with a rim standing somewhat higher than the island except in one place where it opened into a sea or larger lake. It reminded him of the volcanic crater he'd once seen on a trip to Hammerfell.

To the left, beyond the rim, the land rose up in rugged mountains.

"Don't you see the how beautiful she is, this city?" Sul snapped. "Can't you see the canals, the gondoliers?" He stabbed his finger out across the bay. "Don't you see the great cantons, each building a city in itself? And here, right here—the High Fane, the palace, the Ministry of Truth—all for you to gaze upon that you might wonder."

Attrebus bowed his head a bit. "I'm sorry, Sul. I meant no disrespect. I'm sorry for what happened here."

"You've nothing to be sorry for as regards to this place," Sul said. "But there are those who must account."

His voice sounded harsher than usual.

"You might have warned me about the fall, back in Hircine's realm," Attrebus said, hoping to lighten the mood.

To his surprise, it seemed to work. A hint of a grin pulled at Sul's lips.

"I told you it was harder to get to," the Dunmer reminded him.

"Just a tiny bit harder, I guess."

"It's done now."

"I wish Lesspa—" He stopped, realizing he didn't want to talk about that. Not long ago he'd had his arms around her waist, felt the breath in her, heard the savage joy of her cry. To think of her, torn and cold, her eyes staring at nothing . . .

"We'd be dead now if it weren't for her," Sul said. "The Khajiit didn't hold them for long, but it was long enough. We could
have died with her, but then what about Umbriel, Annaïg, your
father's empire? You're a prince, Attrebus. People die for princes.
Get used to it."

"It wasn't even her fight."

"She thought it was. You made her believe it was."

"And that's supposed to make me feel better."

Sul's softer mood broke as quickly as it had formed. "Why in
the world would any of this be about making you feel better? A
leader doesn't do things to make himself 'feel better.' You do what
you should, what you must."

Attrebus felt the rebuke almost like a physical blow. It left
him speechless for a moment. Then he nodded.

"How do we find this sword?" he asked. He waved his hands
about. "I mean, in all of this ruin . . ."

Sul studied him angrily for a moment, then looked away.

"I was a servant of Prince Azura," he said. "Insomuch as
I serve anyone, I suppose I still serve her. I wandered for years
through Oblivion until she gave me haven in her realm, and there
I slowly went mad. For a daedra prince, she is kind, especially to
those she takes a liking to. She knew I wanted vengeance, and
she gave me visions to help me achieve it. I did her services in the
other realms. I settled problems for her, and in the end she promised to let me go, to act on what knowledge she had given me. She
didn't. She decided to keep me, one of her favorite playthings."

"And so you escaped her, as you escaped Vile's realm."

"Yes. And yet, even though I am no longer in her realm or
direct service, she still sends me the visions. Sometimes to aid,
sometimes to taunt, never enough to be fully helpful. But she has
no love for our enemy, and because of that I trust her more often
than not."

"And she showed you where the sword is?"

"Yes."

Attrebus frowned. "You were here before, when you escaped Oblivion. Why didn't you find the sword then?"

"This is all controlled by Argonians now," he said, "although they obviously don't live here. But they do have some ritual associated with this crater, what is now called the Scathing Bay. I arrived here during the ritual, so after running through half the realms of Oblivion, I had to keep running until they gave up, somewhere in the Valus Mountains. After that I . . . delayed coming back here. It's not easy to see this."

"I can understand that," Treb said.

"You can't, really," Sul replied. "Wait here. I need to do something. Alone."

"Even if you find the sword, how do we get across this boiling water?"

"Don't worry about that," Sul said. "I've been here before, remember?

Occupy yourself. Keep an eye out for Umbriel. I'll find the sword."

———

He watched Sul pick his way across the island until he vanished behind an upjut. He looked off across the waters south, toward where Umbriel ought to be, but saw nothing but low-hanging clouds, so he sat down and went through his haversack, looking for food.

He was chewing on a bit of bread when Coo cried softly. He pulled the mechanical bird out, and to his delight found himself staring at the image of Annaïg's face. Her eyebrows were steepled and she looked pale, and then her eyes widened and she started to cry.

"You're there!" she mumbled.

"Yes," Attrebus said. "I'm here. Are you all right?"

"I didn't cry until now," she said. "I haven't cried since before any of this began. I've kept it locked . . . I—" She broke off, sobbing uncontrollably.

He reached forward, as if to comfort her, but realized, of course, that he couldn't. It was heart-wrenching to watch such pain and not be able to do anything.

"It's going to be fine," he ventured. "Everything's going to be fine."

She nodded, but kept crying for another long moment before finally regaining control of her voice.

"I'm sorry," she said, still sniffling.

"Don't be," he said. "I can only imagine what you've been through."

"I've tried to be brave," she said. "To learn the things you'll need to know. But I have to leave this place now. I thought I was fine until I saw you. I thought I wasn't afraid anymore. But I am."

"Who wouldn't be?" Treb soothed. "Can you? Can you leave?"

"I've re-created the solution that allowed me to fly, and I've found a way to Glim—and he's found a place where we can get out. I . . . I don't think I can wait until you reach us. We're leaving tonight."

"But that's perfect," Attrebus said. "I'm in Morrowind. I think you're coming straight to us."

"You're in our path?"

"My companion thinks so."

"Well you can't stay there," she said. "I told you what it does."

"Don't worry about us," he said. "When you escape, I'll find you. I'll let you know which way to fly. Yes?"

She nodded.

"I thought you might be dead," he said. "I kept trying to contact you—"

"I lost my locket," she said. "But I got it back."

"So you're leaving tonight?" he asked.

"That's the plan," she said, wiping her eyes.

"And are you alone right now?"

"For the moment," she said. "Someone might come, and then I'll have to hide the locket."

"Fine, I'll understand when you have to go. But until then, tell me what's been happening. Tell me how you are."

And he listened as she told him her tale in her sweet lilting voice, and he realized how very much he had missed it. Missed her.

———

Sul trudged to the other side of the island, trying not to let his rage blot out his ability to think. It wasn't enough that the ministry fell; the impact caused the volcano that was the heart and namesake of Vvardenfell to explode. Ash, lava, and tidal waves had done their work, and when that was calmed, the Argonians had come, eager to repay what survived of his people for millennia of abuse and enslavement.

Of course, those that had settled in southern Morrowind were likely regretting it now, as Umbriel moved over their villages.

That didn't help, though, did it?

He looked again at the size of the crater. How fast had the ministry been traveling? Did she feel anything? Had Ilzheven known who killed her?

Find the sword. Kill Vuhon. Then it would be over.

He remembered the ingenium exploding; it had expanded and distorted first, and then all he had known was a sort of flash. Then he and Vuhon were elsewhere, in Oblivion.

In his vision, Azura had shown him that again, shown him Umbra hurling the blade through the vanishing portal—and then the scene changed, and he'd seen the sword, lying on shattered stone. He saw it covered by a few feet of ash.

But he and Attrebus had come through the weak spot left by
the portal, just as he had a few years earlier, just as the sword must
have. It was a tricky spot, because the ingenium had been exploding at the same instant the ministry finished its ages-long fall, so
rather than a spot or sphere, the rift was more like a shaft, most
of it underground. If he hadn't seen the sword on the surface, he
would have imagined it entombed beneath his feet.

But it hadn't been where he'd seen it; there wasn't enough
ash, and then there was what looked like an excavation. He
hadn't had time to notice that when he appeared in the midst of
the Argonians, but this time it took only a few seconds to realize
that someone had already taken Umbra.

He could almost hear Azura laughing, because she knew
what he had to do next.

———

His lover formed like a column of dust, like the whirlwinds in the
ashlands, tightening in circumference as her presence intensified,
until at last each delicate curve of her face drifted before him. Only
her eyes held color, and those were like the last fading of a sunset.

"Ilzheven," he whispered, and the eyes flickered a bit brighter.

"I am here," she said. It was a mere wisp of sound, but it was
her voice, the only music he remembered from that long-ago life.
"I am always here. A part of this." Her face softened.

"I know you, Ezhmaar," she said. "What has happened to
you, my love?"

"Time still passes for me," he replied, angry at his voice for
the way it quavered. "Much has happened to me in its grip."

"It is not time that has hurt you so," she said. "What have you
done to yourself, Ezhmaar?" She reached to touch his face, and
he felt it as a faint, cool breeze.

"Is it still there?" she went on. "The house where we learned each other? In the bamboo grove, where the waters trickled cold from the mountains and the larkins sang?"

His throat closed and for a moment he couldn't answer.

"I haven't seen it since we last were there together," he finally managed. But he knew it couldn't be. Not as close as the valley had been to the volcano.

"It is still here," she said, lightly touching her chest. "That place, my love—our love."

He touched his own breast, but couldn't say anything for fear of undoing himself, just when he most needed all of his strength.

"I don't have long, Ilzheven," he said. "I need to ask you something."

"I will answer you if I can," she said.

"There was a sword here, in the ash. It fell after the impact. Can you tell me what became of it?"

Her gaze went off past him and stayed there for so long he feared he couldn't hold her present any longer. But then she spoke again.

"Rain exposed the hilt, and men found it. Dunmer, searching this place. They took it with them."

"Where?"

"North, toward the Sea of Ghosts. The bearer wore a signet ring with a draugr on it."

He felt his grip loosening. Ilzheven reached for him again, but her fingers became dust and blew off on the breeze.

"Let it go," she whispered. "Do no more harm to yourself."

"You don't understand," he said.

"I am part of this place," she said. "I know all that happened, and I beg you for the love we shared, let it go."

"I cannot," he said, as her face was erased by the wind. He stood there for a long time, fighting his shame, hardening his heart. It would not do for Attrebus to see him like this.

But it had been so good to hear her voice. He missed that most of all.

———

"I have to go," Annaïg said suddenly. "I hear someone coming. Keep well."

"Take care," he said, "don't . . ." But she was already gone. He held the bird for a few more moments, thinking that perhaps she'd been mistaken and they could resume their conversation.

After a few minutes he gave up and replaced Coo in his sack. Then he looked off what he guessed to be south, where the crater opened into what must be the Inner Sea, if he remembered his geography lessons correctly.

Something about the scene struck him as peculiar—other than the boiling of the water and all—but at first he couldn't place it. Then he realized what he was seeing was the top of a mountain, peeking through the clouds.

Peeking through the *bottom* of the clouds.

"Oh, no," he whispered.

From Annaïg's description, he'd thought he would see it coming, even with the clouds—where were the flashing threads, the larvae diving down? But that would only happen if something alive was below it, and there wasn't anything living here, was there?

He smelled boiled meat and tracked his gaze back to the water.

Things were coming out of Scathing Bay.

———

North, beyond the Sea of Ghosts, Sul reflected. That probably meant Soulstheim. That would have to be overland or by sea, then. He didn't have a handy path through Oblivion to reach the islands. He wondered if all of the inner sea was boiling.

He heard Attrebus shouting.

Swearing, he drew his sword and ran toward where he'd left the prince. He nearly ran into him on the rise.

"It's here!" Attrebus shouted. "The damned thing is already here!"

Sul gazed toward the water, at the lumbering monsters that had once been living flesh. It would be hard to tell what most of them had been if it weren't for their tails.

"That way off of the island you were talking about?" Attrebus asked.

"The way we came," Sul replied. "We have to fight our way back to the spot where we arrived."

"That's . . . not good. Do you have any arts that will allow us to swim in scalding water?"

"No."

Sul saw that he was scared, and that he was trying not to be.

"The longer we wait, the harder it will be," Sul said. He reached into his sack and produced his ointment, redabbing their brows. "We cut a path to our arrival point," he said. "That's all we have to do. Just stay alive that long."

"Let's go, then," Attrebus said.

TEN

———

When Colin heard the tap of hard-soled shoes, he whispered the name of Nocturnal and felt the shadows around him; felt the moonlight press them down through the marble of the palace to kiss the camp, gritty cobblestones, felt them enter his eyes and mouth and nostrils until he was a shadow himself. Felt them drape across the woman who emerged into the courtyard from the office of the minister.

He padded after her. She was cloaked and cowled, but he knew her walk; he'd been watching her for days. Not for long at a time, because he had cases to attend to. Marall had been right about that—he'd been pulled from the business concerning Prince Attrebus immediately.

But he wasn't quite willing to let it go, was he? He couldn't even say why.

So he'd found the woman Gulan had spoken to that last time, an assistant to the minister. Her name was Letine Arese, a petite blond woman of thirty years. He'd learned her habits, how she moved, when she left the ministry evenings, where she went after.

Tonight, as he'd expected, she was breaking all of her patterns. Leaving at eight instead of six. Going northeast toward the

Market District instead of heading for the Foaming Flask for a drink with her sister and assorted friends.

She wound her way through the crowds of the market district, and Colin became less a shadow and more a nobody—there, avoided if necessary, but not really remarked. After a time she left the arteries for the veins, and then capillaries, where once again it was him and her and shadow.

She came to a door and rapped on it. A slit opened; soft words were spoken. Then the door swung out a crack and she entered.

He quickly examined the building. There were no ground-floor windows, of course—not in this neighborhood, but the house had three stories, and on the third he made one out. He couldn't see ladders or drainpipes to climb, but the building next door was so close he was able to brace his arms and legs and go up it as he might a chimney.

———

Annaïg just managed to hide the amulet before Slyr came out of the corridor. The other woman looked around, puzzled.

"Who were you talking to?" she asked.

"To myself," Annaïg replied. "It helps me think."

"I see." She stood there for a moment, looking uncomfortable.

"Do you want something?" Annaïg inquired.

"Don't kill me," Slyr blurted.

"What the Xhuth! are you talking about?" Annaïg demanded. "You were there—you heard Toel. If I had wanted you dead, you would be dead."

"I know," she cried, wringing her hands. "It didn't make any sense. The only thing I can think of is that you want to do it yourself, when I'm not expecting it. You could probably think of something really inventive and nasty. Look, I know you're probably mad at me—"

"'Probably' mad at you?" Annaïg exploded. "You tried to kill me!"

"Yes, I see now how that might upset you," Slyr said. "To be fair, I wasn't expecting to have to deal with any sort of . . . Well, *this*."

"Yes," Annaïg said, measuring her words. "Yes, I understand that because you imagined I would be dead. Now I'm not, and because you haven't a decent bone in your body, you assume no one else does."

In that instant, her anger constricted violently into the most vicious rage she'd ever known. She felt a sudden jerk on her wrist and then something slid around her pointer finger and stiffened.

Qijne's filleting knife. Of course—all she needed was to *really* want to kill someone. And she could. Two steps . . .

"Please, don't joke with me," Slyr pleaded. "I can't even sleep, I'm so miserable."

Annaïg willed her heart to slow. "What are you talking about?" she asked. "You've been sleeping with Toel."

Slyr blinked. "I've been procreating with Toel," she admitted, "but you don't imagine he lets me stay in his bed all night! I've been sleeping in the halls, terrified of what you're going to do next."

"Next? I haven't *done* anything to you."

"You didn't poison the Thendow frills this morning?"

"They were poisoned?"

"Well," she hedged, "not that I could tell. But I heard you were down there, *handling* them, and that doesn't make much sense unless you were up to something. And you knew I was supposed to make the decoction of Thendow—"

"You aren't dead, are you?"

"Of course not! I made Chave do the Thendow."

"Unbelievable," Annaïg said. "And did Chave die?"

"You're clever enough to make something that would only affect me—I know you are. My hairs are all over our room."

Annaïg rolled her eyes. "I'm not going to kill you, Slyr. At least not today."

But then she remembered her appointment with Glim, and she shot the other woman a nasty smile.

"But there's always tomorrow."

"I'll do anything," Slyr said. "Anything you ask."

"Perfect. Then go away and don't talk to me again unless it's pertaining to our work."

It was probably twenty minutes after the woman left that the knife slowly withdrew back to Annaïg's wrist.

———

The kitchen wasn't still at night; the hobs were there, cleaning, jabbering in a language she didn't know. She had wondered about that, from time to time. Everyone she had spoken to claimed that everyone came out of the sump, went back to the sump, and so forth. But what about the hobs and scamps? Were they "people" in the sense that chefs and skraws were? Or were they like the foodstuff that came from the sump and the Fringe Gyre—things that grew and reproduced in a normal sort of way?

Maybe Glim knew. After all, he'd been working in the sump.

The hobs gave her curious looks as she passed through the kitchen. She wasn't worried—she doubted they would say anything to their masters, but if they did, it would be too late.

Before entering the pantries, she stopped and looked back, and for a moment she almost seemed to see herself, or a sort of ghost of herself, the person she might have become if she'd followed Toel's advice instead of her heart. The ghost looked confident, effective, filled with secrets.

Annaïg turned and left her there, to fade.

The dock, unlike the kitchen, was very quiet, and dark, and she had no light. She stood there, waiting, starting to feel it all unravel. What if it was all a trap of some sort, a trick, a game?

But then she heard something wet move.

"Glim?"

"Nn!"

And he was there, his faintly chlorine scent, the familiar rasp of his breath, his big damp scaly arms crushing her to his chest.

"You're getting me wet, you big lizard," she said.

"Well, if you want me to leave . . ."

She hit him on the arm and pushed back. "Daedra and Divines it's good to see you, Glim. Or almost see you. I thought I had lost you."

"I found Qijne's body," he said, "and the others from her kitchen—" He choked off into a weird, distressed gasping sound that she hadn't heard since they were both children.

"Let's not talk through our chance," she said, patting his arm. "Plenty of time to talk later."

Glim snorted. "No one is going to try and stop us," he said. "No one here can conceive of leaving the place."

"Toel would stop me, if he knew," she said. "So let's not dally."

And so Glim guided her onto one of the big dumbwaiter things, and shortly they began ascending,

"I've never been up this," Glim said. "But I suspect it's a lot easier than the route I've been using. And you won't have to breathe underwater."

"Which is nice," she replied. "Although I've got that covered, if it comes to it." She patted her pockets.

"Do you?" he asked. His voice sounded a bit odd.

"What's wrong?"

"Nothing," he said. "Nothing that matters now."

———

They arrived at a dock not unlike the one they'd left, but Glim found a stairway that took them up and out to the Fringe Gyre. Both moons were out, making a glowing ocean of the low clouds that came up almost to Umbriel's rim. The gyre fanned below them, as fantastic a forest as she could ever imagine. And behind—the dazzling spires of Umbriel as she had never seen them—at night from the highest level. Even Toel was far below her. One tower rose higher than all of them by far, a fey thing that might have been spun from glass and gossamer. Who lived there? What were they like?

She took a deep breath and turned firmly away. It didn't matter.

Then she handed Glim his dose.

"Drink," she said. "Your desires guide you, do you understand? We want to be as far west of here as we can get."

"I'll just follow you," Glim said.

She took his hand. "We'll go together."

And they drank, and they dropped away from Umbriel, and flew over the lambent clouds.

———

Sul furrowed his brow and mumbled something under his breath. The air before them shivered and coruscated, and suddenly a monstrous daedra with the head of a crocodile stood between them and the walking dead. It turned to face Sul, its reptilian eyes full of hatred, but he barked something at it, and with a snarl it turned and rushed into their attackers.

Sul waded in behind the thing, and Attrebus followed. He hacked at the rotting, boiled corpse of an Argonian; he hit its upper arm, and Flashing sheared through the decomposing flesh as if it were cheese, hit the bone, and slid down to cut through the elbow joint. The thing came on, heedless of its loss, and he had to fight the urge to vomit. It reached for him again and he cut off its head, which of course didn't stop it either, so he next chopped at its knees.

The next one to come at him had a short sword, which it jabbed at him in a thoroughly unsophisticated way. He cut the arm off and then slashed at its legs, so it fell, too.

What surprised him was how fast they were. Somehow he'd imagined them slower. He and Sul weren't fighting forward anymore, but had their backs to the Dunmer's summoning and were trying to keep from being surrounded. They were still moving toward their arrival point, but not very quickly, and the dead were now thick on all sides. Attrebus and Sul wielded their weapons more like machetes than swords, chopping as if to clear a jungle path of vines—except the vines kept coming back.

Treb knew it was over when one of them fell and caught him around the leg, holding on with horrible strength. He chopped down at it, and one of those in front of him leapt forward and grappled his sword arm.

Then he went down in a wave of slimy, slippery, disgusting bodies. He had time for one short howl of despair.

I'm sorry Annaïg, he thought. I tried.

He waited for the knife or teeth or claws that would end him, but it didn't happen. In fact, once they had him and Sul immobilized, they stood them both back up. Attrebus renewed his struggles, but quickly found there wasn't much point.

"What are they doing?" he asked Sul.

But his answer didn't come from the Dunmer; everything seemed to spin around, and the bleak landscape of Morrowind vanished.

———

The window was barred and latched, but he had a small magic

for that, and soon he was standing in someone's bedroom, which fortunately was empty. He found the stairs and made his way down until he barely heard voices. He sat in the darkened stairs, beat down his worries, focused, and *listened*.

" . . . would have known?" Arese was saying.

"Anyone," a male voice rumbled. "Anyone who knows you failed to pass on Gulan's warning concerning the prince's activities."

"That is a limited number of people," she said. "What about the woman, Radhasa?"

"I've not heard from her. She was supposed to lie low after the massacre—else how could she explain her survival? This note isn't signed."

"Why on Tamriel would a blackmailer sign their name to a note?"

"I see your point."

"But if not her, that leaves me with you," she said. "Or someone else in your organization."

"Impossible."

"I argued against using you people in the first place," she snorted.

"The job was done."

"The job was not done. Attrebus lives, and someone has implicated me in the bargain."

"You've no proof Attrebus lives," the man asserted. "That's only a rumor."

"Wrong. A courier arrived from Water's Edge this morning with news that he is alive. It went straight to the Emperor. He's keeping it quiet, but troops have already been sent."

That's news, Colin thought. He'd written the "blackmail" letter himself, to draw her out, but he hadn't heard anything about a courier.

"Well, then," the man said. "I don't leave a job unfinished. I deal with it, at no extra charge."

"That won't do. Not now."

The man laughed. "Now, let's not get silly," he said. "If you don't want me to finish the job, fine, but you're not getting your money back. Don't forget who I am."

"You're a glorified thug," Arese replied. "That's who you are."

"I love your type," the man snarled. "You pay me to do murder so you can pretend your hands are clean, so you can continue to think yourself better than me. I have news for you—you're worse, because you don't have the guts to put down your own dogs."

"I wouldn't say that," she replied, a colder note in her voice.

"You're not threatening me."

Colin heard several doors open, and he could all but see the man's guards coming in. But then he heard something else, a sort of ripping sound accompanied by a rush of air and glass shattering. Every hair on his body pricked up.

The next thing he heard was something human ears were not meant to receive, the human brain not meant to interpret, the primal feral sound of which the lion's roar or the wolf's growl were faint shadows. Harsh yellow light shone up the stairs, and then darkness.

Then the screaming began, very human and beyond all terror. Colin began to shiver, then to shake. He was still shaking when the last of the screams abruptly choked off and he felt something ponderous moving through the house. Searching.

———

When light returned, Attrebus first thought he was plunging through a shimmering sky, but it took only a moment to understand that although he was in the air, he wasn't falling, but supported. The shimmer was glass—or what appeared to be glass—and it was all around him; was in fact what held him up in so strange a fashion that it took a moment to sort out *how*.

Some forty feet below him was a web that might have been two hundred feet in diameter. It looked very much like a spider's web, anchored to three metallic spires, an upthrust of stone, and a thicker tower of what appeared to be porcelain. Below the web was a long drop into a cone-shaped basin half full of emerald water and covered with strange buildings everywhere else. The web was made of glasslike tubes about the thickness of his arm. Every few feet along any given tube another sprouted and rose vinelike toward the sky. These in turn branched into smaller tendrils so that the whole resembled a gigantic bed of strange, transparent sea creatures—and indeed, most of them undulated, as if in a current.

Attrebus was about ten feet from the top of the bushy structure, where the strands were no thicker than a writing quill, and these were what held him up. They clustered thickly on the soles of his boots, pressed his back and torso and every part of him except his face with firm, gentle pressure.

He tried to take a step, and they moved with him, reconfiguring so he didn't fall. They cut the sunlight into colors like so many prisms, but it was nevertheless not difficult to see in any direction. He noticed Sul a few feet away, similarly borne.

"You did it!" he shouted. The crystalline strands shivered at his voice and rang like a million faint chimes. "We got away."

"I didn't do anything," Sul replied, shaking his head. "I never got close enough to the door to escape into Oblivion."

"Then where are we?" Treb asked.

"In my home," a voice answered.

Attrebus looked higher up and saw someone walking down toward them, the transparent tubules shifting to meet his feet.

He appeared to be a Dunmer of average size, his gray hair pulled back in a long queue. He wore a sort of loose umber robe with wide sleeves and black slippers.

"Amazing," the man said. "Sul. And you, I take it, are Prince Attrebus. Welcome to Umbriel."

"Vuhon," Sul snarled.

The only strange thing about the man's appearance, Attrebus noticed, were his eyes—they weren't red, like a Dunmer's; the orbs where milky white and the surrounds black.

"Once," the man said. "Once I was called that. You may still use that name, if you find it convenient."

Sul howled, and Attrebus saw his hand flash as when he'd fought and burned Sharwa, but the balefire coruscated briefly in the filaments and then faded. Attrebus ran forward, lifting Flashing, but after a few steps the web suddenly went rigid like the glass it resembled, and he couldn't move anything below his neck.

"Please try to behave yourselves," Vuhon said. "As I said, this is my home." He let himself slump into a sitting position a few feet above them, and the strands formed something like a chair.

"You've come here to kill me, I take it?" he asked Sul.

"What do you think?" Sul said, his voice flat with fury.

"I just *said* what I think—I merely phrased it as a question."

"You murdered Ilzheven, destroyed our city and our country, left our people to be driven to the ends of the earth. You have to pay for that."

Vuhon cocked his head.

"But I didn't do any of that, Sul," he said softly. "*You* did. Don't you remember?"

Sul snarled and tried to move forward again, without success.

Vuhon made a languid sort of sign with his hand, and the glassy vines rustled. A moment later they handed up to each of them a small red bowl full of yellow spheres that did not appear to be fruit. Vuhon took one and popped it in his mouth. A faint green vapor vented from his nostrils.

"You should try them," he said.

"I don't believe I will," Attrebus said.

Vuhon shrugged and turned his attention back to Sul.

"Ilzheven died when the ministry hit Vivec City, old friend," he said. "And the ministry hit Vivec City because you destroyed the ingenium preventing it falling."

"You were draining the life out of her," Sul accused.

"Very slowly. She would have lived for months."

"What are you talking about?" Attrebus demanded. "Sul, what's he saying?"

Sul didn't answer, but Vuhon turned toward Attrebus.

"He told you about the ministry? How we devised a method to keep it airborne?"

"Yes. By stealing souls."

"We couldn't find any other way to do it," Vuhon allowed. "Given time, perhaps we could have. At first we had to slaughter slaves and prisoners outright, as many as ten a day. But then I found a way to use the souls of the living, although only certain people had souls—well, for simplicity's sake, let us say 'large' enough. We only needed twelve at a time, then. A vast improvement. Ilzheven was chosen because she had the right sort of soul."

"You chose her because she wouldn't love you," Sul contradicted. "Because she loved me instead."

"We were always competitive, you and I, weren't we?" Vuhon said, almost absently, as if just remembering. "Even as boys. But we were friends right up until the minute you burst into the ingenium chamber and starting trying to cut Ilzheven free."

"I meant only to free *her*," Sul said. "If you hadn't fought me, the ingenium would never have been damaged."

"You put yourself and your desires ahead of our people, Sul. And all you see is the result."

"You're twisting it all up," Sul said. "You know what happened."

Vuhon shrugged again. "It's not important to me anymore. Did you find the sword?"

"What sword?"

Vuhon's eyes narrowed. "I suppose you didn't find it. My taskers certainly haven't." His voice rose and his calm broke. Attrebus suddenly seemed to hear boundless anger and violence in the Dunmer's tone. "*Where is it?*" he shouted.

"What do you want with it?" Attrebus asked.

"That's none of your concern."

"I think everything about you is my concern," Attrebus snapped back. "Whatever happened in the past, you're many thousands of times a murderer now. All those people in Black Marsh . . ."

Vuhon sat back, seemed to relax. His voice became once again maddeningly tranquil.

"I can't really deny that," he admitted.

For a moment Attrebus was stunned by the casual confession. "*But why?*" he asked finally.

"Look around you," Vuhon said. "Isn't it beautiful?"

Almost against his will, Attrebus once again took in the sight of Umbriel.

"Yes," he was forced to confess.

"This is my city," Vuhon said. "My world. I do what I must to protect it."

"Protect it from what? How does destroying my world save yours? Are there no souls to feed on in Oblivion?"

Vuhon seemed to consider that for a moment.

"I'm not sure why I should waste my time telling you," he replied. "I'll most likely have to kill you anyway."

"If that's so, why haven't you done so?"

"There are things you know that might be helpful to me," Vuhon replied. "Or, if you could be convinced, do for me."

"Convince me, then," Attrebus said. "Explain all of this."

Vuhon ran his thumb under his lips and shrugged.

"Sul told you how we were cast into Oblivion? How we met Umbra, and the deal I made with him?"

"Yes," Attrebus replied. "And how you tortured him."

Vuhon's grin turned a little nasty. "Yes, but I grew bored with that. I could never torture him as much as he tortured himself."

"A problem I won't have with you," Sul said.

"Ah, Sul. You really haven't changed."

The red bowls were gone, replaced by skewers of slowly writhing orange caterpillars.

"Vile had made it impossible for Umbra to leave his realm, and after your escape, Sul, he tightened his walls further so that I couldn't leave either, even if I'd had the means. The only way to escape was to circumvent his restriction, to remain in his realm, at least in a way. I built my ingenium, I powered it with Umbra and the energies he had stolen from Vile. I turned our city, wrapped those circumscribed walls around it. Twisted it like a sausage maker twists a casing to form a link, the way a child might an inflated pig's bladder to form a double ball. Twisted it until it broke loose, like a bubble."

He bit one of the caterpillars, and it exploded into a butterfly, which he caught by the wing and devoured.

"That was a long time ago," he went on. "We've drifted through many realms and places beyond even Oblivion. We cannot leave the city—Vile's circumscription still surrounds it. Nor would I want to leave it—I've come to love this place I built. To survive in those long spaces between the worlds, we had to become a little universe of our own, a self-sustaining cycle of life and death and rebirth, a continuum of matter and spirit—all powered, manipulated, mediated by my ingenium. We've moved beyond the inefficiency some call 'natural,' and in doing so approach perfection. Everything here is in a real sense a part of everything else, because all flows from the ingenium."

Sul—off to the right and in the corner of Treb's vision—made a sudden gesture with his hands. Without turning his head, Attrebus shifted his gaze the tiniest bit. The Dunmer's lips moved in an exaggerated fashion.

Keep him talking, Attrebus thought he was saying.

Attrebus put his full focus on Vuhon, who didn't seem to have noticed.

"Not so self-sustaining," he countered. "Your world feeds on souls from the outside world."

Vuhon nodded. "I said we 'approach' perfection. Beyond Mundus, our need for sustenance is minimal. In some places, not necessary at all. Here, on this heavy plane of clay and lead, much more is required."

"Then why have you come here?"

"Because this is one place that Clavicus Vile cannot pursue us, at least not in the fullness of his power."

"Then you've won," Attrebus said. "You're free. Why are you still running? Surely there must be some way to land this thing—in a valley, a lake—someplace?"

"It's not that simple," Vuhon answered. "Vile can still work against us. He can send mortal followers to assassinate me, for instance." He nodded pointedly at Sul.

"Sul's not an agent of Clavicus Vile," Attrebus protested.

"Do you know that? He was in Oblivion for a long time. And he hates me enough to make whatever bargains he thinks will get him his revenge. But that aside—Umbriel isn't fully in your world yet."

"Yet?"

Vuhon shook his head. "No, we remain a sort of bubble of Oblivion in Mundus, and as such we're vulnerable. But I've found a way to change that, and to be free of Clavicus Vile forever."

"And you need this sword of Umbra to do that?"

Again, that sudden uncharacteristic rage seemed to rise up in Vuhon.

"No," he all but snarled.

"But you *do* want it," Sul said, breaking his long silence. "It can still undo you, can't it? Where is Umbra, Vuhon? You said he powers your ingenium. If Umbra is re-imprisoned in the sword, what becomes of your beautiful city?"

Vuhon seemed to be actually shaking with rage. He closed his eyes and drew long deep breaths. When he finally did speak again, it was in even tones.

"We didn't come just for the sword," he said. "I came to repair the rift into Vile's realm, and now that's done. Umbra wanted to find the weapon, and we shall still look for it, but we have other agents that can do that. If you know where it is, I will find out, I promise you. But it's time to turn my attentions elsewhere."

"Why didn't you use these other 'agents' of yours in the first place?" Attrebus asked.

"They couldn't have sealed the rift. Besides, this little meander gave me time to build my army. It's already marching, you know. The walkers need not remain near Umbriel—they can go where I choose." He scratched his chin. "And here is where you might prove yourself useful to me, Prince Attrebus," he said.

"Why should I want to do that?" Attrebus asked.

"To preserve your own life, and the lives of many of your people. And to finally be the man you want to be."

A little spark traveled up his spine. "What do you mean, 'the man I want to be'?"

"I mean I suspect that your adventures have probably caused you to learn that much of your fame is based on fraud."

"How do you know that?" Attrebus asked, backing away. "If you've just come from Oblivion . . ."

"Don't you see?" Sul shouted. "He has someone inside the palace. That's who tried to have you killed."

"Is this true?" Attrebus challenged.

"Your fame was the problem, apparently. My ally feared you might create popular demand to attack Umbriel before we were ready, and to make the siege more bitter."

"Siege?"

"Regrettably, I must attack the Imperial City. I suspect they will resist."

"Why must you attack the city?"

"I need the city," Vuhon said. "Specifically, I need to reach the White-Gold Tower. Then all of this can end. The dying can stop, and I can bring Umbriel to rest somewhere. If you want to save lives, all you need do is convince your father not to fight—better yet, to evacuate."

"My father spent his life putting the Empire back together. There's no way he would surrender the White-Gold Tower. I certainly couldn't convince him."

"You could try. It's the offer I'm making you. I have gifts for you, the kind that only a god can bestow. You can return to Cyrodiil and lead your people to safety. You can be a real hero."

Attrebus looked at Sul, then back out at the city.

"What about Sul?"

Vuhon ate another butterfly.

"Sul is mine. I'll learn what he knows and then he will die."

"If you murder Sul, I'll never help you."

"Think carefully, Prince. I could have lied to you and told you he would live. I didn't. If you don't help me, you'll die, too. And then I will still take what I want at whatever cost of life is required."

———

Annaïg felt sheer exhilaration as she rushed through the air. The first time she'd been too terrified to even begin to enjoy it. This time she felt it was the most wonderful thing she'd ever done.

She glanced back at the receding bulk of Umbriel. Nothing was following them. No one seemed to have noticed, and no one would until Toel came looking for her. By then she and Glim would be a hundred miles away.

She gripped Glim's hand harder, just a friendly squeeze, but something about it felt strange. She glanced at over at him.

At first she thought he was surrounded by a stray wisp of cloud, but then she saw it was *him*, starting to bleed like a watercolor that had been spilled on.

And, looking at her hand, so was she.

————

Attrebus fell silent for a long moment. Sul could practically see the thoughts turning in his head. The boy he'd rescued from kidnappers wouldn't have thought about it at all—he had believed himself the hero the ballads spoke of, and that man would never turn on a companion.

But he knew that Attrebus was a little more pragmatic now. He might even be capable of making the right decision, to sacrifice him, buy himself time.

It didn't matter. He couldn't die, not before he killed Vuhon. And Vuhon had made a mistake just now.

And Attrebus had given him almost all the time he needed.

Sul closed his eyes.

"How long do I have to make my decision?" he heard Attrebus ask.

"Not long," Vuhon said. "Sul, what are you—"

Pain jagged through Sul, crippling, nightmarish hurt that once would have paralyzed him. But he'd felt it before, and worse, and all he had to do was reach through it, past their confinement, through the walls between worlds to find it there, waiting. Angry.

"*Come!*" he commanded.

"You shouldn't have told me we were in Oblivion!" Sul shouted.

And all around them glass whinged and shattered.

———

Colin had to run. Out the window, down the street, away. Everything in him screamed for him to run.

That's how mice die, the small sane part of him thought. They see the shadow of the hawk, they run . . .

He remembered the man he'd stabbed again, the confusion in his eyes as the blade struck him, the desire to live, to breathe just a little longer. Had he been the hawk then? He hadn't felt like one.

A boy was once born with a knife instead of a right hand . . .

He felt tired. He wanted to give up, get it over with. But there was a rot in the core of the Empire, in the palace itself. And only he seemed to care.

So he drew himself in, held the darkness to him closer than a lover, and tried to clear his mind as he heard the thing come around the corner.

He felt its gaze touch him, but he kept his own on the floor, knowing that if he saw it, he would lose all control. The stairs creaked beneath its weight, and he felt it brush by him. It paused for a long moment, then continued up.

A few moments later it came down, turned back around the corner. After what seemed an eternity, he felt the air wrench again, followed by the quiet opening and closing of the door. The house was still.

He sat there, unable to move, until the smell of smoke brought him out of it. Heart thudding, he ran downstairs.

The fire was already everywhere on the ground floor, but he could still see that the bodies looked almost as if they had exploded. It would take hours to figure out how many of them there were.

He went back up and out through the window. He wished he'd been able to search the house, to find some clue as to Arese's reason for wanting the prince dead.

And for that matter, why she hadn't killed the prince herself.

A few questions in the right places would tell him which crime lord had just died, but that was moot at this point. No, he'd found out what he really wanted to know—Arese arranged the massacre.

The next question—the most dangerous one—was whether she was working alone, or just the point of a larger knife.

———

Attrebus had the barest glimpse of something horrible before he found himself suddenly free of both detention and support; he was falling. He reached out desperately and caught one of the broken tubes, which was whipping about like a dying snake.

He turned his gaze up and saw the thing again, a phantasmal mass of chitinoid limbs and wings that felt like scorpion and hornet and spider all together. A lot of the strands—including those holding him—had been shattered by its arrival, but plenty were groping at it now from farther away, trying to wrap it up as it surged toward Vuhon. It tore through them, but they slowed it down.

Vuhon—still supported—stood, and a long whip of white-hot flame lashed out at the thing. One of its claws fell off, but the same attack sheared through the protecting tubes.

Attrebus was now below and behind Vuhon, and the tendrils seemed to have forgotten him. He sheathed Flashing so as to free both hands. The tube he held was now swaying rhythmically; when it came nearest Vuhon, he grabbed another and began climbing toward him. The nearer he got, the easier it was, for the web was still thickest beneath the enemy.

Another flaming chunk of beast fell past him, and he tried to climb faster. If Vuhon was distracted by the thing, he might have a chance, but if he wasn't, that whip of flame would turn on him.

He was still twenty feet away when what passed for the daedra's head came off, and Vuhon's quick gaze found him. Suddenly the tendrils became rigid again, and Attrebus howled in frustration.

That was when Sul came hurtling down from above and smashed into the glassy foliage that held him. Attrebus had a glimpse of him, of the blood on his lips and the drooling from his nose, and then Sul's wiry hand pushed through to grasp his shoulder. The Dunmer's eyes were tortured and his voice cracked.

"Not now," he said.

The falling-everywhere-at-once sensation hit him again, and Umbriel vanished.

EPILOGUE

———————————

Annaïg sat with Glim for an hour weeping, turning her gaze out to a world that wouldn't have her anymore.

"I don't understand," Glim murmured. "We weren't born here."

Annaïg looked at her friend's forlorn face, sighed, and wiped away her tears.

Enough of that, she thought.

"I don't understand either," she said. "But I'm going to."

"What do you mean?" Glim asked.

"We can't leave. We have to go back, and I have to figure out how to—cure this, fix it, whatever's causing this."

"Everything doesn't have a cure or a fix," Glim replied. "Sometimes there really isn't any going back."

No," she said softly, thinking of Lilmoth, of her father, of a life now more like the memory of a dream than anything that had ever been real. She had been dreaming, hadn't she? Playacting. This was the first real thing that had ever happened to her.

"No," she repeated. "Glim, we go forward. But I promise you, forward will one day take us away from here. Just . . . not now."

And so they sat together for a while longer before going back down to the dock, and there they said their goodbyes.

Coming out of the pantry, she stopped at the threshold. Even the hobs were gone now, and the kitchen—for another few hours—would be truly silent.

And she imagined she saw herself again, that ghost of her with that faint smile on her face, looking confident, effective, filled with secrets.

"Okay," she said, softly. "Okay."

And she entered the kitchen.

About the Author

Born in Meridian, MS, in 1963, GREG KEYES spent his early years roaming the forests of his native state and the red rock cliffs of the Navajo Indian reservation in Arizona. He earned his B.A. in anthropology from Mississippi State University and a master's degree from the University of Georgia, where he did course work for a Ph.D. He lives in Savannah, GA, where, in addition to full-time writing, he enjoys cooking, fencing, the company of his family and friends and lazy Savannah nights. Greg is the author of *The Waterborn, The Blackgod,* the Babylon 5 Psi Corps trilogy, the Age of Unreason tetrology (for which he won the prestigious "Le Grand Prix de l'Imaginaire" award), and three *New York Times* bestselling *Star Wars* novels in the New Jedi Order series.

Welcome to Vegas.

New Vegas.

Enjoy your stay.

"It will dominate the skyline like a
mushroom cloud."

- Eurogamer

fallout.bethsoft.com

a ZeniMax Media company

Fallout®: New Vegas™ © 2010 Bethesda Softworks LLC, a ZeniMax Media company. Bethesda Softworks, ZeniMax and related logos are registered
trademarks or trademarks of ZeniMax Media Inc. in the U.S. and/or other countries. Fallout, Fallout: New Vegas and related logos are registered or registered
trademarks of Bethesda Softworks LLC in the U.S. and/or other countries. Developed in association with Obsidian Entertainment Inc. Obsidian and related
logos are trademarks or registered trademarks of Obsidian Entertainment Inc. All Rights Reserved.